# I WANT YOU GONE

A PSYCHOLOGICAL THRILLER WITH A NERVE-
SHREDDING TWIST

MIRANDA RIJKS

Revised Edition 2019
INKUBATOR BOOKS

www.inkubatorbooks.com

First published as "The Obituary" by Miranda Rijks (2018)

# 1

'I'm so sorry. This isn't me bailing out, really it isn't! My daughter, she's being hysterical.' I hold up my mobile phone. I have ignored her calls twice, but now maternal panic has kicked in. I excuse myself, twisting away from the small round table to listen to her messages. I can barely understand what Mel is saying.

It is my second date with Ben Logan and I want to be there. He is balding, square-jawed and wears those black-framed glasses that used to adorn the noses of geeks but now are on trend. And he is a doctor. A catch. And we make each other laugh.

'Your daughter?'

'Eighteen, first term at university, first term away from home. She's finding it hard to settle.'

He leans back into his chair and nods. 'Go, it's fine.'

'Go, go?' I frown. 'Or go and take the call and come back when you're done?'

'Hopefully the latter.' There is something delicious about his grin.

I stride away from the table, wondering if he is watching

me, checking out the size of my backside. I debated wearing the black skirt, turning this way and that in the mirror earlier in the evening. The seams are precariously stretched, but I don't have anything else that matches my new pale pink silk blouse. I nearly stumble and grab onto the edge of a table, catching a glass of wine as it topples, muttering my apologies to a young couple who stare at me, their faces plastered with disdain. At the front of the pub, I stand underneath an awning, which is just wide enough to protect me from the autumnal wind.

'What is it, Mel?' I sigh. Earlier today, she left me messages about being lonely, not having enough to do, not under-standing her tutorial assignment, not having a single friend in the world, regretting choosing Manchester University, pondering whether she should take a year out. And I am getting bored. Is it permissible to say that about one's own daughter?

But this time it is different. She is sobbing.

'Thank God, Mum! I was so scared. And especially when you didn't answer the phone.'

'Slow down, Mel. What are you talking about?'

'Your Facebook page. It says you're dead.'

'What?' I snort with laughter.

An elderly man in a flat cap, walking a miniature schnauzer, stops and stares at me. The dog is attached to one of those extendable leads, and it ambles right up to me and lifts a leg. I scuttle sideways just in time. The man pulls the dog, and urine trickles down the pavement into the gutter.

'Your Facebook page. You're dead. You died yesterday. All these people are leaving comments about how shocked they are, sending their condolences. You're not dead though, are you?'

My laugh tapers into a snigger. 'Not the last time I checked.'

'Then why?'

'I have no idea. Perhaps they've got the wrong Laura Swallow.' I stamp my feet up and down, jiggling to keep warm.

'More likely your account's been hacked.'

I can picture Mel rolling her eyes, instructing me to improve my online security. She is studying business at university and spent the summer shut in her room, huddled over her computer when she should have been outside in the fresh air.

'When did you last go onto Facebook?' she asks. The sniffing has stopped.

'Three, four weeks ago, maybe.'

'OMG! That long ago?'

'I only look at Facebook to check up on you, and as you've blocked me, what reason do I have for wasting time on social media?'

'Oh, Mum, you're such a loser.'

'Thank you, darling.' I sigh. I am used to the derogatory comments. 'I'm out for a drink with a friend, so if you don't mind...'

'You need to change your password. I'll re-friend you.'

'I will change my password tonight. I promise. Bye, darling.'

THE EVENING LOSES some of its sparkle after the conversation with Mel. I stare at the way Ben's lips move, the thin top lip eking out a little to the side, twitching slightly as if a tiny nerve is caught. Faded acne scars on his neck are like miniscule pockets – probably miserable reminders of his youth.

'Would you like to come?'

'Sorry,' I say. I haven't heard the beginning part of the question.

'You're upset about something your daughter said. It's quite all right. Why don't we reschedule? I was wondering if you'd be free to join me at the theatre on Friday evening?'

I take my phone from my bag and pretend to look at the

calendar. Of course I am free. Fridays through to Sundays are wide, painful, gaping holes of loneliness. Whenever possible, I grasp the opportunity to do weekend shifts at work, but those opportunities have faded away over the past few months. Cuts, lay-offs, reduced pay: all perfectly normal in this era of Brexit.

'Thank you.' I put my phone on the table. 'That would be lovely.' How very civilised. I can't remember the last time I went to the theatre, or even the cinema, for that matter.

He polishes off his beer and gently places the glass back onto the table. I finish my white wine and we grin at each other awkwardly.

He offers to drive me home, but I decline. It is, after all, only our second date, and I am not sure if one quick drink even counts as a date.

HOME USED to be an airy modern house on the outskirts of Cranleigh. It was where Mel grew up, where I tended the garden and made hearty Sunday lunches for Ian and our extended families. Often called the largest village in England, Cranleigh has it all: M&S on the high street, plenty of quirky, independent shops, a village green and a true sense of community. And we were part of it. That was until one Friday evening shortly after Mel turned fourteen, when Ian announced he had fallen in love with a colleague and wanted a divorce. I begged and wailed and blamed myself. I withdrew, then I got angry, and eventually and reluctantly, I accepted our marriage was over and it was up to me to determine the second half of my life.

During the last two years, home has been a two-bedroom top-floor flat in the centre of Horsham. The building used to be a bank and it still has some of the quirks of its former glory, which were sold to me as 'a blend of character features and high-quality modern living'. The pneumatic tube system winds its way through the communal corridors, now devoid of money and filled up with dust. I miss not having a garden and frequently curse the neighbours for making too much noise or leaving bicycles or prams in the lobby, but it is my little home and I feel safe there. I have a quaint view over rooftops, and when the sun sets on a late summer's day, I squint my eyes and pretend that the squat church spire is the Duomo in Florence and the modern, grey and brown tiles of the office blocks are the ancient terracotta roofs of Renaissance buildings. I imagine the Ponte Vecchio is just around the corner, and if I so chose, I could take my chilled wine down to the river and watch the mighty Arno weave and flow downstream. The River Arun is perfectly lovely with its overgrown leafy banks and its resident wild ducks. It's just nothing like my Florentine dream.

WHEN I ARRIVE BACK from my truncated date, I am ravenous. I had assumed that our early evening drink would lead on to supper and perhaps a bit more. Did I eat any lunch? I can only recall munching half a bar of chocolate mid-afternoon. I swing open the fridge door and am greeted by two eggs, a quarter pint of milk, half a bottle of white wine and a lemon. I groan. Omelette with toast it will have to be. Again. At least when Mel was living at home, I made an effort to buy groceries, to cook.

I switch on the television and half watch, half listen to the news as I make my paltry meal. Afterwards, I get up and find my canvas bag dumped next to the front door as I hastily returned from work and then left again. Firing up my laptop, I carry it to the living room, kick off my shoes and slump onto the sofa, balancing it on top of my favourite furry, aqua-blue cushion. Ian would never have countenanced a furry cushion.

I type in my password. The password box wriggles from

side to side and stays stubbornly blank. I try again. Nothing. I check that the caps button isn't on, and I type my password slowly, saying the letters and numbers out loud. And still the machine doesn't fire up.

'What the hell,' I mutter. Letting the laptop drop onto the sofa, I grab my handbag. Where is my phone? I tip the bag upside down, and all the detritus accumulated from the past few months litters onto the floor: pennies, scraps of tissue paper, a lost lipstick, receipts and dust. But no phone.

'Shit!' I throw my head back and yell. I cannot lose my phone!

I nearly hadn't bothered installing a landline when I moved into the flat, but Mel had insisted. Surprising really for one so young and techie. It is just as well I did. It takes a while to find the handset, which has made its way, rather bizarrely, under my bed, and a lot longer to ring directory enquiries and track down the phone number of the pub where Ben and I had our curtailed drink.

It rings and rings and I nearly give up, but then an exasperated female voice answers.

'Sorry, love, nothing's been handed in. What model is it?'

'An iPhone 5.'

'Not a chance. It'll have been swiped and long gone. Suggest you put a block on it.'

With no phone and a laptop that has died on me at exactly the wrong time, how the hell am I meant to 'put a block on it'? I need to call someone. I pace my small living room, three measly steps each way, desperately trying to retrieve phone numbers from my malfunctioning brain. 773248 mocks me again and again. My old telephone number. Ian's telephone number now and whoever his latest squeeze might be. I am not going to call him. I will try my friend Anna. She is social media savvy.

I punch in some numbers.

'Wrong number.' He hangs up. I try again, changing the last digit from a seven to a one.

'Hi, Anna, can you go onto Facebook for me?' I ask as her breathy voice says hello.

'Why?'

'My computer's broken and I've lost my phone.'

'Why Facebook? You don't approve of social media.'

'Apparently I'm dead!' I chuckle. 'Mel rang me about it. Can you read me what it says?'

'Wow!' I can hear her clip-clopping across her travertine-tiled kitchen floor. A few long moments later, she returns. 'What am I looking for?'

'My timeline? I don't know.'

'I'm looking at you, and the last time you posted was – bloody hell, Laura – seven months ago! Nothing since. Hold on whilst I search if you've been tagged in anyone else's posts. Nothing. Was Mel taking the mickey?'

'No, she was really upset about it.'

'How odd. There's nothing untoward that I can see.'

'Perhaps it was the wrong Laura Swallow after all. I suggested that to Mel, but she thought my account might have been hacked.'

'She's not, you know, taking anything, is she?'

'What... No. I don't think so.'

Anna is silent.

'Nothing to worry about, then,' I say. 'How are you anyway?'

We chat for a few minutes about nothing in particular. I tell her about my non-date. She doesn't ask his name and I don't mention it, but she does tell me to be careful, how she's heard of all these dating horror stories. I cut the conversation short then. After pouring myself a large glass of wine, I run a bath and soak in lavender-scented bubbles for a very long time, watching them pop and amalgamate into little bubble islands until I almost fall asleep.

## 2

Friday. After an uneventful, early morning viewing, it is nearly 11 a.m. by the time I arrive back in the office. I have parked my car in my private parking space in the underground car park in the centre of town. I pay an obscene annual charge for the privilege and often wonder if it's worthwhile. Undoubtedly it would be cheaper to take taxis everywhere for the amount my car costs me, but a rural estate agent without a car is a rural estate agent without a job.

Slate Wilders is the largest agency in Sussex, and as the Horsham branch is also the head office, the premises are sprawling. The public see the double-fronted windows abutting the high street, but the building extends far back and there are two office floors above. When I'm in the office, I sit at a desk the furthest away from the windows on the second floor. Sometimes I love my work; mostly I'm just grateful I have employment. After fourteen years away from the workplace and with no relevant experience, I was lucky to be offered the job. My old friend Jenny pulled a lot of strings.

The front door rings with a little tinkle when it opens, and normally most of my colleagues would look up. They're all hungry to pounce on a potential buyer or renter, eager to bolster their meagre earnings with a commission or two. Sometimes their faces drop when they realise it's a colleague and not a punter walking through the door, but generally those on the phone give a little smile or a wave; those not doing much say hello. They're a friendly bunch.

This Friday morning, when I walk in, not a single person on the agency floor glances up at me. I sense something is wrong. Every step I take up the stairs, my heart sinks a little lower. Fridays are lay-off days. By the time I have reached the middle of the stairs, I am convinced it will be my head on the block today. How will I cope without a job? Ian's maintenance payments have stopped now that Mel has gone to university. And my savings are paltry, to say the least. I won't be able to pay the mortgage; I'll lose the flat and then what? Most of my friends have children still living at home, houses overflowing with overgrown children. It's only Anna who is childless and mostly husbandless. But there's only so long I would be able to stay with Anna. Jim will come home and I'm sure he would be unimpressed to have one of Anna's waifs and strays staying over. I will be on the streets then.

'Laura, can I have a word?'

I put my bag on my desk and fling my coat onto the back of the chair. That is quick. Was it really necessary to accost me the moment I reached the top of the stairs? My boss, Peter Fielding, must have been stalking me. He has a room all to himself at the front of the building with windows affording a fine view of the high street.

I follow him into his brightly lit office and stand in front of his messy desk overflowing with brochures and magazines and invoices. He sits down.

'How much notice will I get?' I ask.

'What?' He has a nasally voice.

'I assume you're laying me off?'

'Sit down, Laura.' He waves his stubby fingers at me.

I sigh as I sink into the leather armchair. It is slightly lower than his and I wonder if he likes the superior view it gives him of his adversaries.

'Have you seen this?' He holds up the *Gazette*. It is the latest edition, the one that is printed late on a Thursday evening and arrives on the news-stands in the early hours of Friday morning. We get fifteen copies delivered to the office every Friday, enough for each agent to check their listings, to appraise themselves of what the competition is doing. Not that the newspaper is so important anymore with the advent of Rightmove and Zoopla.

'No, I haven't seen it.'

I try to recall what listings I wrote earlier in the week. Have I made a spelling mistake or put the wrong price on a property? My mind is blank. I think back to yesterday; an ordinary day albeit a day without my phone or laptop. Peter hands me the newspaper. It isn't open at the property listings pages but at the back: the obituaries. I pause for a moment. Who died? Do Peter and I know someone in common?

'You are Laura Swallow, born on 10 January 1967 with an ex-husband called Ian and a daughter called Melissa?'

'Yes.' My hand is shaking slightly as I take the paper.

'Second down on the left. I think someone has done something very malicious.' Peter clears his throat.

I look at the paper and follow Peter's instructions.



*LAURA RUTH SWALLOW, née Carson, passed away suddenly on October 28 after suffering fatal injuries in a car accident. She is survived by her ex-husband, Ian, whom she divorced in 2013, and her daughter, Melissa. In life, there was no notable contribution, nothing remarkable. In death, there will be celebration.*

.  .  .

My obituary.

Peter is looking at me expectantly. I open my mouth to speak, but no words come out. What is this? Who has written this? I look at it again, but the letters swim and become illegible.

'Are you ok?'

'No. Not really.'

'You don't look as shocked as I thought you would.' Peter flips his pen between his fingers.

Really? How shocked should I look?

'Someone posted that I was dead on Facebook. My daughter rang me in hysterics on Wednesday, but by the time I checked, there was nothing there. I thought she had the wrong person.'

'It's not a very nice prank,' Peter says. The understatement of the year.

'How did you come across it?' I ask.

'Young Rob on lettings found it. His gran died last week and he was checking the listing. Yours is underneath.'

That explains why everyone downstairs avoided looking at me.

Peter clears his throat again. 'Do you know who did this?'

I shake my head. Little me, why would anyone do this to me? I don't have any enemies, do I? I look at it again. *'No notable contribution.'* How cutting. But I *have* made a contribution, haven't I? I have raised a beautiful, confident, capable girl. Perhaps Mel isn't confident right now, but then few kids would be during their first few weeks at university, away from home. I have done my bit for charity. Not so much these days, because I can barely afford to look after myself, let alone anyone else. But when I was living the life of luxury with Ian, I raised money for the church, I wrote articles for the arts festival, I did my fundraising bit for Mel's school. Nowadays, I support myself financially and am no burden on the state. I am a good friend, and before he divorced me, I was a faithful wife. Why do I deserve this? And who will be celebrating my death?

'Are you sure there's nothing you're holding back?'

I stand up; my legs are wobbling. Tears well in my eyes.

'No! I've got no secrets, nothing. I don't know what this is all about!' I wave the newspaper in front of me.

'Do you want to take the rest of the day off?' Peter's voice has softened. He isn't the sort of bloke who copes with tears.

'No, I'm fine.' I stand up straight and wipe my eyes with the back of my hand.

'In which case, would you like to do a couple of viewings?'

This is, of course, a rhetorical question.

'There is a lovely new build near Storrington and The Rectory, which you've already visited over Pulborough way.' He hands me the glossy brochures detailing both houses. I know The Rectory well. I have visited it twice and drafted the wording for the sales listings.

'You'll need to leave straight away. The potential buyers are a Mr and Mrs Drover. They specifically asked for you to do the viewing. Apparently, you showed them around a property before. Said how professional you were.'

I shake my head. The name doesn't mean anything, but that doesn't bother me. I am good at recognising faces and lousy at remembering names. And it is nice to know that some clients appreciate me. Perhaps I am further from the being-let-go precipice than I had imagined.

'No need to come back to the office afterwards. I expect you'll have things to do at home.' Peter turns towards his computer. I am dismissed.

When I dropped my bag on my desk, I didn't notice the padded envelope with my name typed on the front. I rip it open, tip it up, and out falls my mobile phone. My lost mobile phone with its photograph of Mel on the back cover. I stare at it. How did the person who found it know it was mine? Perhaps

Ben retrieved it and dropped the envelope off at the office? I check inside for a note. There is nothing. If it had been Ben, he would have left a note, surely? But if it wasn't him, then how would anyone have known it was mine? The phone is locked. I unlock it and check the call list. The last calls made and received were between Mel and me, exactly as I remember.

Yesterday I put a block on my phone and rushed to Carphone Warehouse in my lunch hour, purchasing a new phone because, of course, my paltry finances had not stretched to taking out insurance. I had been eligible for an upgrade, but I declined, sticking to my old contract and choosing an earlier, cheaper model. Then I had rushed to the computer repair shop, where the assistant had tut-tutted as he opened my old laptop. He had promised to do his best to recover my data. But with no laptop, I haven't been able to back up my data to the new phone.

As I am peering at my lost and found phone, Jenny appears.

'You're looking remarkably healthy for a corpse.'

'Ha ha!' I grimace.

'What's it all about?' She perches on the edge of my desk, causing it to creak alarmingly.

'You mean the obituary, I suppose.'

Jenny nods.

'It's not strictly an obituary,' I muse. For a moment, I wonder why I'm being so calm. Perhaps I'm having an out-of-body experience? I shake my head. 'It's a death notice, actually. Death notices are paid for; obituaries are written by staffers about famous people.'

'Ah yes. I had forgotten that you were a journalist back in the day. I didn't know you wrote obituaries though.' Jenny smiles, pushing up the sleeve of her pale grey jacket to scratch her arm.

'I freelanced for several broadsheets and wrote obituaries for about eight months.'

I was proud of my career when I was younger. Sometimes I think it's ironic that I have been a member of two of the most untrusted professions: journalists and estate agents. I know some people think both are distorters of the truth. I prefer to call myself a wordsmith with an optimistic spin.

Jenny is my friend. We met years ago when our kids attended the same primary school. When she went back to work and I stayed at home, our paths diverged, and although we stayed on each other's Christmas card lists, we never met up. After Ian left and it became apparent that I would need to find myself a job, someone, I can't even remember who, suggested contacting Jenny. She is a director at Slate Wilders and a keen supporter of middle-aged women re-entering the workplace. It helped that she also went through a divorce a few years back. Jenny gave me my break, offering me part-time work for three months, which then morphed into a permanent full-time contract.

Two years ago, at Slate Wilders' Christmas lunch, Jenny and I sat next to each other, having a thoroughly jolly afternoon. She invited me to join her book club. I am a private reader with eclectic taste and a propensity for remembering storylines and forgetting titles and author names. I went along to that first get-together simply to be polite to my colleague. Sycophantic as it may sound, I was sufficiently insecure in my job to think my rejection of her social invitation might affect my chances at work. Now, the thought is hilarious.

Jenny's house is quaint, crooked and charming. I was nervous, and for the first hour, it seemed I was correct to be so. There were four or five other women who took the literary analyses utterly seriously. One of them read a bad sex scene out loud. Jenny caught my eye and we both burst into childish sniggers. The others stared at us with contempt. Jenny cocked her head towards the kitchen, and I followed her. We collapsed with hysteria, snorting wine from our noses. Her kitchen was a visual delight with florid pink walls and a small turquoise Aga.

'I love the décor,' I gasped through my giggles. She filled up my wine glass until it overflowed, and we laughed some more. It was silly, undignified and totally unappreciated by the other women. One of them emerged from the living room and asked us to be quiet.

'You're in my bloody house!' Jenny spluttered.

'We'll leave, then, shall we?' The woman had a tight face; I wasn't sure if it was from Botox or meanness.

'Yes, I think that would probably be a good idea.' Jenny put her hands on her hips and grinned.

It clearly was not the answer the woman expected, because she stood there, rooted to the floor, staring at Jenny, her mouth opening and closing like a fish. Five minutes later, with much audible huffing and puffing and whispering, the front door slammed, and Jenny and I were left alone with a large supply of alcohol.

'Thank heavens for that!' she said.

And so began a friendship that, for me at least, has become increasingly important. We meet for supper at least once a month and frequently catch up for a quick drink after work. These days we're bonding over our mutual re-entry into the world of dating.

'Give me a call anytime you'd like to talk.'

'Thanks, Jen. I've no idea what's going on. I need to process it.'

'I'll ring you over the weekend. You can tell me about your date with your hunky doctor, and I'll give you the low-down on my Match.com likely-to-be disaster.'

'I'm keeping my fingers crossed for you,' I say.

## 3

I t is not far to Storrington, but still a long enough drive for me to ponder the words on the death notice and work myself into a frenzy. Putting to one side the whole incomprehensible horror of it, I mull over its elements one at a time.

The first is my supposed death in a car accident. This is particularly cruel. My sister died in a car accident less than four years ago. We had been close. Becky was the youngest child in our family, the glue that bound us all together. All she ever wanted was a husband and a house full of children. It never happened. She married at twenty, but he was playing away. With men. They divorced, and she spent the rest of her too-short life single and childless.

Becky doted on Mel. We weren't very good at baby-making, the three of us Carson kids. Donny, our elder brother, emigrated to Australia, and although he may have scores of offspring for all we know, he has never settled down. After Mel was born, Ian and I tried to have more children. When I was thirty-nine, we spent thousands on two rounds of IVF. They both failed. And then I went through an early menopause. The failure to have more children was a cause of desperate heartache for me and undoubtedly was a major contributor in the breakdown of our marriage.

During the past couple of years, I have spent much time musing on whether Becky ever experienced true happiness. It's a question I will never be able to answer, and the not knowing gouges away at me. I pray she did, but as far as I know, her heart was broken and she never allowed it to fully heal. Would her death have been any easier to bear if she'd had a loving family, a partner and children? Probably not. The circumstances of any road traffic death are devastating, but Becky's were particularly traumatic. My grief has shredded my life, more so than the disintegration of our marriage. I am scared of driving. Not surprising, really. Being a passenger is the worst. Looking in the mirror and seeing a lorry bearing down on me, driving faster than the car I am in, gives me palpitations. Meditation, breathing – it all helps.

I am doing my deep breathing and counting as I turn off the A24 onto the A283. Counting in, holding my breath, and easing my breath out slowly just about stops my eyes from welling up with tears. I am on a road I used to enjoy, with sweeping views across to the South Downs, pockets of woodland and the snaking River Arun, but today I could be anywhere. My lower belly aches, the forebearer of period pains, which in my post-menopausal state is a cruel joke my body plays upon itself. It is as if my abdomen clenches in mockery of my barrenness whenever I think about Becky, whenever I think about the babies that never were. This leads me on to thinking about death: mine in particular. Have I really made no notable contribution? Perhaps not to society at large, but surely I have made a contribution to my circle of friends and family?

With an unusual lapse of concentration, I swerve a little into the centre of the road and am rewarded by the brutal hooting of a white van driving in the opposite direction. My fingers grip tightly around the steering wheel. Who is it that is being so cruel? And who is going to celebrate my death? I can't imagine celebrating anyone's death, however much I despised them. Relief perhaps they've passed away, but celebration? Not that I hate anyone. Someone once told me that hate is so close to love, it shows that you care. Disdain is much stronger. I can't think of anyone who hates me or anything that I might have done to provoke a strong negative emotion. Even Ian, who undoubtedly resented me for kicking up such a fight over the settlement of our divorce, never actually hated me. I am convinced about that.

I pull up outside a red brick new build, with vivid emerald turf laid around the front and a bright chalky pebble drive. The house is stark, bare of plants and curtains and other paraphernalia that softens a house into a home.

'Laura?'

'Yes.' I drop the brochures as I get out of my car. He leaps forwards to pick them up, wiping them discreetly on his smart jeans before handing them back to me. I look up, flushed and unsettled. I don't like my clients to arrive before me; it doesn't give me time to open the house up, check it is in a viewable state, switch the lights on, and let in some fresh air.

'Edward Drover,' he says, proffering a hand.

I shake his hand and then stride ahead of him, fumbling with the locks and eventually getting the front door open. The empty house has that freshly painted smell that I find almost nauseating and an artificial brightness from the startling white walls and bare light bulbs that trigger headaches.

After walking around the soulless downstairs, Edward Drover stops and sighs. 'I'm sorry, but this house isn't doing it for me. We prefer a property with features and ideally a good view. Can we move on to the other house, the one in Pulborough?'

I am relieved. It doesn't do it for me, either.

'Yes, of course,' I say. 'I'm sure you'll love The Rectory. It is laden with period features and has amazing views across the river to the Downs.'

The viewing has been so quick I haven't even ascertained if he knows the area, so with him tailgating me in a shiny black Range Rover, I drive more slowly than normal. Built of mellow stone with a Horsham slate roof, The Rectory is my favourite house of all the ones I have shown in the past few months. It is large but not grand, with a fabulous sweeping drive and some of the best views in Sussex. It has a treasured feel about it, with owners who indulge their love of gardening and who have modernised the house with flair. As we walk into the flagstoned hallway, Edward Drover lays a hand lightly on my arm. I jump.

'Laura,' he says expectantly.

I swivel around. It is abnormal for clients not to call me Mrs Swallow and doubly unusual for them to touch me.

'You don't recognise me, do you?' His teeth are unnaturally white. Should I recognise him?

'I'm sorry, I'm having one of those days,' I mumble.

'I'm Ed Drover.'

I try to rearrange my features into ones of recognition, but I can't place this man. I reckon he is about my age but better preserved. He has a full head of greying hair and a casual but smart look about him that only the super-rich manage to fully achieve. I assume that is what designer labels achieve. I don't own any.

'Eddy from Westwood Grammar?' He peers at me and then it becomes obvious.

'Oh, my God, Eddy! I'm so embarrassed!' I put my head in my hands and turn my back on him. What a day.

'I was sure I recognised your photograph on Slate Wilders' website, which is why I asked for you to do the viewing.'

My face is burning. Eddy Drover. 'Little Eddy' as he had been known in those days, and how cruel I had been, stoking up gossip. I had known he fancied me; he asked me out enough times, and after one particularly alcohol-fuelled school disco when he had sidled up to me yet again, I had bent down and snogged him.

'What's that in your pocket?' I had asked when we both came up for air. 'Is it a pencil?'

He had blushed scarlet and had disappeared rapidly into the dancing throng. Afterwards, whenever he saw me, he had skedaddled. I had been horrible. I insinuated that Eddy was, ahem, little.

Now, at six feet, he has grown up, and I doubt there is much little about Eddy. Not his stature, not his presence or his bank balance, assuming he has the money to purchase a pricey property such as The Rectory. Thirty-odd years later, it is my turn to redden.

'Is Swallow your married name?' He politely ignores my embarrassment.

'Yes. Divorced now, though,' I say unnecessarily. 'How about you?'

He holds out his left hand, displaying a ring finger adorned with a gold wedding band.

'Married, three kids. Our youngest is ill, so Annabel had to stay at home this afternoon. We'll return for viewings together.'

'What do you do now?' I ask unimaginatively.

'I have my own IT company. Life has been good to me.'

I have no answer to that, so I lead him from room to room, searching in vain for suitable things to say.

'I love the house. I'd like to return with Annabel.'

'Great!'

'I look forward to seeing you next time.'

I smile but intend to palm off that viewing on a colleague. I don't need to meet Annabel or find out how marvellous life is for Eddy. And then my mobile rings and I am saved from an awkward goodbye.

'Take it.' He waves as he steps out of the front door.

'Laura, still on for tonight?'

It is Ben. And I have forgotten. How could I have forgotten? My date, a visit to the theatre. I hesitate.

'Do you want to take a rain check?' I can hear the disappointment in his voice.

'No, absolutely not,' I say. 'I'm looking forward to it.' And in that moment, I am. In front of me are an unexpected couple of hours to get ready. An evening out with the delectable Ben is exactly what this supposedly dead woman needs.

'By the way, did you drop off my mobile at the office?'

Silence. 'Sorry, not me. Did you lose it?'

'Yes, but it's not a problem, as I've got it back again.'

'Can't wait to see you!' he says and hangs up.

I grin. As I drive back to Horsham, my stomach is calm and I am filled with positive anticipation for the night ahead. Ben is smooth and charming. I wonder if he is this eager with all the women he dates. I promise myself I will go slowly. I have no intention of getting hurt. But at the same time, I am bemused about my mobile phone. How could it have reappeared on my desk unless someone knew it belonged to me? If someone is tech savvy, could they bypass the security code? Slate Wilders is in my phone, listed as work.

I shudder. If that is the case, someone has found out a great deal about me, potentially knows where I live, who my friends are, and perhaps has even read my emails. I must check my online banking when I get home. The last thing I can afford is for someone to wipe out the meagre sums in my bank account. I will have to mention it to Mel, tell her to be on the lookout. But then I change my mind. I don't want her worrying about me. Worrying about something that is most probably nothing.

# 4

I have agreed to meet Ben in the foyer to the theatre, twenty minutes before the performance is due to begin. This time I am wearing a dress, another wardrobe staple, navy blue and nipping in at the waist. It suits me. I wear it for smart work do's or not too smart cocktail parties (of which I think I have attended one in the past four years), teamed up with a chunky fake gold necklace that Anna gave me for my last birthday. I had admired it in the window of a boutique in town months earlier and was over the moon that she bought it for me.

The foyer is thrumming with people and I have to search to find Ben. I wonder if I have been stood up, but no, here he is, in a navy jacket and pale blue tie, leaning down to kiss me on the cheek, his spicy aftershave giving me olfactory delight.

'You look stunning,' he says.

I glance away, embarrassed.

'Let's go and find our seats, shall we? I've pre-ordered us drinks for the interval.'

Ian never pre-ordered drinks in the interval. On the rare occasions we visited the theatre, he sneaked in a bottle of water in my handbag, which we shared, or occasionally stretched to a vanilla ice cream in one of those little tubs.

The performance is a reworking of Alan Ayckbourn's play *Body Language*. If I had known that it was a farce about the swapping of a fat woman's head on a thin woman's body and vice versa, I might have chosen to go with Anna or Jenny, not on a date with Ben. Yes, it is funny and Ben roars with laughter. I am more subdued. I find it hard to shift my thoughts from the events of the day, and when I do, I just liken myself to the unattractive, fat journalist in the play because of course I am nothing like the thin glamour model.

'Are you enjoying it?' he asks me eagerly during the interval.

'Yes,' I say, but he raises an eyebrow, and I think he knows that I'm lying.

'It's amusing, but the acting isn't great,' he says. I concur because I can't think of anything meaningful to add.

During the second half, Ben leans in towards me more frequently, and I feel a welcome frisson of electricity each time his arm brushes against mine. I can't remember the last time I felt that. Probably in the early years of my relationship with Ian.

As the curtain falls and the cast of actors take their first round of bows, he whispers into my ear, 'Let's nip out now before we get caught up in the crowd.'

Ignoring the tutting and sighs of the folk on our aisle, we squeeze out and run up the steps behind us. He makes as if to grab for my hand as we emerge blinking and shivering into the night air, but then seems to think better of it and shoves his hands into his pockets.

'I've booked us dinner. Are you hungry?'

'Yes,' I say, wrapping myself in my black woollen winter coat.

I am relieved we don't have to walk far. The emotional roller coaster of the day has caught me in its web, leaving me tired and hungry. The restaurant is bijoux, just fifteen tables. Our little table for two is snugly positioned towards the back. Ben pulls out a chair for me and I sink gratefully into the plush seat. I stifle a yawn. He raises an eyebrow.

'Sorry.' I wince. 'It's been one hell of a day.'

'Let's order a drink and then you can tell me about it.'

Ben is a good listener. To begin with, the intensity of his gaze is disconcerting, but as I get into the flow of recounting the horrors of the death notice and the vanishing Facebook post, I feel a warmth and comfort from his all-encompassing attention. His eyes rarely wander off my face. I like this man. A lot.

'I've heard plenty of crazy things in my time, but nothing like that. I'm so sorry this is happening to you.' He reaches across the table and takes my hand.

'Tell me more about you,' I say.

'Not that much to tell. After my wife died, life was tough for a few years. The boys were twelve and fourteen, and it was hard being a single dad and being a consultant, working crazily long hours. My mother was amazing. Is amazing. She brought up the boys, really. Marcus is in his third year of medical school – taking after his dad, even though I tried hard to discourage him – and William, my eldest son, is trying to make it as a singer-songwriter. The boys are so different, but I couldn't be more proud of them both.'

Emboldened by a couple of glasses of wine, I ask, 'How long have you been dating?'

'Two years. I couldn't think about it until the boys left home, and I can't say I've enjoyed it. I tried internet dating, but it's not for me. It was such a relief to meet you the old-fashioned way!'

'I quite agree.' We grin at each other. It is one of those elastic moments where if we hadn't got a table laden with food in between us, the elastic would tighten and bring us together for a kiss. As it is, a waitress appears and tops up our wine, snapping the moment.

'Tell me about your work.'

'I'm a neurologist and I treat diseases of the central nervous system. Multiple sclerosis, epilepsy and the like. Sadly, it's rare I can cure my patients, but I can ease their suffering and stop symptoms, if we're lucky.'

There is a crash, a splintering of glass. Then a yelp. We both turn around. Ben leaps to his feet and comes nose to nose with a woman.

'Laura, is that you?' There is a quiver to her voice as she looks from me to the shattered wine glass on the floor and back again.

'Yes! Hello, Emily, how are you?' I smile at her. She is looking svelte in a black sleeveless dress, her arms finely toned, unlike my arms, which have to stay hidden beneath long sleeves. 'It's so lovely to see you! It's been way too long. Let me introduce you to Ben.'

'Emily's daughter, Sasha, was best friends with Mel throughout junior school,' I tell Ben.

Ben stands up again and holds out his hand, but Emily ignores him. I frown. She is normally polite, friendly. It is as if the blood has drained out of her already pale complexion. She grips the edge of our table. I wonder if she is going to faint.

'I thought you were dead.' Her hand is in front of her mouth, her eyes wide. 'I rang Sasha tonight, told her to get in contact with Mel, to send our condolences. I was going to call Ian tomorrow.'

'No, I'm not dead. Sitting here having a lovely dinner!' I try to laugh, but it sounds fake.

'Someone at the newspaper made a mistake.' Ben comes to my rescue. 'We're investigating it.'

I like the 'we' in that sentence.

'Awful,' Emily says. 'So awful. I'm just glad you're okay. I must get back to our table.' She throws us both a tight smile and hurries away, stepping haphazardly over a waiter who is sweeping up Emily's broken wine glass. Her party of six lean forwards, whispering, surreptitiously glancing towards me and then hastily looking away when I catch one of their gazes.

'Can I get you a dessert?' our waitress asks.

'You're upset,' Ben murmurs, reaching for my hand again. He turns to the waitress. 'Thank you, but just the bill.'

She nods and leaves.

'I'm going to take you home and give you a large glass of whisky.'

'I don't like whisky,' I mutter.

'Brandy, then. Come on, we're going.'

Ben takes my hand and leads me through the restaurant, avoiding Emily's table of six, even though we have to walk the long way around. I am grateful for his thoughtfulness. A taxi appears and Ben leaps out, waving his arm energetically. He opens the door for me, and I slide in, weariness making my bones ache.

'Forty-one Springfield Avenue,' Ben says.

'Actually, do you mind if we go to mine?' My nerves are frayed, and although Ben appears to be charming, authentic and everything I am looking for in a man, I have a pang of unease about going to his house.

'Of course not.' He squeezes my hand reassuringly.

We sit close together on the back seat of the taxi, knees touching. But whereas before, I felt those bolts of electricity, now I can't concentrate on Ben. All I can think about is, who wrote the post on Facebook? Who placed that death notice in the newspaper?

It is as if he is reading my mind.

'You work for an estate agency. They must have good contacts with the local paper. Perhaps you could get them to investigate who placed the obituary?'

'Yes, I'll ask Jenny tomorrow. She's my friend and a director of the firm. They'll have records, I'm sure.'

As the taxi pulls up outside my apartment building, Ben makes as if to get out. I am not in the mood.

'I'm sorry, Ben, but do you mind if we call it a day for now? I'm really tired and emotionally overwrought. I'd love to see you again though if you're up for that?'

After the words tumble out of my mouth, I mentally pinch myself. That was a very bold statement for me. Either he is going to think I'm forward, or he is going to run a mile.

He smiles and squeezes my hand. 'Yes, of course. I understand. How about brunch on Sunday if you're free?'

This man is keen. I feel fabulous and the worries evaporate briefly.

'I'd love to.'

He leans over and brushes his lips on mine. My stomach performs cartwheels.

～

THE NEWSPAPER IS LYING on the kitchen counter, where I dropped it before going out. I pick it up again and read it, even though I know the words off by heart. I pour myself a very large glass of gin and tonic and collapse onto the sofa. Shutting my eyes, I try to think, but I am brutally jolted out of my blurred reverie by my phone chiming. My breath quickens. It is 12.30 a.m., not a time of morning when I normally receive phone calls.

Mel.

I answer, my heart beating hard.

'What's the matter, love?'

She is hysterical again. It is hard to make out what she is saying.

'Have you been drinking?' I ask.

Her words become more coherent as the misery gives way to anger. 'I don't fucking drink, Mum! You know that,' she sobs. 'I haven't even been out tonight. I hate it here and I've got no friends.'

'Is that why you're calling me in the middle of the night?'

'No,' she spits. 'I got a message from Sasha. She thinks you're dead.'

'Ah, yes. I saw Emily this evening.'

'How can you be so calm!' she screeches. Not giving me time to respond, she continues, 'Did they see the Facebook post?'

'Yes, I assume so.' I don't need Mel to know about the death notice in the local Sussex newspaper. At university in Manchester, she is several hundred miles away and couldn't possibly see it.

'I checked. It's not on Facebook anymore. It's horrible. Hard-core. Why would someone do that?'

'I don't know, love. But shouldn't you be asleep?'

'For God's sake, Mum, I'm an adult. Stop telling me what to do. Going now. Bye.'

And she hangs up.

I shriek out loud and hope I haven't awakened the neighbours. At least Mrs Steel, who lives downstairs, is largely deaf. It's at times like this that I curse Ian. I need him now, to discuss how to support Mel, to calm me down, to hold me in bed so I can fall asleep feeling safe and loved. Instead I pour another gin and tonic, one I don't need and shouldn't drink, and I let the tears fall, tears of frustration but largely tears of self-pity.

## 5

I awake late, my mouth furred over, my head heavy. After taking a long shower and drinking two mugs of black coffee, I call the office and ask to speak to Jenny. It is her weekend on, mine off.

'How is my favourite corpse this morning?'

'Very funny,' I say flatly. 'Actually, that's why I'm calling. You know the team at the *Gazette*, and I was wondering if you could ask one of your contacts how I can find out who placed the death notice.'

'I'll ask the question, but I don't suppose I'll get an answer. Data protection and all of that.'

'They didn't do a very good job checking their facts, did they?' I spit.

'No, but I don't think it's a good idea to come down heavily on them. Actually we can't afford to. This business depends on us having a good relationship with the local paper. I'll give the deputy editor, Gordon Farmer, a call on Monday.'

My shoulders sink. Of course. I will have to wait until Monday. And of course, Slate Wilders is more important than me. I am annoyed with Jenny. I know her job is to look out for the business, but she could be more supportive of me, couldn't she?

AFTER COMPLETING my normal Saturday morning chores, which involve sticking a load of laundry into the washing machine and doing a quick whizz around the flat with the vacuum cleaner, I lock up and make my way to Aroma Mocha. It is a little coffee shop in a crooked timber-framed building on the cobblestoned market square in Horsham, set back from its more grandiose neighbours: on one side a large gargoyle-adorned Portland stone building housing a ubiquitous mobile phone shop, and on the other side a large house with a white plastered façade and duck egg blue window frames.

Anna and I meet for a latte and a sticky bun – or in Anna's case a skinny latte and no bun – on a Saturday, whenever I am not working. Very occasionally we meet in my lunch break. Anna never stops asking to meet at lunchtime. It's as if she can't remember that I have a full-time job. She always sounds somewhat peeved that I prioritise work over lunch with her. From time to time I wonder if she has other friends. She never mentions them.

Anna was Becky's friend. I assume we met at the occasional drinks party over the years, but I don't remember her. Our friendship blossomed after Becky's death. Living in Horsham, she was there for me at a time when most people disappeared. She lets me witter on about my memories of Becky; she helped me with the practicalities of moving into my new flat whilst I was trying to impress in my full-time job. She never seems to mind when I bad-mouth Ian or complain about work. She's one of those people who make you feel important and, for that, I love her.

She is sitting at our regular table by the window, nursing a small cup, looking beautiful as always. Her dark brown hair falls in soft waves to her shoulders, creating a startling contrast to her pale skin. I often think that Anna looks like Snow White. Once, I told her that. She roared with laughter and asked if I was the evil stepmother or one of the seven dwarves.

'Hi, sweetie.' She stands up to air-kiss me, tugging down her pale grey cashmere jumper.

Years ago, I kissed her on the cheek. Anna visibly recoiled and wiped her face with the back of her hand. Neither of us said anything, but afterwards, I followed her lead. No actual touching.

'Tell me all the gossip.' She rubs her hands eagerly, her diamond engagement ring sparkling in the low light.

'Some really weird things have been happening. I'll just grab a drink.'

I order my coffee and bun and sit down, unwinding my long woollen scarf and shrugging off my navy anorak.

'That's terrible,' she says in a hushed whisper, her eyes bright and round as I tell her about the death notice. 'Have you got a copy with you?'

I don't need a copy. Everywhere I look in town, the local paper mocks me. Previously, I never noticed the boards standing outside newsagents or discarded copies on park benches or forlorn papers on coffee shop tables. And to prove the point that they are ubiquitous, a copy of the *Gazette* lies on the chair of an empty table right behind Anna.

'Behind you.'

She leans back and swipes the paper.

'Towards the back,' I instruct as she starts to flick through the paper.

Her head is down as she reads it, her Friday morning coiffured hair in front of her face.

'Oh God,' she says, a look of horror mirroring my own

dismay, dismay that hasn't eased much. 'That's awful, Laura.' Her hand shakes a little as she lifts her cup of coffee to her lips.

Things affect Anna. She can't watch news stories of famines or natural disasters or murders. 'They give me nightmares,' she explained. A couple of years ago, she showed me a book entitled *The Highly Sensitive Person* by Elaine Aron. 'If you want to understand me, read this,' she said, waving the book in front of me. I never got around to reading it.

'Who would do such a thing?' she muses.

'I don't know, but I intend to find out.'

'How?'

'A colleague is going to contact the paper on Monday to try to discover who placed the notice. I just can't work out who hates me that much.'

She opens her mouth as if to say something and then shuts it again.

I tip my head to one side and raise my eyebrows.

'Ian?' she murmurs with a slight inflection.

I sigh. I knew she would say Ian. It's not his style. Besides, he doesn't hate me; sometimes I wonder if he still loves me, just a little bit. If he had shown some of the sensitivity and kindness to me that he wrapped me up in after Becky's death, perhaps we would still be married. Or perhaps not, because he would still have fallen in love with someone else. But most importantly, I am utterly certain that Ian would never knowingly do anything to hurt Mel.

'Maybe that's why the Facebook post was taken down so quickly. He realised Mel might see that, but he knows she'll never see the obituary, not now she's so far away in Manchester,' Anna muses.

'Unfortunately she did find out about the obituary. She rang me in pieces last night. I pretended that the person who told her about it read the Facebook post. I don't want to worry her any more than necessary. It's hard being away from home for the first time.'

'Poor girl,' Anna says. 'Other than that, how is she?'

'Struggling. I think she expected to make lifelong friends in the first week, be out partying every night, breeze through her studies and, of course, fall head over heels in love. It hasn't panned out quite like that.'

'Talking about love, have you been on another internet date? I'm rather envious of you, internet dating.'

'I did go on a date, but it wasn't via the internet. I met up with Ben Logan again.' I shuffle uneasily.

'Oh!'

The normally loquacious Anna falls silent.

'You don't mind, do you?'

'Of course not,' she says unconvincingly.

'I just wondered if it might be awkward with him being your doctor...'

'He's hardly going to share my medical secrets with you.' There is a hard edge to her voice. It has worried me that Anna might feel uncomfortable with me dating her consultant, and it appears I am right. She bites the side of her nail, and a drop of blood appears.

'Do you have any medical secrets?' I ask and immediately regret the question. Anna's epilepsy is not something to joke about. 'Anyway, I just wanted to thank you for introducing me to the delectable Dr Ben. We went to the theatre, had dinner, and then...'

Anna leans forwards. 'And then...' she repeats.

'He dropped me back home.'

'Did he come in?' she asks.

'No.'

I don't think that the brush-on-the-lips kiss is worth mentioning.

'Probably just as well nothing much happened,' Anna says, leaning back in her chair and sucking the side of her thumb.

I frown. 'Why?'

'I told you before, he's got a reputation. I wouldn't want you to get hurt.'

'I'm the queen of hurt,' I say. 'Anyway, tell me about your week.'

ANNA DOESN'T WORK, doesn't need to work because she has a handsome husband who earns a fortune working in Dubai. She travels a lot, meeting Jim in exotic places across the world. In the last couple of years their property portfolio has extended to a chalet in the Alps and a villa on the Algarve. She has shown me the photographs and the property particulars, but there is little hope I will get to see their holiday homes, as I can't even afford a flight. Anna has done very well for herself.

Anna and Jim do not have children. A long time ago, I shared my fertility problems with her, hoping that she would open up to me. But she didn't. 'We chose not to have children,' she insisted. 'I love Jim, and he's enough for me'.

From time to time, I wonder how Jim can be enough for her. They probably only see each other once a month, although perhaps that is the secret to their marital success. I have met him twice: once when he was on his way out of their beautiful house, hurrying to the airport. The second time was a chance meeting on a balmy summer's night at Friar's Hall Hotel. Mel had got herself a washing-up job there, just for three weeks in the school holidays. To her disgust, I didn't allow her to return home alone in the dark and insisted on collecting her, and so it was that I had parked up and was loitering near the entrance. I had a fine view of the guests in the dining room, and there was Anna seated at a table of eight with Jim at her side. He is an exceptionally handsome man: chiselled jaw, dark eyes, clean cut, as handsome as a catalogue model. Her hair was pinned up on top of her head, but she looked bored, staring into the distance, straight at the window, as if she could see right through me. I stepped backwards. I felt like I was prying, but I wanted to see her, my friend. And then she had stood up and collected her purse, and I watched her disappear out of the room. I had casually wandered into the reception area and downstairs into the ladies'.

'What are you doing here?' she asked as she came out of the cubicle. There wasn't an iota of warmth in her greeting.

'Collecting Mel. Are you enjoying your dinner?'

'No.'

'Is it a corporate do, for Jim's work?'

'No,' she said. 'Excuse me, I must go back.'

She had left then. It was as if she had forgotten who I was. I had asked her about the dinner when we next met, but she had shrugged away my question, saying it had been a boring fundraising dinner and changing the subject to questions about Mel.

Although Anna doesn't work for money, she does describe herself as having a job. Sort of. She does stuff for charity and organises fundraising dinners and the occasional masked ball.

## 6

Three weeks ago, on what was perchance another of my free weekends, she rang me in a panic.

'I've organised this art exhibition that's happening in Brighton tonight. Two of my assistants have dropped out at the last minute. Could you come and help? And drive me there and back?'

It was the least I could do after all the support Anna has given me. She doesn't drive. She can't, with her epilepsy. She hasn't even got a licence. Although she rarely complains, I know she hates how she has been stripped of her independence, how she has to rely on taxis and the goodwill of friends. It's not often I have to act as chauffeur; she only asks me when all other options are exhausted. She knows all too well that I don't like driving.

The art exhibition was held in a disused warehouse in an edgy part of Brighton. It was a beautiful evening. The light was low and the sea shimmered a silvery blue, while the sky was painted with streaks of pale oranges and pinks. Anna was regaling me with names of artists I had never heard of and how the auctioneer was coming down from Christie's in London especially for the evening. She reeled off names from the guest list, Lady this and Lord that, names that meant nothing to me.

'We're hoping to raise one hundred thousand pounds tonight,' she said casually.

'Goodness,' I exclaimed.

'It's going towards an MRI scanner for the hospital, particularly for use in the neurology facility.'

'A good cause,' I mused. I have never liked to ask Anna too much about her epilepsy. I have tried over the years; only once did she semi-open up to me.

'Have you had epilepsy all of your life?' I asked.

'Nope,' she said. There was a heavy silence and then she surprised me by saying, 'It was the result of an accident ten years ago.'

'What happened?'

'A car accident. Drunken driver, smashed up my car. I walked away without a scratch on my body, or so I thought. But it turns out I got brain damage.' She pulled a ridiculous face.

'You're the least brain-damaged person I know,' I said, and then wanted to take back my words, inappropriately joking about something that is never a laughing matter.

'It gave me epilepsy. I had my first fit forty-eight hours after the accident.'

'I'm so sorry.'

'It's one of the reasons Becky's death affected me that much. I got lucky.'

We were both silent, but she was looking at me, her pale blue eyes impassively taking in my face. I've never seen anyone have an epileptic fit, but I decided to Google what to do if someone has one. I needed to be the friend to Anna that she was to me.

'It's under control,' she said, and then she changed the subject.

THE WAREHOUSE WAS VAST. Brick walls extended upwards towards a ceiling of industrial steel rafters and large aluminium pipes. The pictures hung on the walls with plenty of space around them, while sculptures were dotted in the centre of the space. In between were tables clad with black cloths on which stood massive white floral arrangements. Waiters dressed in black manoeuvred between the crowds of people, proffering trays of champagne and sushi. I was responsible for selling raffle tickets, although at fifty pounds a pop, they were the most expensive raffle tickets I had ever encountered.

After an hour or so, my bag was bulging with cash. The artworks were, in my opinion, ghastly. Most of the paintings were massive, larger than a whole living room wall in the average middle-England house, featuring large splodges of colour, or in some cases no colour at all. Having sold all the raffle tickets, I was excused my duties and was nursing a glass of champagne, standing in front of the only painting that featured people. The crudely depicted woman was wearing a lacy emerald dress and sported scarlet lips so engorged, they looked as if they were going to burst open. She was sitting on the shoulders of a man who stood naked, his penis massive and erect, so big it almost reached his chin. It was a grotesque painting, and as I stood staring at it, I couldn't contain my giggles. I looked around me to see if anyone had noticed, and unfortunately someone had.

'You don't like it, do you?' he asked in a whisper.

'No!' I replied. 'I've never seen anything quite so dreadful. Not close-up, anyway.'

'I'm very disappointed because I'm the artist.'

'I'm so terribly sorry,' I stuttered as I stepped backwards. 'I know nothing about art...' I could feel my face turning puce.

'Only joking!' the stranger said.

'That was horrible of you!'

'I know.' He looked ashamed. He removed his trendy glasses, and I noticed his startling almost amber-coloured eyes. 'I don't know what came over me. I'm truly sorry, and for the record I think all the artwork here is hideous. Will you forgive me and let me get you a top-up of champagne?'

I put my hand over my glass. 'It's kind of you, but I'm driving so sticking to this.'

'I'm Ben and very embarrassed!' He put his hand out and I shook it. He had long fingers and clean-cut nails.

I introduced myself and then we fell silent for a few long moments before both speaking at the same time. Gradually, we felt our way through some awkward pauses, and then the conversation began to flow, and we shared our ignorance of art and our love of theatre and music. He asked me if I was attending with a partner, and I said I was with a girlfriend and then had to explain that she was a friend and not a lover and that I was single and heterosexual, and he said, so am I. We both burst out laughing. We were interrupted when someone tapped the side of a microphone and announced that the auction was about to begin.

'I've got to be at the front now,' Ben said. 'Have you got a business card? I'd like to see you again, if I may?'

And I could have said no, but I didn't. I fumbled in my purse and found a card and handed it to him, and then he disappeared into the throng, and I stood there wondering what had just happened and who he was.

When there were loud cheers and the auction was all over and the crowd had started to thin out, I went to look for Anna. She was standing by a hefty alabaster statue, seven feet tall, and I could see her talking to someone. Her forehead was furrowed and her hands made rapid circular motions; she then ran them through her hair. When I was a couple of feet away, I could see her eyes were wet and she was blinking rapidly. I stepped forwards.

'Are you all right?' I asked.

And then I realised she was talking to Ben.

'I'm fine, thanks. It's these damned lilies. I'm so allergic to them.'

I frowned. I hadn't realised Anna suffered from allergies. I was sure I had seen lilies in her house over the years.

Ben stepped backwards as Anna pulled me towards her.

'Meet Dr Ben Logan, he's the best neurologist in the country. Dr Logan, this is my best friend, Laura Swallow.'

'We've already met,' I said, grinning, happy to be officially introduced to Dr Ben Logan and equally chuffed, although perhaps a little surprised, to be called Anna's best friend. Ben's nod towards me wasn't as enthusiastic as I expected. I won't be hearing from him again, I thought disappointedly. And then I realised: he probably can't socialise with someone close to a patient. There must be a code of ethics about something like that. That was an explanation, but it didn't dispel the regret. I liked this man. It was the first time since the divorce that I had felt a real connection. I sighed. Goodbye, Dr Ben Logan.

He turned to Anna. 'Thank you, Mrs Moretti, for your incredible fundraising. The new scanner will make such a big difference to our department. It was a pleasure to meet you, Mrs Swallow, but please excuse me. I have an early clinic tomorrow morning.'

I watched him as he strode away, and then I flung my arm across Anna's shoulders. 'You never told me you had such a hunky doctor.' I laughed. Anna wobbled slightly on her vertiginous heels.

'I haven't heard the word *hunky* in about thirty years,' she said. 'Come on, let's go.'

When we were back in my car and I was edging us through

the vibrant Saturday night throngs flooding Brighton's streets, I asked, 'What's he like, your doctor?'

She was silent for a moment. I wondered if she had heard the question, but then she asked, 'Why?'

'I had a really nice chat with him and he took my card.'

'Is he looking to move house?' Her voice was edged with surprise.

I glanced over. Anna was staring out of the side window, and in the darkness, I couldn't see her face.

'He's a good doctor,' she said, 'but I don't know about his personal life. I've heard rumours that he's worked his way through the nursing staff and he's married. I considered changing consultants when I found out about that but eventually decided not to. He has helped me get my epilepsy under control, and I just can't take the risk of moving to another doctor.'

'Oh,' I said. My shoulders slumped with dejection.

'It was a great night though, wasn't it?' Anna's voice moved up a few tones. 'The artworks were fabulous, don't you think?'

'You did an extraordinary job, raising all of that money!'

'It's not just me,' she said modestly.

We fell silent for a while. I put my foot on the accelerator as we drove north onto the dual carriageway. Out of the corner of my eye I could see Anna's knuckles shining white as she grasped the edge of her seat, her left foot jumping up and down. It did nothing to help me relax. A nervous driver and a nervous passenger didn't make for a relaxing journey. I could feel a nerve twanging in my jaw and a painful tightness across the back of my neck. I was about to switch on the radio, tune into some calming music, when Anna spoke.

'I'm going to ask Jim to buy one of the paintings,' she said. 'The one of the woman and the man with the massive dick.'

'Are you serious?'

'Of course! It will look stunning in our bedroom.'

We didn't talk after that. I hoped I would never have reason to go into Anna's bedroom.

BACK IN THE COFFEE SHOP, I have finished my latte and bun and am debating whether to buy another. Anna's week has been uneventful, and I zone out for a while as she tells me about her new manicurist and a ketogenic recipe that she is excited about trying. Despite Anna's description of me as her best friend, I wonder if a chasm is opening up between us. Her interests, her worries, seem increasingly materialistic and shallow. I catch myself in my judging mode: 'you're jealous' says the little voice in my head. Perhaps I am a bit. Anna has so little to worry about. She can buy whatever takes her fancy; she only has herself and Jim to think about. Although we were never flush with cash, I never worried about money when I was married to Ian. But now my clothes come from charity shops and every penny is budgeted for. Then I remind myself. Money cannot buy good health, and Anna suffers from more than one serious medical condition.

She leans forwards, making the table wobble and jolting me out of my reverie. 'Are you still on that dating website?'

'Um, no.'

'You should go back on it.'

'Why?'

'I really don't want you to get hurt. I don't think you should see Ben again.'

I do not tell her that I am meeting him for brunch tomorrow.

## 7

I t is 10.30 a.m. on Sunday morning and I am half dressed. The telephone rings. My paltry selection of jumpers and shirts are piled on top of the bed as I try on everything I own in a vain attempt to try to achieve the Parisian chic, laid-back Sunday morning look that I aspire to. As I don't possess a striped Breton jumper or a crisp white cotton shirt or a selection of silk scarves, I know I am doomed to fail. My pale blue go-to jumper that is starting to bobble up from over-wearing is the only top I haven't yet tried on. Inevitably, it will be the jumper I will wear. A disappointment. Standing in my bra and jeans, I fumble around trying to find the phone underneath the pile of clothes, my heart sinking. I suppose it is Ben ringing to cancel.

But it isn't. It is Ian.

'Is everything ok?' I ask, slightly out of breath.

'Mel's upset.'

'Yes, I know. She hasn't settled at uni and my death notice just made things worse.'

'She mentioned something about that, but none of it is important.' Typical Ian, I think, brushing away other people's woes. 'I told her I was having a baby. Well, not me obviously. Charlene, she's having a baby. We're having a baby.'

'What!' I screech. 'You're going to be a father again, at your age! For God's sake, Ian, that's disgusting.'

'Not the correct reaction, Laura. Congratulations are in order.'

I sit down on top of my pile of clothes and take a deep breath. 'I'm sorry, Ian. Can we please start again? Congratulations to you and...'

I can't remember her name. But I do remember the conversation I had with Mel a few months ago.

'You should start dating,' she had said.

'Why?'

'Dad's going out with someone who works at the doctor's surgery.'

'Is she a doctor?' I asked, instantly feeling threatened.

'Nah. Receptionist, admin or something. I haven't met her.' Mel had rolled her eyes and changed the conversation.

'Charlene. She's called Charlene. And we're getting married. We want Mel to be chief bridesmaid, but she went apoplectic on the phone.'

This news shouldn't shock me, but it does. Ian left me for another woman, and by all accounts, he's had a series of girl-friends in the intervening years. It was an inevitability that he would settle down with someone sooner rather than later, as it was evident he struggled being alone. But there is a tactful way of sharing emotional news and this is not it. It makes my blood boil.

'Is it really surprising, Ian? You're her dad. You ring her when she's feeling low anyway and spring on her the fact that she'll be getting a stepmother and a sibling. She's been an only child for eighteen years. Once again, you have been selfish in the extreme. The very least you could have done was tell her face-to-face.' And you could have warned me in advance, I think to myself.

'Fuck off, Laura. You are so bloody sanctimonious. You could try to be happy for me, just for once.'

'And what about me? You dumped me for another woman. We couldn't have more children, because of me, and now you're ringing up gloating about your virile sperm. How do you think this makes me feel?'

'As always, you twist everything to be about you. Goodbye, Laura.'

He hangs up.

I sit on the bed, shaking. Perhaps I was a bit out of order, quite a lot out of order, but this is the man I was married to for fifteen years. This is my daughter's father. And he has just rung up casually to announce he is getting married and is having another child. How am I meant to feel? How must Mel feel? My poor baby. A shiver ripples through me, and hastily, I shrug on my pale blue jumper. I take a deep breath and call Mel. Surprisingly, she answers immediately.

'Hello.' Her voice is small.

'Darling, I've just heard Dad's news. I'm so sorry.'

She sniffs.

'Has it come as a terrible shock?'

'Not really. Charlene is okay, I suppose.'

'I thought you hadn't met her?' I am taken aback.

'Yes, a couple of times in the summer. They were revoltingly lovey-dovey. She's half Dad's age and was trying pathetically hard to be my friend. I didn't tell you because... I didn't tell you because I didn't want to hurt you. Sorry, Mum.'

'You've got nothing to apologise for, darling. How do you feel about having a baby sister or brother?'

'A half sibling,' she retorts. 'Mum, that's not why I'm upset. Well, a bit about that, but mainly it's...' She pauses as if she is summoning up the courage to say something dramatic. 'That Facebook thing saying you're dead, it's up there again. Someone called Joel Smith posted it. Have you got a friend called Joel Smith?'

'No,' I say. 'The name means nothing.'

'Go onto your page and you'll see it. It's horrid and...' She starts crying again.

'My sweetheart, it's all too much, isn't it? Do you want to come home?'

She snivels. 'No. I'm in the netball team and we've got a match this afternoon. And I've got lectures tomorrow and a tutorial on Tuesday.'

'That's great you're in the netball team!' I say, relief coursing through me that Mel is engaging with university life.

'Not *the* netball team,' she corrects me. 'It's the sixth team, the worst players in uni. But at least I'm in it.'

'I'm proud of you,' I say.

'Can you get that Facebook post taken down?' she asks.

'I'll investigate,' I promise. 'But don't worry about it; things will be fine.'

I hear some giggling in the background. 'I've got to go now!' And Mel hangs up. As is so often the way with her, her mood morphs into ebullience just moments after being sombre.

Without a laptop, I struggle onto Facebook on my phone. I scroll from here to there, but I can't find the post or any reference to Joel Smith. What I do discover is a friend request from Edward Drover. I hesitate. Should I accept it? Do I want him to know about me, and equally, do I want to know about him? How I loathe social media. It seems to be the source of so much misery and angst. I am still sitting on my pile of clothes, my face unmade, my finger hovering over the accept button when the doorbell rings. I jump up and, in doing so, click accept. Decision made. I look at the clock and swear. It will be Ben and I am not ready.

'Can you give me five minutes?' I speak through the intercom.

'Um... it's pouring rain. Any chance you could let me in?'

'Oh, sorry,' I say, pressing the button to open the front door. I unlatch my flat door and rush back into the bedroom to shrug on my pale blue jumper, then dash into the bathroom, hastily rubbing foundation across my uneven complexion and attempting to put on mascara with a shaking hand.

'Hello?'

'Come in!' I yell, trying to recall if I have cleared away my breakfast things.

After running a comb through my hair, swiping lipstick across my lips and dousing myself with perfume, I stride into the living room, and there is Ben holding a Waitrose bag in one hand and a large bunch of flowers in the other.

'Oh!' I say, a little disappointed by the sight of the Waitrose bag.

'It's a miserable day out there, so I thought I'd make brunch for you here. Is that too presumptuous of me?' He removes a bottle of champagne and holds it aloft. 'If it's not convenient, we can still go out, or I can cook at mine.'

I stumble for words. 'The kitchen is a mess; I would have cleared it up. I'm...'

He leans forwards and gives me a peck on the cheek. The scent of his aftershave is intoxicating; I have a good nose, overly sensitive, Ian used to say, and I detect a mixture of musk, pomegranate, pepper and lemon wafting from Ben's neck.

I inhale again.

'Show me where to go.' He grins and my mood lifts.

My kitchen is postage-stamp small, alternately described as bijou or cosy in my new estate agent lingo, and certainly not large enough for two people to cook in. It is awkward, showing him what is where, trying to help him put the food into the fridge. We brush up against each other a couple of times. It is electric and very disconcerting. As I step out of the kitchen, he grabs my arm. I resist slightly.

'Is everything all right, Laura?' he asks, his amber eyes burning.

'Yes.'

'In which case, may I?' He pulls me towards him and kisses me. Hard.

'Go and put your feet up,' he instructs as he releases me, breathless and overwhelmed. 'I'm going to make us scrambled eggs with smoked salmon and lashings of guacamole on toast.'

'Sounds delicious,' I say as I settle on my cream sofa, tucking my feet up under me.

'But first, you need champagne.' I hear the cork pop and then he appears with a full glass.

'Tell me how the past two days have been.' He disappears back inside the kitchen. Although I can't see him, at just a few paces away, I can hear him, and so I tell him all about Mel and Ian and the reappearance of the Facebook post.

'I've got my iPad with me, so we can have a scout around after brunch.'

But we never do.

Because after brunch, which is prepared with great panache and is far tastier than anything I could have made, we polish off the bottle of champagne and then somehow we end up in a tangle of limbs on the sofa, and then he asks where my bedroom is, and the pile of clothes on my bed becomes a pile of clothes on the floor.

And then I burst into snivelling tears.

I can't do it.

It is precisely five years and eight months since I last had full-blown sex, and as much as I want to, I can't. Despite my pulling the curtains, it is daylight outside, and in the pale grey light, my roll of stomach flab and meagre but sagging breasts are on full display. I know my face is still attractive, my eyes bright and my hair luxuriant, but my body disappoints me. I look at Dr Ben Logan, the curling dark hair on his chest, his well-toned limbs, and every self-doubt I have ever had pours like an overflowing jug of wine into my head.

'I'm so sorry,' I whisper, the sheets pulled high over my chest, my tear-stained face in my hands. 'It's too soon.'

Ben pulls me towards him and wraps his arms around me. He kisses my cheek and whispers into my neck, 'I'll wait.'

'I sound like a virginal teenager not a fifty-year-old mother,' I hiccup.

'It is only our fourth date.' He strokes my leg. 'It's fine. Tell me more about you.' He leans back in the bed, one arm under his head, the other flung across my untoned stomach.

'What would you like to know?'

'Your heartfelt wishes and your greatest fears.'

'Nothing too deep, then,' I say sarcastically.

I hope he will laugh, but he doesn't. 'I'm serious. I want to know about you,' he says, poking my flab. I edge away slightly and pull in my stomach.

I sigh. 'I want my daughter to be happy and fulfilled. I'd like to go to the Maldives. I'd like to have my own business, perhaps as a relocation agent so I can travel all over the world. I guess I'd like to win the lottery too.' I pause. I'd like to be in a long-term, secure relationship as well, but I have no intention of articulating that. 'What about you?'

'Similar to you, I suppose. I want the boys to be settled. I love my work, so nothing to change there. And I want to share my life with someone and take them to the Maldives.'

We are both silent for a while. I feel awkward with this intimacy. I move, as if to get up to go to the bathroom, but he tugs me back.

'Don't go. Tell me about your fears.'

I am uncomfortable now. I lie there, rigid. Ben must sense it, because he carries on talking.

'Okay, I'll go first. I am terrified of dying before my sons have truly flown the nest. I want them to be happy in relationships, be sure in their careers. They've lost their mum; they can't lose their dad.'

'Tell me about your wife,' I say, relaxing back into the soft mattress. I take his hand under the sheets.

'Sadie and I met at medical school. She was the love of my life. Perhaps I shouldn't be saying that?' He turns to me, his breath warm on my neck, and strokes my hair.

'Of course you must say that,' I reassure him.

'She was vivacious, a great mum, totally chaotic to live with but an amazing doctor. She specialised in paediatrics. Life was always fun, if not slightly manic, with Sadie. It was January and she'd received a call to say one of her little patients was deteriorating fast. Sadie being Sadie, she jumped in her car and raced to the hospital. She didn't make it. The car spun on some ice and that was that.'

'Oh God,' I whisper. 'I'm so sorry.' I let go of his hand. I can feel myself trembling. I shut my eyes and take a deep breath. 'My sister died in a car accident. Well, not exactly a car accident: she was run over.'

I don't mention Anna's car accident, but I'm thinking about it too. How likely is it that the three of us have all suffered such tragedies? Do tragedies subconsciously bring people together? Or perhaps they're not that uncommon and it's just a matter of averages. Statistics were never my strong point, and those statistics seem too macabre to investigate.

It is Ben's turn to be still and then, abruptly, he sits up in bed. 'You suffered the same heartbreak. Maybe that's why we feel this connection.'

Do we? I think. I don't say anything. My connection to Ben is physical, isn't it? At least I thought it was until I chickened out. I like him, but do I want to be connected to him because of tragedy?

'What happened?' he asks.

I can feel my lower lip quivering and know that if I speak, the tears will come.

'It's fine,' he says. 'You don't need to tell me now.' He slides back under the duvet and holds me in his arms tightly. Eventually, my limbs soften and I relax, feeling secure for the first time in years and years. Perhaps he's right about this connection. After several long minutes, his breathing becomes deeper and slower, and I turn my head to look at him. His eyes are closed. I look at this stranger in my bed, with his long eyelashes and cleft chin, and wonder why he has chosen me. I am a slightly damaged, slightly overweight woman with a broad smile and high cheekbones who likes to drink too much. When I am sure that he is fast asleep, I slip out of his arms and go to the bathroom.

When I emerge from a long shower, Ben is sitting up in bed, reading the back cover of *The Other Woman's House* by Sophie Hannah.

'You're dressed?' His expression is one of disappointment.

'Can we carry on another time?' I ask.

'Of course.' He smiles ruefully.

Ben leaves soon after. I can't work out if I am happy, lonely, confused or exhausted, and eventually decide I am a mixture of all these emotions. Thank goodness for Netflix. I spend the rest of the evening watching rubbish television.

## 8

It is Monday mid-morning and I am exhausted. The emotional upheavals of the past few days have wrung me out: the downs of the Facebook post and death notice, Ian and his announcements along with the distress everything has caused Mel, as well as the highs, namely Dr Ben Logan. His amber eyes stare back at me when I look at my computer screen, my phone, and when I gaze out of the window; I feel his light touch on my skin. I know I am behaving like a love-struck teenage girl, but I just can't stop thinking about him. And then physically, I am knackered. I am not used to going out, drinking lots of alcohol; well, perhaps the latter statement isn't strictly true, nevertheless...

When Jenny sidles up to my desk, I find it difficult to focus on her. 'Two things to tell you,' Jenny says. 'Firstly, an Edward Drover wants you to do a viewing of the house you showed him on Friday. Four p.m. this afternoon.'

'Can someone else do it?' It is the last thing I feel like.

'We're really short-staffed today, Laura.'

'Ok.' I swallow a sigh.

'Secondly, I'm afraid my contact at the *Gazette* isn't able to help. He said the notice was sent in the post along with cash for payment. He remembered it because it's been ages since anyone has paid by cash or even sent something by post. Normally it's all done online.'

'Haven't the guys at the *Gazette* abrogated their responsibility by not checking the death notice's validity?' I frown.

'It's a moot point. You probably know better than me the difference between a death notice and an obituary. I think the local rag is just eager to get whatever income it can. I don't suppose they've got the resources to check out every notice or advert that comes their way.'

'So there's nothing they can do to help me track down who wrote it?'

She shakes her head.

'He suggested going to the police, but I'm not sure what crime you'd be reporting.'

I sigh. 'Apparently it's been posted again on Facebook. I haven't had the chance to look.'

'Bloody hell,' she says, smoothing down her grey skirt. She glances around to make sure that no one is listening. 'What I really want to know is, how was the date?'

'Fabulous. We spent most of yesterday together too.'

She raises her eyebrows.

'How was yours?'

'Disaster as always. His profile picture was taken at least thirty years ago, assuming it was his photo. He looks like he's at least fourteen months pregnant, but I could cope with that. What I couldn't cope with was the monologue about his ex-wife. He is obsessed with her. It was Mary this and Mary that and "my bitch of an ex". I asked how long ago he got divorced. Twenty-two years! Twenty-two bloody years ago! I excused myself after the main course and was home in time to watch *The X Factor*.'

'I'm sorry,' I commiserate.

'Don't be. I'm more worried about what's going on with you. Want a drink this week? I can do Tuesday or Wednesday.'

We agree on Wednesday and she disappears downstairs.

On the dot of 1 p.m., just as I am about to take a bite out of my sandwich and start browsing Facebook, my mobile rings. It is Anna.

'I just heard the news,' she says melodramatically.

'What news?'

'Ian and that floozy, Charlene.'

'You know her?' I am surprised.

'I've seen her around. She works at the surgery and goes to the Club.' She means the exclusive health club and spa she visits most days, where they charge an obscene annual membership fee for the privilege of exclusivity.

'How do you know who she is?'

'She's been on Ian's arm a few times, so I checked her out.'

'You didn't tell me,' I snap.

'I was trying to protect you.'

What is it with everyone trying to protect me?

'Are you okay?'

'Yes. Thanks.' I soften.

'Any progress on tracking down who placed the obituary?'

'No. I gather the Facebook post is up again though.'

'Oh no! What are you going to do about it? It's horrid, Laura.'

I sigh. 'I don't know. Besides, I can't do much because my laptop is still being repaired.'

'I can bring mine around this evening if you like. Jim is away.'

Jim is always away, I think. I wonder whether Jim plays away when he's away. I've asked Anna a couple of times whether she misses him, but she turned her lower lip down and said, 'A little, I suppose.' I felt she was giving the answer she expected others wanted to hear as opposed to the truthful answer. The thing with Anna is, she can be unexpectedly prickly, so on personal issues such as the state of her marriage, I never push too hard.

As much as I enjoy Anna's company, tonight, I would prefer to be alone. The only thing I feel like is snuggling up in bed, watching some trashy TV and having an early night. 'That's sweet of you, but I'm really tired...'

'I won't accept no for an answer.'

IT IS GETTING dark by the time I pull up at The Rectory. The nights have drawn in so quickly. It is my least favourite time of year, not just because of the shortening days and worsening weather, but because everything bad that has happened in my life has taken place in those few weeks in the run-up to Christmas. It was when Becky and our mum died, three years apart, when my last IVF failed, and when Ian announced he was leaving me.

The statistics suggest that most marriages fail over Christmas, that divorce lawyers are the busiest in January. But Ian landed his bombshell during the Christmas party season. If he hadn't wanted me to accompany him to his Christmas do, he could have come up with some excuse. But as it turns out, Ian is only good at lying when he isn't directly challenged. So one Tuesday evening, after a silent supper, when Mel was upstairs doing her homework, he stuttered out the words he had obviously been practising.

'I'm sorry, Laura, but I'm leaving you. I've fallen in love with someone else.'

I thought he was joking at first, but then I noticed his deathly pallor and his shaking hands. There was nothing funny about it. And it was even less funny when he announced that he didn't want me to tell anyone until after Christmas, as it wouldn't be fair to Mel or his parents to ruin the whole family's Christmas. More fool me, I went along with his suggestion. I thought that it would buy us some breathing space during which I could attempt to change his mind, make him fall back in love with me. It didn't work because there is nothing less attractive than a desperate partner. I know that now. I also know that I will never, ever be so submissive again. I learned a great deal about myself during that miserable time.

As I climb out of my car, external lights flood the drive. Eddy's black Range Rover is already there. He isn't in it. I walk to the front door and open it, swiping a fob over the alarm panel on the wall. I do my usual: quickly walking around the house, switching on lights, checking that it is in a viewable state, all the time listening for the doorbell. Eventually I walk back to the front door and poke my head out.

'Hello, Laura!'

I jump out of my skin. He is standing right in front of me, dressed in a pinstriped suit, with a red tie at his neck. How has he appeared from nowhere like that?

'You gave me a fright!'

'I'm sorry.' He leans forwards and gives me a kiss on the cheek. I stumble backwards in shock, but he reaches for my arm and steadies me. He walks past me then, into the house, and stands in the hall, gazing upwards at the old wooden staircase.

'It's beautiful, isn't it?' he murmurs.

I wait for someone else to step inside, but it seems that he is alone. I try to regain some composure. Shutting the door, I ask, 'Isn't Annabel with you?'

'What? Oh no. She's working today. I thought I'd have another look myself.'

I feel a deep unease. That kiss, banal in itself, was nevertheless completely inappropriate. Perhaps that is what has caused the little hairs on my arms to stand up on end. It isn't the first time I have felt uncomfortable on a viewing; it's an inevitability of the job, being alone with strangers in a third party's house. But something doesn't feel quite right. As Eddy is wandering ahead of me into the living room, I take my phone out of my bag and slip it into my jacket pocket.

'The fireplace, it's stunning. I assume it works?'

'Yes, it does.'

'Who owns this place?' He glides over to the grand piano and picks up a silver-framed photo. Happy families. Lots of smiling faces of blond, cherubic children.

'An older couple whose children have grown up now. I believe the photos are of their grandchildren. The owners are looking to downsize.'

He turns to me, a grin on his face. 'Relax, Laura. You seem uptight this afternoon.'

I step backwards and trip on the edge of an antique Chinese rug, steadying myself by gripping a worn, rose-patterned armchair. 'I wasn't uptight until you said that.' My laugh sounds forced.

He raises his eyebrows. 'I can't tell you how happy I am to see you today. I read the obituary someone wrote about you on Facebook along with your daughter's post stating that you are alive and well. Must be very unpleasant for you.'

'Yes.'

So he is stalking me, virtually at least. What does he want from me? Does he still like me, as he did forty years ago? It seems unlikely. Not only is he married, but he is in considerably better shape than me. On the other hand, it is possible, I suppose. It takes me back to my twenties when, as a trainee journalist, my love interests were either famine or feast. Months would go by when no one would show any interest, and then suddenly, along came two or three at once. Perhaps I give off extra pheromones when I am in a relationship with someone. Maybe that is happening now. I wish Ben were with me; strong, handsome, charming Dr Logan. Ben, with whom I have a connection.

I change the subject.

'Have you sold your current house?' I ask.

'No. We're putting it on the market shortly. Can I look upstairs again?'

'Of course.'

I follow him up the stairs and into the master bedroom. The curtains are pulled and the bed neatly made up. I hover near the door as he wanders around, opening the built-in wardrobe doors, peering into the en-suite bathroom. He swivels quickly and takes a few long strides towards me, his eyes fixed on my face.

'I think you are remarkable,' he says, his long face serious. 'And I can't believe you haven't made any noticeable contributions.'

A chill passes through me. Not only has he read the false death notice, he has learned the words. He reaches for my hand and pulls me forwards. I resist, but he is stronger than me. Much stronger.

'I want to kiss you, Laura. I've never forgotten you. I've always been hopeful, and now fate has brought us together again.'

'No!'

I twist my hand from his grasp, fear coursing through me. Is he going to rape me, here in this beautifully decorated bedroom with its antique rose curtains and matching bedspread? He is a married man with three children, with a wife called Annabel. He is respectable with his own business and he drives a large fancy car. I always told Mel that wealth and status mean nothing, absolutely nothing. But did I really believe that? For sure, I do now. What is happening? He steps forwards again and I bolt down the corridor.

'Oh, Laura, I would never hurt you!' he says, sadness streaking through his words.

I look at him over my shoulder and there is disappointment written all over his face.

'Laura, I'm so sorry.' He puts his hands together as if in prayer.

'I thought you were happily married. To Annabel,' I spit.

'I am married, but not happily. I don't know why I said that last time. We're splitting up, which is why I'm looking for a new house.'

'That was totally inappropriate behaviour.'

'Yes, it was. Please forgive me.' He looks down at his shiny brogues. His shoulders sink and I can see the diminutive boy in him all over again.

'I would like you to leave now,' I say, gripping the stair rail tightly.

'Of course,' he replies. He slips past me, down the stairs, and doesn't look back. The front door snaps shut quietly behind him. I stand at the top of the stairs for a few more minutes, waiting until I hear the roar of his car, the crunching of tyres on the gravel and the sound of his engine disappearing down the drive. And then I burst into tears.

## 9

The relief of being home, snug and secure in my own little space, is overwhelming. I pour myself a very large glass of red wine and collapse on the sofa. Then I pick up my fluffy cushion, burrowing my nose in it, sniffing hard to seek out any residue of scent left by Ben. There is none. I switch on the news and then turn it back off again. Too depressing. And then the doorbell rings. I jump, adrenaline coursing through me. But I can't move. The doorbell rings again. I remind myself of the beauty of apartment living. Thanks to my video intercom, I can see who is at the door, but they can't see me. Carefully, I place my glass on my driftwood side table and pad over to the little screen attached to the wall. Am I fearful that Eddy has tracked me down? Or worried that Ian is coming after me? Or hopeful that Ben has appeared for an improved repeat of yesterday? I breathe out a sigh of relief. It is Anna.

She arrives in my flat in a whirlwind of chatter and bags, flinging off her red coat, stepping out of her high heels, depositing her MacBook on the table, and slipping into the kitchen with two Harrods carrier bags.

'I've brought us supper and wine,' she says. 'I see you've already started. Pour me a glass, will you?' she instructs. Two meals provided by someone else on two consecutive days is a first for me. I smile.

'From Harrods?' I joke.

'If only Harrods had an outpost in Horsham, I wouldn't be considering moving back to London.'

'Are you?' I ask, surprised.

'I would go in a jiffy, but Jim doesn't want to. He likes living in the semi-countryside. What he forgets is how difficult it is for me, not being able to drive. In London I would just get Ubers everywhere or walk. I can but dream!'

'I would miss you,' I say.

'If I moved to London, I'd buy a house with an annex where you could live. You'd like that, wouldn't you?'

I am glad she has her back to me. It is such a strange comment, and I'm sure my surprise must show on my face. I follow her into the kitchen. Somehow there seems to be more space in my little kitchen when Anna is in there. Of course she is much smaller than Ben, but it is more than that. It must be the easy familiarity that we have acquired so rapidly in our relatively new friendship.

'You're looking pale.' She peers at me, pursing her crimson lips.

'I've had a hell of a few days and a shitty afternoon.'

'What happened?' She takes a large swig of wine from the glass I have handed her.

'A bloke I knew at school tried to kiss me during a house visit.'

'Bloody hell!' she screeches. She shakes with laughter until she sees my not-amused expression. 'Are you all right?'

'Yes. He didn't do anything else and he left when I told him to, but it shook me.'

'I'm not surprised! My poor little Laura.' She moves as if she is going to hug me, but she just taps me on the arm, as if she were patting a mongrel dog. 'What's he called?'

'Eddy Drover.'

She frowns and bites the side of her lip.

'Do you know him?'

'No. No, the name doesn't ring any bells.'

'He has his own IT company in town,' I add.

'Nope, I don't know him. Are you going to report him to the police?' Anna asks.

'For trying to snog me? No. Besides, we're probably quits now. I was horrid to him at school.'

'I suppose you're not used to having men chase you,' Anna mumbles, seemingly more to herself than for my benefit.

I raise my eyes, but she has her back to me.

'Perhaps you gave off the wrong signals. You are rather out of practice. Men respond in two ways to desperation: running a mile in the opposite direction or taking advantage of you. They're just animals, really.'

'Wow, Anna. That's a pretty stinging statement towards me and a very misogynistic viewpoint.'

'Sorry. But you are out of practice. Your hair needs to be sorted by a good colourist, and I've been desperate to take you out shopping for a new wardrobe for ages.'

'I can't afford it,' I say wanly, returning to the living room.

'It's all a matter of priorities,' she says. It isn't the first time Anna has riled me, but after my tumultuous few days, I am annoyed.

'Ben Logan doesn't seem to mind about my lousy hair colour or my ancient clothes.'

A crash comes from the kitchen and then silence.

'What?' she asks eventually.

'I slept with him,' I say. I wonder why I have lied. Well, I sort of slept with him. We made out even if we didn't have full-blown sex.

For a moment I wonder if she has heard me, but of course she has. She starts making a lot of noise in the kitchen, opening and closing cupboards, clattering crockery on the counter, boiling the kettle. I sigh. Anna is having a little hissy fit. I have experienced this before and reckon it is best to let her work through it in silence. I switch the television back on. But I can't concentrate, and after about five minutes, I get up. Leaning against the doorframe, I am conciliatory.

'You're annoyed I'm going out with your doctor.'

'Yes.' She doesn't turn around.

'I'm sorry, but I like him, and I don't see how it's going to compromise your doctor-patient relationship. He would never talk about his patients.'

'No.'

'We will never discuss you. Ever.'

She still keeps her back to me, so I return to the sofa and collapse into it, sighing dramatically.

'I just don't want you to get hurt,' Anna says from the kitchen. Her voice is taut.

'I'm a big girl, Anna. I appreciate your concern, really I do. And I promise I won't come running to you if I do get hurt.'

She appears then, her cheeks rosy, her hands wringing a tea towel. 'Oh, darling! Absolutely you must come to me when you get hurt. I wouldn't want it any other way. I'm just trying to protect you, that's all.'

'Fair enough. But I don't intend to get hurt.'

'Of course not. Now come and get your food, and then let's have a nosey around Facebook and see if we can find that bastard Joel whatever he's called.'

ANNA'S FINGERNAILS tap away at the keyboard rapidly. She tuts and huffs and taps some more.

'I can't see the post at all when I'm logged in as me. There are a few Joel Smiths around here, but I'm not sure any are likely to be your culprit. They're mainly too young or live miles away.' She tips her head back to finish off the dregs of wine at the bottom of her glass. 'It would be good if I could log in as you or as Mel. Do you have her login details?'

'Good heavens, no!' I laugh. 'She defriended me until last week. But I'll see if I can remember my details.'

'Unfriended me, actually,' Anna mutters. She gets up from the chair and I take her seat. Unfortunately, I log in automatically from my old laptop, so, after three failed attempts at remembering my password, it times out.

'You're such a luddite!' Anna huffs. 'Here, let me help you reset it.' She leans over my shoulder to reach the keyboard, and I get a strong inhalation of her rosemary-scented hair.

My mobile phone pings.

'That will be the pin to reset your password,' she says.

In the end I shift off the chair, hand over my mobile, and she takes over again.

'What password are you likely to remember?' She dismisses my suggestions. 'They're all too obvious. Let's go for Ian Bastard spelled like this: !an8a5tard. Can you remember that?'

'Write it down for me, please.' She scribbles it on the back of a torn envelope. But I reckon I can remember it. Clever Anna.

And then we are logged in. As me. Anna spends some time reading through things, scrolling all around. I refill her glass of wine. I am on my third.

'I can't see anything,' Anna says. 'There's no obituary post and you aren't friends with anyone called Joel Smith.' She leans back in her chair, her bare feet pushing up against the wall. Her toenails are painted navy blue.

'Did you see the post?' she asks.

'No.' I get up and pace around the living room.

'Is it only Mel who has seen it?' she asks.

'Yes.' I pause a moment. 'And Edward Drover. The creep who tried to kiss me today.'

'Not the most reliable of witnesses, then,' Anna says.

'But Mel is reliable,' I say.

'Really?' Anna sounds doubtful. 'Firstly, she's a teenager. Secondly, with all of these panicked phone calls and sobbing, is she really reliable?'

'It's my daughter you're talking about,' I say. But Anna is right. Mel isn't in the best of states right now.

'But she wouldn't have made it up!' I have to defend her.

'No. But she might have got the timing wrong, or the name of the person. I don't know.' Anna shrugs and stands up.

'Can I report it to Facebook?' I ask.

'What is there to report? If the post has been deleted or the user removed, there's nothing there anymore.'

'I guess so.' I sink dejectedly into the sofa. Someone wants to scare me, and I have no idea who it is and no means of tracing them.

'Cheer up, long face.' Anna pulls a silly face, which doesn't quite work. 'Someone has played a mean prank on you, but that's it.'

'Someone who knows that my sister died in a car crash. Not many people know that. It's so cruel.' I close my eyes. My head is pounding and my limbs feel like lead. And it is only Monday evening, I can't envisage how I am going to get through the week.

'Why don't we have a girls' pamper day at the club? How about Friday?' Anna collects the dirty plates and carries them through to the kitchen. I know her. That will be the extent of her tidying up.

'I'm working every day this week.'

'Saturday?' she asks, coming out of the kitchen. I envisage the mess she has left. Considerable.

'I'm working.' I scowl.

'Sunday?'

'Jim's not back this weekend?'

'No. He's back in a fortnight.'

'I would love to, but I've already promised to see another friend.'

Anna turns her back on me to put on her shoes, then flings her coat over her shoulders. 'The other friend being Ben, I suppose,' she mutters.

'No, actually,' I say lightly. 'My old friend Jenny, from work.' It is a lie. Of course I am reserving Sunday for Dr Ben Logan.

## 10

It is Tuesday afternoon and very quiet. My phone rings, startling me out of a gentle reverie.

'Someone for you,' Hannah says.

'Who is it?' I ask, but she has already transferred the call through.

'Laura?'

It is Ian. He sounds strangely tentative.

'Is Mel ok?' I ask, my stomach clenching. I have received two WhatsApp messages from her during the past forty-eight hours, but we haven't actually spoken. I take that to mean she is feeling happier, more settled, less homesick. Or perhaps Ian is calling to apologise for our conversation about his pregnant girlfriend. But no. He wouldn't call me at work about that. Besides, there's a nagging thought in the back of my head that it was me who was out of order during our telephone conversation.

'Mel is fine. Why? I don't know.' He stumbles over his words. 'I'm not calling about Mel.'

'So why are you calling?' I can't help the sharp edge to my words.

'Could you come around for a drink after work?'

'I would rather not.'

'It's important, Laura. I wouldn't ask if it wasn't.'

'I could do without driving all the way to Cranleigh. I'm tired. Can't you come to me?'

'No. Please come to mine.'

I sigh. I remind myself what the counsellor said. 'You don't hate Ian. You hate what Ian has done.' How can I hate Ian? I think I did hate him for a bit, maybe that first year after he announced he was leaving. But this is the man I loved for the best part of my adult life, the man who gave me my glorious daughter. I should have moved on. I have moved on; it's just that Charlene and the baby have thrown me. I need to be the bigger person, so I agree. Six p.m. at his house.

IAN'S HOUSE is four doors down from our old house. It has the same red brick façade, the same white framed windows and integrated garage. The only difference is it has three bedrooms rather than four and a smaller garden, and it's on the wrong side of the road, nearer the main road as opposed to the river. We bought our house off plan. It excited us to be the first owners of a home, to be able to decorate it any way we wished, to have a say in something that would be standing for decades. Ian's dad told us we were foolhardy. Those developers, they'll rip you off, he said. There were some minor snagging issues, but they didn't rip us off. We had a lovely home and it sold for considerably more than we paid for it.

Twelve years ago, Downbridge Lane was to be a small development of twenty new homes, and so it stayed for five years. I walked Mel to her primary school, and when she went to secondary school, the bus stopped at the bottom of the lane. But then the local council identified a need for more housing, and several developers got on board, and soon the area morphed from a mini hamlet to a small town full of cloned little houses with miniscule gardens and insufficient places to park. I loved our home for the first five years, but when the cranes moved in and the roads clogged up, I fell out of love with the location. Ian didn't.

I often wondered why Ian didn't offer to buy me out. It would have been much more economically sensible, saving him estate agency fees and taxes. I assume he insisted we sell up and split the proceeds just to upset me. He misjudged that one. I was distraught because he had torn our little family apart. I was devastated because he had lied. A home can be recreated anywhere, so long as there is love.

What had been a little country lane is now set deep within a modern housing estate. It is a veritable maze. I have visited Ian's house on several occasions, collecting Mel from sleep-overs, but it hasn't been for a few months and then it had been light. I get lost. My satnav thinks I am driving through a field rather than an estate of closely built houses.

I am red-faced and flustered by the time I pull up outside 17 Downbridge Lane. I don't like to be late, particularly when seeing Ian. Ever since the divorce, I have made an effort when seeing him. I want to make him see what he has lost, so I put on make-up, smart clothes – he isn't to know they were bought from the charity shop – and I stand up straight and smile. But this evening I am tired and emotionally strung out. I haven't touched up my make-up after work, and I am wearing an old suit with a skirt hem held up by a safety pin. To compound my misery, it is pouring rain.

Fumbling with my umbrella, I get out of the car and put my foot straight into a puddle, my shoe immediately filling with freezing water. Swearing, I run up his drive and stand shivering on the doorstep. The doorbell rings with one of those twee electronic melodies. The curtains are drawn, but there are lights on in the house. I wait a few long moments and ring the doorbell again, keeping my finger on the button.

I hear footsteps and then the front door swings open.

I take a step backwards and my eyebrows shoot up to my hairline. I am not expecting her. My mistake: I should be.

'Charlene, I assume?' I put out my hand, but she ignores it. She is adjusting the buttons of her blouson, which stretches across her vast, distended belly. When Ian announced that she was pregnant, I assumed she was in the early stages, not about to give birth.

'Come in,' she says. She shifts to the side and I have to draw in my stomach and slide in sideways to avoid bumping into her.

'Leave your umbrella on the doorstep,' she instructs. The lack of 'please' before or after the sentence grates. I flick droplets of water over the front doorstep.

'He's in there.' Charlene waves her hand towards the living room.

Ian is on the phone, but it isn't Ian that I see. It is the room. Three months ago, Ian's living room had been bland, with magnolia-painted walls and scuffed old leather sofas. There were a couple of pictures on the walls that his mother had given him and numerous photos of Mel scattered on the windowsills and the mantelpiece. The room has had a makeover, a shocking makeover. It looks just like our living room from our old marital home. The walls around the fire-place and windows are painted the faintest of pale blue, and the main wall behind the sofa is covered with a delicate wall-paper featuring exotic birds and butterflies. I fell in love with it and begged Ian to be allowed to spend an extortionate sum on the designer wallpaper. Just the one wall, then, he had conceded. The cream sofas are piled high with blue cushions, and there is a large silver gilt mirror hanging above the fire-place. The only thing that hadn't existed in my old home was the large thick pile rug on the floor and the multiple photographs of Charlene in various stages of undress. Just one photo of Mel remains.

'What's with the room?' I wave my arms around.

Ian turns his back on me. 'I've got to go,' he says to whomever he is talking to on the phone.

'What's with the room?' I ask again as he turns to face me.

'You did a fine job the first time around, so I thought I'd recreate it.' He grins as if it is perfectly normal.

'What about Charlene? What does she think?'

'Keep your voice down.' Ian scowls.

'Doesn't she have a style of her own?' I spit in a whisper. 'Or perhaps she doesn't know that our living room used to look just like this?'

Ian grimaces and wrings his hands. 'Charlene's not that interested in interior décor. I showed her a photo of our house and she liked the living room. Anyway, please sit down.'

As I sit on one of the pristine sofas, I realise it isn't exactly like our old home. Everything is new and perfect, for starters. That won't last long with a baby, I think meanly. The pictures on the walls are unfamiliar, but that wallpaper, that was mine. I am surprised it is still available.

'Why am I here?' I snap.

'Charlie, have you got it?' Ian shouts.

'Coming, darling!' She waddles back into the room holding an envelope.

'Would you like a drink?' she asks me.

The nicety takes me by surprise.

'No, I'm fine, thanks.'

Now I have a chance to have a good look at her. You are so predictable, Ian, I think. With her blonde, gently curling hair and wide-set green eyes, she could be my doppelganger, my much, much younger, prettier sister. I bite the side of my mouth. I had a younger sister, but she wasn't blonde, and although she had an inner beauty, she was not classically pretty. I focus on Charlene. I assume she is mid-thirties, and from the photos I can see she had a stunning figure pre-pregnancy.

The question is, why on earth is she with Ian? With his receding hairline and paunchy front with a hint of man boobs, couldn't Charlene have done better? He is a good man, a kind man to everyone except me, and of course he has a healthy bank balance, increased recently, if Mel's feedback is accurate. Apparently, he was headhunted by the American competitors of the pharmaceutical firm where he is European sales director. He was all set to jump ship, but when his managing director found out, he lured him to stay by doling out share options and a massive bonus. Ian promised Mel a holiday to the Caribbean, but that was before the baby pronouncement. Mel – bless her – recounted all of this. 'You should renegotiate your settlement,' Jenny had advised me when I told her. I had rolled my eyes. The thought of returning to court and going through all that stress again just isn't worth it.

I am tugged back into the room by Charlene speaking to me.

'We'll be having our tea soon. Would you like to join us?'

Tea! She called their supper tea! Ian used to mock people who said that, but as I look at him, I see only tenderness in his eyes.

'Charlie is an amazing cook.' Ian smiles. He rubs his pot belly.

'Thanks for the invite' – I try to be gracious towards Charlene – 'but I've got my supper in the slow cooker.' That is a lie; I don't even own a slow cooker. 'So what did you want to tell me?'

'This arrived,' Charlene says, holding an envelope out to me. 'It shocked us,' she says.

I take the envelope. They are both staring at me. It is addressed to Mr I. Swallow. I extract the piece of paper from inside and open it slowly. I recognise it: a death certificate. My hands start shaking before I can open it properly and read it. I know what it is going to say.

Sinking back down into the sofa, I can feel the blood draining from my face. As the room starts to spin, I wonder if I am going to faint.

'She needs a glass of water,' Charlene says.

Ian hurries out of the room and returns at impressive speed with a small glass of brandy. 'Drink this.' He thrusts it towards me.

I do as instructed. My ex-husband knows me well. Charlene frowns. I pick up the death certificate and read it properly. Death in the sub-district of Horsham in the County of West Sussex. It states my full name: Laura Ruth Swallow. Apparently I died exactly one week ago in Horsham. My occupation is listed as unemployed, and the cause of death is road traffic accident.

'It looks real to me,' Charlene says.

'It can't be.' I sigh. 'I'm sitting here, alive, in front of you.'

'Maybe it's another Laura Swallow,' Ian suggests lamely.

'With the same birthday and in the same town as me. Not very likely.' I put the glass of brandy to my lips, but it is empty. 'It's malicious.'

'We need to help you find out who did this,' Ian said.

'Actually...' Charlene drags out the word, 'tea is ready, so perhaps your amateur dramatics can wait until another day.' She smiles at Ian, her white teeth flashing against her sunbed-tanned face.

'You mean sleuthing,' he says. 'Amateur sleuthing, not dramatics.'

'Whatever.' She leans forwards, fingers slipping into the back of Ian's trousers, and she kisses him on the cheek.

I stand up.

'Thank you for giving me this.' I wave the death certificate.

Ian shrugs Charlene off and walks towards me. We stand there awkwardly for a moment.

'Goodbye, Laura. Take care.' He moves as if to kiss me on the cheek, but I take a step backwards, turn and rush out of the front door.

By the time I get home, I feel as if I have been through several rounds in the boxing ring. I am mentally and emotionally battered, and all I want to do is numb myself with alcohol. I would like to call Ben, but I am proud. He hasn't been in touch since leaving on Sunday, and I have taken that to mean his interest in me has faded. Perhaps my lack of performance in between the sheets sounded the death knell for a relationship that never really began. So much for his pronouncement about feeling the connection between us. I try not to feel a deep disappointment, but I do.

## 11

'**M**r Drover has asked to view Brunning's House,' Peter says. 'Can you meet him there this afternoon?'

'No.'

Peter sucks in air between his teeth and draws his head backwards like a tortoise. He then clears his throat. 'Did you just say no?'

'I'm sorry, I can't show Mr Drover around a house. He tried to make a pass at me.'

Peter swallows a snigger. How dare he! I glower at my boss. I have seen him retreat on many an occasion when directly confronted by Jenny. I put my hands on my hips and try to emulate her stance.

'I can't put myself at risk,' I say, sounding much stronger than I feel.

'No, no, of course not,' he blusters. 'But there's no one else senior enough to do the viewings this afternoon.' Peter rubs his chin. He has a hairless face and I wonder if he ever needs to shave.

'Take young Rob with you. And if there's a real problem, we'll involve the police.'

'No need for that,' I mutter, inwardly cursing that I will need to see creepy Eddy again. I am not sure how the diminutive, adolescent Rob with his acne-covered forehead will offer me any protection. But mainly I am surprised that Eddy returned for more. After my brushing him off, I assumed he would take his house-hunting to another agency. There are plenty others to choose from.

We are in my car.

'Have you been to Brunning's House before?' Rob asks. He is chatty and confident, and I can see why Peter has taken a chance on him, training the lad up straight out of school.

'No,' I say. I am not feeling talkative.

'I have. It's the sort of place I want to live in, in about ten years' time.'

'Right.' I wonder how he is planning on getting from minimum wage to multimillionaire by the time he is thirty.

'I'm sorry about your gran,' I say.

I can see Rob's blush out of the corner of my eye. It makes his acne look particularly virulent.

'And I'm sorry about that horrible obituary written about you. It's dead weird.'

'Dead indeed,' I mutter.

'Sorry. Did you find out who wrote it?' There is an eagerness to his voice.

'No,' I say. 'Tell me about your gran. Were you close?'

'Nah. She was an old bag, grumpy, mean, and my mum hated her.'

I can't think of a response.

'Mr Fielding says that the geezer we're about to show the house to is a bit of a creep. Is that right?'

Wow! Mr Fielding was rather out of order for saying anything to Rob. I hope we don't get ourselves into a 'situation'.

'I'm sure Mr Drover will be polite and proper today,' I say. 'Because I'm with you.'

We fall silent for a while. I concentrate on the road and try to stop the nerves from swirling in my stomach at the thought of seeing Eddy again. They are not the butterfly, tingling type of nerves that I get when I think of Ben, but rather the foreboding, bristling-of-hair variety that occurs when I tune into my intuition. These nerves are nearly always the precursor to something bad happening. I try to be logical and calm. Of course I am on edge. Eddy Drover groped me; someone is threatening my life via social media, the newspaper and a death notice. And I have no idea who would want to do that to me. Right now, Eddy Drover seems like the only potential culprit.

Rob splices my negative thoughts. 'Is he the son of Luke Lolly Drover?'

We are at a set of temporary traffic lights near West Chiltington. They turn green, but I don't notice because Rob's words have just turned on a switch in my brain.

Yes. And I have totally forgotten. The bad boy of rock living off the proceeds of a one-hit song. How could I have forgotten? A lorry hoots behind me – a loud, deep blast that makes me jump. I jam my foot on the accelerator and we leap forwards. A legacy from Becky's death is a profound fear of letting lorries get too close to the rear of my car. Even if it means breaking the speed limit, I have to put a decent distance between us. We speed along the bypass.

'How on earth do you know about Luke Lolly Drover? He was dead before you were born!'

'Yeah. But Mum was a fan and she played that rubbish song "Gimme Luv Bruv" on repeat all through my childhood. She told Dad she only married him 'cos Luke Lolly was dead. It's wicked that we're going to meet his son. Mum'll be well stoked.'

'I suggest you don't say anything.'

I can't look at Rob, but I can sense him rolling his eyes at me. 'I'm a professional,' he says. We'll see, I think.

Eddy Drover never let on that he was Luke Lolly's son when we were at school. As a late developer and the class nerd, life was tough enough for him as it was, without everyone knowing that he was the offspring of a local hero; even if that local hero had written just one decent song and had drunk himself to death by the age of sixty. His dad never showed up at the school gates or at parent-teacher meetings. If he had done, we would all have known about it. Still, I wonder how Eddy kept it quiet. Perhaps his parents had split up? In fact, I only realised that Eddy was Luke Lolly's son years later when I wrote his obituary. Shit. I wrote his dad's obituary! How had I forgotten?

'You all right?' Rob asks.

'Yes.'

'You've gone ever so pale.'

'I'm fine,' I snap.

I wrote his father's obituary. But what did I write? Was it kind or acerbic? Probably the latter. And how could Eddy have ever found out it was me who wrote it? Obituary writers never have bylines; their names are kept well out of print. Has Eddy written my fake obituary as revenge for the one I wrote about his father? And if so, why wait twenty years? I need to find the box file where I have stored all of the clippings from the articles and obituaries I wrote in my early twenties. I can't even remember where it is. Did I bring it with me to the flat? If I left it behind, Ian may well have binned it. We tried to be civil about the splitting up of our affairs, but it was hard. Ian let me have everything I wanted; guilt, I suppose.

We pull into Brunning's House. It is even more grand than The Rectory, and I wonder if Eddy can afford somewhere like this, whether he is living off the proceeds of his deceased father's success or whether he has made his own millions. Unlike The Rectory, it is a newly built house, timber-framed with lots of glass and uplighters that throw shadows and highlight the complex oak structure. Entry to the house is via a complicated technological set-up involving fingerprints and security codes. I am glad I have Rob with me, who seems totally unfazed by it.

'Have a look around,' Rob says, sinking into a vast white leather sofa.

'Oy, it's not your house,' I chastise him. 'Get up! They've probably got security cameras everywhere.'

Rob jumps up and pats the sofa down behind him. I chuckle to myself. The lad is ambitious; he clearly wants to keep his job. I spend the next ten minutes slowly wandering around the beautiful house, admiring the bespoke modern chandeliers with their coloured orbs and the clean lines of the white kitchen, without a hint of any kitchen appliances sullying the surfaces. All the time I keep a listen out for the sound of Eddy's Range Rover. Eventually I am back in the living room, where Rob is fiddling with his mobile phone.

'He's late,' Rob says unnecessarily. 'How long do you normally wait when clients are late?'

'Half an hour. Depends what the next appointment is. His number is on the client sheet.' I hand Rob the file.

'Can't you call him?'

'No. You can do it.' I have no intention of ringing Eddy, of giving him my mobile phone number.

'His phone is ringing out,' Rob says.

'We'll wait a bit longer.'

Half an hour later when Rob has tried Eddy again and has rung the office to check if he has left us a message, I decide Eddy isn't going to show up. I am relieved but also a little disappointed. I was dreading the awkwardness, but I am also curious as to how Eddy would have reacted to me. Was he intending to apologise or to act as if nothing had happened? Was he going to try his luck again, and if so, what would Rob do?

We switch all the lights off and I watch Rob set the alarms and lock up the house.

'A waste of time and money,' Rob mutters.

'An annoyance of the job,' I say, age having made me more sanguine. On further reflection, I am relieved. Very relieved. I wonder whether Eddy did it on purpose, to make me uneasy. I blow out air slowly; I am beginning to get paranoid. Dusk is falling as we climb into the car. We have a 4 p.m. appointment with some other clients just ten minutes away. I turn the car in Brunning's House's impressive entrance with its sweeping drive and uplighters that cast shadows from the specimen trees, and edge out onto a narrow lane enclosed by tall oak trees and hornbeams. Even without their leaves, the trees make the lane dark and just a little foreboding. A split second after I turn onto the lane, I hear the roar of a large car behind me, and bright headlights light up the road all around us.

'Shit!' I say as I put my foot on the accelerator in a reflexive motion to put some distance between us and the car behind. My heart is pumping hard. I didn't see it coming. Have I just pulled out into another car's path, or was it coming around the corner so quickly I couldn't see it approaching? The car lights are dazzling, temporarily blinding me, and I have no choice but to reach up to angle my rear mirror downwards.

'Bastard has left his lights on full beam.'

'Could be a she,' Rob retorts.

'Humph.' I grip the steering wheel tightly. This scenario is precisely what gives me palpitations. A large vehicle right on my tail. The car revs, as if it is pushing me to go faster. The road is too narrow and I don't know my way. I can't go faster.

Rob turns around. 'Bloody hell, a bit close.'

The comment only makes me more nervous. I think of the death certificate: my death, the result of a car accident. But what about Rob? He is young, bright, ambitious, with a long future in front of him. I need to protect him too. I have to slow down as we reach a T-junction. The car is so close to our rear, I can't see its lights, but they throw light from behind us, out into the road and on the hedge in front. Its engine is throbbing and it sounds as if the driver is putting the car into full throttle and then holding back, trying to push me forwards, like a racing car ready to pounce. I stop and peer to the left and the right. Darkness. I don't indicate. If the car behind me doesn't know which way I am going, perhaps it won't follow me. I'm getting ridiculously paranoid. I pull out quickly, turning to the right. Almost too quickly, as the wheels of my car spin ever so slightly and the rubber screeches. My heart is thumping as I correct the car. I put my foot on the accelerator and speed away. I glance up to the rear mirror. There are no lights behind me.

'Bloody hell,' Rob says again. 'You practicing to be a rally driver?'

'No. I'm sorry.' My paranoia is making me reckless and I need to be careful.

We have two more viewings to do and all I want is to snuggle up under the duvet at home.

'I'd like you to take the lead on these viewings,' I tell Rob as we arrive at a well-lit house in a newly built cul-de-sac in Southwater.

'Really?' he says, a big grin lighting up his face.

As he gets out of the car, he stands up straight, shrugs his shoulders back, and pats down his jacket. I smile to myself.

## 12

As soon as I get home, I pull down the loft ladder and switch on the light. It is one of the advantages of having the top-floor flat; I get additional storage and lots of it. And I certainly need it. As Ian was generous about letting me take whatever I wanted, I took far too much, and most of it doesn't fit into the flat. Candlesticks and photo frames and vases, all the chattels we acquired as wedding presents and superfluous items bought on holidays, I shoved into boxes and straight into the loft. I didn't have the energy to sort through the memorabilia of my life. I sigh. There are lots of boxes and none are labelled.

I climb back down the ladder and find some tape, scissors and a black pen and pull on an additional sweater. It's cold up there in the attic. There is a single hanging light bulb and it smells dank and dusty. I shiver. Trying to be systematic, I start at the rear of the attic, opening up each box, then sealing it back up again, writing on the box a description of the contents. There are boxes of Mel's school reports, baby toys, old ski wear that I'll likely never use again, my record collection – now useless, as I don't have a record player – boxes and boxes of stuff from when we cleared out my parents' house, and a box of keepsakes from Becky.

I hesitate when I open that, my fingers twitching, my heart sinking, but no. I don't have the strength to look through it. I will have to some time, I suppose, but not today. After what seems like hours later, but is probably only twenty minutes or so, I find what I'm looking for. The box full of newspaper cuttings. It is heavy and difficult manoeuvring it down the ladder. I bump it down from one step to the next and eventually let it drop to the floor below. Pushing the ladder back up, I switch the light off and shake the dust from my sweater and out of my hair.

It's time for a glass of wine and a jacket potato.

The cuttings are in no order, not that it would make any difference, as I don't remember when Luke Lolly Drover died. I am impressed with the collection. I wrote quite a few obituaries, including one for Michael Hutchence. He was a far bigger celebrity than Luke Lolly. Death by suicide has a higher ranking, a greater shock value than death by liver failure. I remember Hutchence's obituary was checked and rechecked for style and substance by my boss and the editor. I doubt Luke Lolly's went through the same rigorous vetting procedure. I remember now how I didn't get the big one of that year. Not surprising that it was our editor himself who wrote Princess Diana's obituary. At the time, I was livid. The arrogance of youth. I reach the bottom of the box file, but Luke Lolly Drover's obituary isn't here. I don't understand. I remember writing it, remember thinking how interesting that he was a local star. So why wouldn't I have kept the cutting when I have kept every other piece I've written? How frustrating. Did I give it to Mum, perhaps? She might have been interested, as he was a local celebrity. I curse. I will need to search the British Newspaper Library, and I can't even do that online, as I'm still without my laptop.

THE NEXT MORNING I am summoned in to see Peter Fielding yet again. I know something is wrong because he refuses to meet my eyes, but all I feel is a sense of resignation.

'Sit down,' he barks. 'We've received an official complaint.'

'Sorry?'

He speaks louder, as if I am a dimwit. I know, from over-hearing him speak to other members of staff, that he increases the volume of his voice the more angry and frustrated he becomes. Resilience is not Peter Fielding's strong point.

'This letter!' He waves it in front of my nose. 'I will read it to you. *Dear Mr Fielding, I have thought long and hard about whether to write to you or not, but eventually I felt compelled to do so. Last week I was shown around a property by your employee Mrs Laura Swallow, whom I knew from my youth. We have not seen each other in thirty years. When we were upstairs in the house, she made an inappropriate sexual pass towards me. I was deeply shocked and left immediately. I made an appointment to view another property. When I saw Mrs Swallow's car in the drive, I left, as I did not want to see her again. I trust you will take appropriate action. On this occasion, I will not be referring the matter to the police. Yours sincerely, Edward Drover.*'

'The bastard,' I spit. 'He is a liar.'

'Is that so?' Peter narrows his eyes.

'Surely you must believe me over him?' I leap to my feet. 'You've known me for nearly three years and I've never lied.'

'I will give you the benefit of the doubt on this occasion, as it does seem very much out of character. But the reputation of this business is everything to me, and I am not prepared to risk it.'

'But...'

He waves me away.

Back at my desk, I am fuming. I am too old to be treated like this. How dare Peter talk to me as if I am a child! I am not sure who I am more angry with: Peter for insinuating that I might be to blame, or Eddy for sending such a blatantly false letter that he knew would have negative repercussions. I am meant to be writing some property particulars, a job which usually flows easily, but I can't concentrate. The fury boils inside me, burning like acid. I can't remember the last time I felt such injustice. Should I speak to Jenny? Get her to intervene? Or is that putting her in an invidious position? I type bastards, bastards, bastards on my keyboard and then delete the words. It doesn't make me feel any better.

My mobile buzzes on my desk. It's Ben. Seeing his name lifts my mood as if it has been attached to a helium balloon and I get immediate relief from the fury. Perhaps he hasn't been scared off after all?

*'Sorry haven't been in touch. Been a hell of a week. A bit last minute but my clinic has been cancelled. Are you free today/tonight?'*

I weigh the phone in my hand and bite the side of my mouth to try to stop the grin that I can feel working its way across my face. Having been the most diligent of employees for the past two and a bit years, I decide in that moment that my commitment and allegiance to Slate Wilders has been misplaced. Bugger Peter. I'm going to skive off.

*'I can do lunch. 1pm outside John Lewis?'*

The John Lewis and Waitrose store is a short walk away but sufficiently far from the office for me not to be spotted by Peter or Jenny.

*'Perfect. Will pick you up in the car. Bx'*

AT TWELVE THIRTY I send Jenny an email saying that I have a doctor's appointment and might be late back into the office, but I have no viewings booked for the afternoon. Then I dash into the ladies', pull a brush through my hair, put on a slash of rose lipstick, grab my coat and hurry downstairs.

I walk quickly through the centre of town and cross over Albion Way through the car park, arriving outside the glass-fronted building on the dot of one o'clock. My face feels flushed and my heart is beating a little too fast. A sleek silver car pulls up alongside me. Ian would be impressed. Mentally I kick myself. Ian's judgement doesn't matter anymore. I've been thinking of my ex-husband far too much during the past few days.

'Hop in, Laura!' Ben grins at me. 'I've booked us a table at The Dog and Duck.'

# 13

The pub has low-slung beams and dark grey wainscoting with interesting prints of ladies dressed in old-fashioned attire hung on the whitewashed walls above. Ben selects a table that is almost private, hidden by warped, dark oak beams. I sit nearest the roaring open fire; Ben faces the entrance.

'They're prints by Václav Hollar,' Ben says as I look at the pictures. 'He was a Czech artist from the 1600s, who at one time was a servant of the Earl of Arundel. Those women are ladies of the night, and see that?' He points at numbers at the bottom of each print. 'Those are how much the women charged!'

'For someone who proclaims to have no interest in art, you have a great deal of knowledge!'

'I am a font of useless knowledge. I do very well in pub quizzes, but when it comes to practical stuff, current affairs and the like, I'm useless.'

'I don't believe that!' I say.

Further proclamations of modesty are interrupted by the waitress wearing a long dark grey apron, the same colour as the walls.

'What can I get you?' She is all smiles.

I order chanterelle risotto and Ben selects the sea bass. After a quick look through the wine list, he chooses a bottle of Sauvignon Blanc.

The waitress pours me a large glass. Lunchtime drinking is permissible if you don't have to work in the afternoon, I reassure myself. We eat, we talk, we laugh and we flirt. The restaurant fills up and a crowd of people jostle at the bar; the noise levels increase and I am glad we are cocooned in our little alcove. He asks about the obituary, the Facebook post. I tell him about Eddy Drover, omitting my teenage antics. And I tell him about the death certificate.

'How easy are they to come by?' I ask.

'They're difficult to fake,' he says, his face furrowed with concern. 'Sometimes they are stolen. The penalty is considerable if you're caught, a custodial sentence even. Do you know anyone who works in a doctor's surgery?'

'The only medic I know is you.'

'Not guilty,' he says, grinning. I laugh.

'Are you going to report it to the police?'

'I don't know.' And then I remember. 'Actually, I do know someone else who works in a surgery.'

Charlene. I am sure Anna said she worked at a doctor's practice. Or was it Mel who told me? But Charlene wouldn't do anything like this, surely? It should be me being foul to her, not the other way around. She's got my man. And from what I could glean, she's hardly the brightest biscuit in the cookie tin. It is so unlikely. The trouble is, the more I talk about my faceless predator, the more I become suspicious of everyone I know and the more scared I become. Even the soothing effects of the wine are failing to cut through the fear. The worry must be evident on my face. I decide to change the subject.

'Anyway, tell me more about your sons.'

'First, would you like a brandy?'

'It's the middle of the day.' I laugh. 'Are you going to?' I am tempted.

'No, I'm driving.'

'Can I get you two anything else?' the smiley waitress asks. 'A coffee or an Irish coffee perhaps?'

'An Irish coffee would be lovely.' I flutter my eyelids coyishly, aware I have already drunk enough. In for a penny, in for a pound. Besides, it's been years since I've had an Irish coffee.

I excuse myself and go to the toilets, surprised that I seem quite able to walk in a straight line. Perhaps I'm not tipsy after all. My ability to absorb alcohol is improving the more I drink. Not a good thing. On my return I have to ease my way through a tight throng of noisy people. Christmas parties come early, I guess. I see what I assume to be my Irish coffee on the bar, waiting to be collected by our waitress. It looks delicious, topped with a large dollop of wicked frothy cream.

I take my seat back at the table and Ben beams at me. My coffee arrives and I take a sip, savouring the sublime combination of some of my favourite ingredients. Shortly afterwards, Ben pays. I stand up but have to grab the back of my chair. I feel extremely light-headed. We walk slowly to the car, but rather than sobering me up, the cold air hits me and makes me dizzier. Cars appear double, blurred at the edges. How strange! I must have drunk way too much. How bizarre that I was okay only minutes earlier. There can't have been much whiskey in the Irish coffee.

I grab Ben's arm to stop myself from stumbling. He says something to me, but I can't work out the words, so I smile. After helping me into the passenger seat, he closes the door and climbs into the driver's side. I am so woozy. As he starts driving, the countryside spins, curling into increasingly tighter coils, and then I feel an utter exhaustion, a weariness in my limbs and a wooziness in my head that is bizarre, unsettling, uncontrollable. Could I be having a bad reaction to the lunch? It doesn't feel like food poisoning. He's a doctor. Ben will know. I try to ask him, but the words don't come out. My eyelids are so heavy, I can't keep them open. I can hear Ben say something, but I don't know what he says; I can't make out the words.

And that is the last thing I remember.

## 14

When I awake, I am in my bed. It is dark outside, but the curtains are open. My mouth is parched dry and my head is pounding as if I have a migraine. I feel a sense of panic. Something is wrong, seriously wrong. I turn my head towards my bedside clock. It is 7.37 p.m. Why am I tucked up under my duvet so early in the evening? I feel nauseous and leap out of bed, slipping and then pulling myself up against my bedside table. I make it to the bathroom just in time before being violently ill. As I sit on the bathroom floor, shivering uncontrollably, I notice with shock that I am wearing my bra but nothing else. How can that be? I wash out my mouth, my head pounding, and pull on my dressing gown. What has happened? I stagger back to bed, shivering, aching all over, and try to remember.

Fragments of memories return. I had lunch with Ben; I skived off work; he drove me home; he came in... But then my memory disappears as if it has been thrown off the edge of a cliff. There is a black void. Am I naked because we had sex? Oh God! Did I pass out? But the flat is quiet. Is Ben here? Is someone else here?

With a thumping heart, I drag myself out of bed again and stumble into the living room expectantly. The flat is empty. I make it to the kitchen and pour myself a glass of water, grabbing onto the kitchen counter to stay upright. Everything appears to be as it should be. Except for me. There is something wrong with me. Ben must have left me a note; after all, he brought me back here. I look around for a piece of paper or scribbles on the back of an envelope, but there is nothing. My head is pounding and I feel sick again. It doesn't stack up. Ben is a doctor. Surely he wouldn't have left me if I was ill? Has something else happened? And then the horrific thought hits me.

I must have been raped.

I am freezing cold, shaking, but I force myself to walk around the flat, to seriously assess whether anything is out of order. My coat is dumped on the floor by the front door; the door is shut but unlocked. My handbag is on the console table in the living room, where I always leave it. The cushions are neatly piled on the sofa. I look around the room, trying to keep my sight level, to stop it from spinning. Everything is in order. I glance into the kitchen. My coffee cup and breakfast bowl are in the sink, where I left them this morning. There are no wine glasses to be seen, no empty bottles.

I open the door to Mel's bedroom with trepidation, but everything is as it should be. Her bed is neatly made with her worn, wool cherry red rug pulled up over it, smoothed out by my hands as I shed tears after she left for university. Her bathroom is untouched. So that only leaves my bedroom and the bed where I was, until a few minutes ago, fast asleep. I hold onto the doorframe as I glance around the room, as if seeing it for the first time. My clothes are scattered across the floor, my knickers discarded in a crumpled ball cast aside on the floor near the curtains.

The duvet is hanging off the side of the bed, but I'm not

sure if I did that in my hurry to get to the bathroom. Has my bedroom been defiled? Have I been defiled? I stagger to the bed and stare at the sheets. Are there any telltale signs of sex? I sniff, but I can't smell anything, and it just makes my stomach heave. I put my hand between my legs and then pull it away quickly in disgust. I don't feel sore. I don't feel any different. Surely I would if I had been raped? I haven't had sex in so long, my body would feel altered.

I remember Anna's words then, how she warned me about Ben. There must have been something she didn't tell me. A rumour, a hint of something bad about him. But how could I have missed it? My intuition is normally good. I was falling for Ben, truly falling for him. And then as I try to order my thoughts, the doorbell rings. I freeze. I have never been so scared of a doorbell. Has he come back? I don't know what to do, so I stay sitting for a long time. I am so very, very cold. The doorbell rings again and then I hear my mobile phone chiming. I walk carefully to the living room and extract it from my handbag, holding it aloft as if it is contaminated. I force myself to look at it, hoping, praying that it's not Ben.

It's not.

'Hello,' I whisper.

'Hey, babe. Why aren't you opening the door?'

'What do you mean?'

'I'm downstairs and you're not letting me in!'

'What are you doing here?'

'Have you forgotten?' Anna's laugh is a tinkle. 'We're going out tonight. I said I'd come and collect you.'

I have forgotten. Totally forgotten. As if my memory has been erased. I glance at the calendar on my phone, and it's there. Anna, 7.45 p.m.

'Hold on.' I teeter back to the living room and press the intercom to let her in. I wait, listening to her footsteps pounding the stairs, and pull my dressing gown around me tightly, until it hurts. When she raps the door knocker, I open the door and step back, as if the air from the communal corridor is going to assault me. She is togged up in her black winter coat, and a red, shimmering scarf around her neck, high-heeled boots and a black, sequinned clutch bag under her arm. I swallow hard to stop her floral perfume from causing another round of nausea.

'What's happened?' she exclaims, stepping into the flat and closing the door behind her. 'Oh, darling, are you ill? You look terrible.'

She takes off her coat and hangs it up on the coat hook.

'You look really dreadful.' She peers at me, but doesn't get too close. I know that Anna is phobic about catching anything.

'I'm sorry. I forgot we were meant to be going out tonight.' My voice is a rasping whisper. I don't sound like me.

'Don't worry. We were only going to that new bar on East Street. You hop back into bed and I'll make you a nice cup of tea.'

I do as I am instructed and hobble back to the bedroom. But then I pause. Is my bed the scene of a crime? Should I get back into it? I sink down onto the carpet next to the bed and burst into sobs.

'What the...?' Anna pulls her stiletto-heeled boots off at the bedroom door and then walks inside. 'What's happened?'

'I think I've been raped,' I murmur.

Her hand flies up to her mouth and she stares at me. 'When? Where?'

'I don't know. Here, I suppose. I had lunch with Ben and then I felt really weird, ill.'

'It was Ben?' She turns around and screeches, 'He's my fucking consultant! He's a doctor!'

I let the tears flow. Anna sinks down to the floor next to me and puts her arm around my shoulders. In all these years, this is the first time she has touched me.

'Let it out, babe,' she says, shushing me as if I were a young child. 'What happened?'

'I don't know. I can't remember anything, but I woke up and I was naked,' I sob and bury my face in my hands.

'Did he give you a date-rape drug, do you think?' she asks, her voice catching and cracking at the horror of it.

'I don't know.' I sniff. 'I feel terrible though.'

'Holy shit. What are we going to do?'

I don't answer. I can't answer. My mind is a frozen blank. She gets up then, suddenly.

'You stay sitting there. I'll make you a nice cup of tea and then I'll call my friend Brad. He's a solicitor. He'll know what to do.'

Anna returns with a steaming cup.

I don't want Anna to call Brad. I don't want anyone to know. It's too horrible to think about. Shameful. But I have no energy and Anna will do whatever she decides. She sits down next to me, stretching her stockinged legs out. Her toenails are painted in her trademark navy and look like little bruises underneath her tights.

'It could have been Eddy, I suppose.' I sigh.

Anna's neatly arched eyebrows rise up to her fringe. 'You were with Ben this afternoon. How could Eddy have done this?'

She's right. As much as I would rather pin this on Eddy, it is unlikely in the extreme. I began to feel ill after lunch. Now I remember sitting in Ben's car, feeling dizzy, exhausted. And I remember Ben supporting me as we came into my flat. But then my memory is a big blank.

'Can you remember anything? Anything at all from when you got home?'

I shake my head.

'Do you feel as if you've been raped?'

I burst into tears again. How would I know? I've never been raped before. Blessedly, I don't know anyone who has. I wipe my eyes and my nose with the sleeve of my dressing gown and sniff loudly. I'm still sitting on the floor of my bedroom, plucking little tufts from the carpet. I reach across and pick up the scalding cup of tea, my hands clasped around the mug. The scorching of my hands feels good. I want my body to hurt.

'Why don't you get into bed?' Anna suggests.

I shake my head. My hair feels lanky, which is weird because I think I washed it this morning. Now I'm thinking of it, I feel dirty all over.

'I'm going to have a shower.'

'Good idea. Do you want me to start running it for you?'

'No.' I place the cup of tea underneath my bedside table and get up slowly. The room is still spinning. Walking carefully to the bathroom, I turn on the shower as hot as it will go. I shut the bathroom door, shrug off my dressing gown and bra, and when the water is steaming, I get under it; the pounding and burning, a relief. I stand there and let the scorching water mingle with my tears, hoping that it will flush away some of the confusion, the shame, the filth. And then suddenly, I scream.

'No!'

I turn off the taps; the water stops.

'What is it? I'm coming in!' Anna is at the door. I see the handle move.

'Stay out!' I say, panicked. I feel violated enough as it is, without Anna barging in on me. I wrap a towel around me, and despite my red, burning skin, I am shivering again. How stupid I am! I shouldn't have had a shower. How will they be able to tell if I've been raped, now I've washed off all the evidence? I try to recall whether I have seen anything on the TV as to what a victim should or shouldn't do. Oh God! I'm a victim. I have never seen myself as a victim. Even when Ian walked out, I didn't sink into that pathetic victim mode. I was angry, embittered, motivated to do something, not a shrinking violet, a walkover. But now. Now Ben, a person I trusted and liked, really liked, has turned me into a victim!

I fling the bathroom door open. Anna has her back to me, but she spins around. The hot, damp steam winds its way into the bedroom, ghostlike.

'I shouldn't have had a shower,' I state.

'Why?'

'Evidence. I've just washed away the evidence.'

'Oh, Laura, darling. I think that's only in films. I just had a quick word with Brad. He said there's not much you can do. Drink lots, and if you want to report it, go to the police station tomorrow.'

I sink onto the bed and then, remembering what occurred on my bed, slip down into my default position on the floor. I whisper the word *police*. No. I can't go to the police. That is too horrific. Too mortifying. What will they think about me, a middle-aged woman, putting herself in the position to be date raped? It's laughable. I'm not beautiful like Anna. I don't have a good figure. Who would want to violate me?

I am still. It's as if I have forgotten to breathe, because then I take a massive gasp of air and splutter. I have been focused on the rape, but what of all the other events of the past ten days? The death notice? The Facebook post? The death certificate? Someone wants to hurt me, or worse still, someone wants me to die. Maybe I will have to go to the police. Dr Ben Logan will have to pay. I can see the headlines. *Leading consultant accused of rape and hate crime!* Who will believe me over Dr Logan? I am a nobody. He is a hero, helping people get better, people like my friend Anna. Can she accept that Ben Logan is a violent, revolting non-person? I think of those warm amber eyes and his polite, gentle manner and wonder how I could have got him so very, very wrong.

'I think you should eat something.' Anna interrupts my thoughts.

'What?'

'I'll make you an omelette or some soup. What have you got in your fridge?'

'I'm not hungry.'

'You need to eat and drink. It will make you feel better.'

'How do you know?' I ask.

'Laura, you're in shock. You're not thinking straight. Let me help you. Why don't you get off the floor and into bed?'

'I don't want to get into...'

'Of course. The sheets. Silly me.'

Anna whips off the duvet, removes its cover and peels off the bottom sheet.

'There's no stains,' I murmur.

'There won't be if he used a condom,' Anna says blandly.

I quiver.

'Sorry. I shouldn't have said that out loud.' She pats my shoulder. She has touched me more this evening than in all the time we have known each other. 'I'll pop these in the washing machine. Where do you keep your fresh linen?'

'Throw them away,' I say. 'Linen is in the cupboard in the bathroom.'

Anna doesn't listen to me. She doesn't throw things away. 'Waste not, want not' is one of her favourite expressions. Despite all her wealth, she takes care of things. But I won't use those sheets ever again. When they are clean, I will put them in the charity box outside the supermarket.

I can hear her padding into the kitchen, switching the washing machine on and then walking into the bathroom, opening the tall cupboard next to the bath. She returns carrying a rose-patterned duvet and pillowcase. I haven't got the energy to tell her that they belong to Mel. It will be comforting sleeping in Mel's sheets. I wonder if they will smell of her or just the fabric conditioner I use too much of. Anna makes the bed, smoothing down the bottom sheet, plumping up the pillows and putting the large duvet in its cover with surprising fluidity.

'I've made you a hot-water bottle.' She pops it under the duvet. The look of concern on her face makes me weep all over again. What would I do without Anna?

I get into bed, and although I feel utterly exhausted, my mind is whirling, and I know I won't be able to sleep. Anna perches on the end of the bed.

'Do you have any sleeping pills?' she asks.

'No.'

'I've got some tramadol in my bag. It should knock you out. You must sleep.'

I don't know what tramadol is, and I don't question Anna. She hands me a small pill and a large glass of water. I swallow both.

## 15

When I wake up, it is dark. My heart is racing and my head is pounding. I reach for my alarm clock. It is 4.10 a.m. That's good. I have slept for many hours. I lie in the dark for a while, but then the darkness becomes oppressive and I need to get up. I switch on my bedside lamp and see a piece of paper under the door. Swinging my legs out of bed, the room sways from side to side. Why do I feel so disorientated, so weird? I place one foot in front of the other and reach the piece of paper.

'Laura, I hope you feel much better after a good night's sleep. Call me in the morning. Ax'

So, Anna has gone. I wish she were still here, looking out for me. I slide one foot in front of the other and make it to the front door. I bolt the door and then, worried that the locks are insufficient, drag a small sideboard in front of it. The exertion is too much. Aching all over, I force myself back to bed and I sleep again. When I next awake, grey light is shining through the curtains. It has just gone 7 a.m.

I need to get up and go to work. But am I in any fit state? I think of Peter Fielding and my meeting with him, which rationally I know was only yesterday morning but feels like weeks ago. Having skived off work yesterday afternoon, I can't not go in today. Peter has got it in for me, and even Jenny won't be able to save me.

I have another shower, a cold one this time. The evidence will be truly washed away, but I don't care. I feel a deep, bone-aching lethargy. The bastard will get away with it because I don't have the energy to fight. I dress in all black and walk wearily into the kitchen. I stand at the kitchen counter, aware that I need to eat. It's as if I am in a treacly fog. I'm not sure if it's the effect of the drugs Ben covertly put in my drink or the pill Anna gave me to sleep. Either way, I am dreading the day, worried about how I am going to keep my eyes open and concentrate on my job.

After two burning cups of strong, black coffee and a slice of toast that tastes like cardboard, I find my bag where it was left last night in the living room. As I am putting on my coat, wearily struggling to get my arms through the sleeves, my mobile phone rings. I expect it to be Anna, so I reach for it and take it out blithely. When I see the caller's name on the screen, I drop the phone. Ben Logan. I stand in the entrance to my flat, shaking. How could he have the gall to ring me after what he did? I am quivering but frozen to the spot, and now I feel fear racing through my veins. What does he want?

The phone stops ringing. I stare at it and eventually pick it up and put it back in my bag, not looking at it, as if the device is contaminated. My lethargy lifts. I need to take action, and my first step must be to see my GP. I laugh to myself bitterly. I don't have a GP, of course; none of us do, unless you're Anna, who has a private doctor she sees at the drop of a hat. It is a lottery who I get to see, and even if I get to see a doctor at all. But that is what I will do, and if the doctor says I should go to the police, then I will, however humiliating that will be.

'New Place Surgery, how can I help you?'

'Please can I have an appointment to see a doctor?'

'Is it urgent?'

'Yes,' I say.

'I'll need to get a nurse to call you back.'

I had forgotten that. The triage system. So not only will I need to tell a doctor what has happened, I will also need to tell a nurse. The shame cascades through me again. I am about to say don't bother, it's fine, but the receptionist has hung up.

I must get going now; otherwise I will be late for work.

It is a cold, clear day. The sky is a milky blue, cloudless, and the air is sparkling. My breath hangs in little visible puffs as I walk through the centre of Horsham, forcing myself to put one foot in front of the other. The sun shouldn't be shining. It should be dark and damp and miserable. My mobile rings as I am three doors away from work. I slip into an alleyway between the shops, near a row of dumper bins. My phone says number withheld. I hesitate but eventually answer it. What a relief that it is the surgery nurse.

'How can we help?' she asks. Her voice has a warm, reassuring timbre.

'I was attacked last night and I need to see a doctor,' I whisper, glancing around to make sure no one can hear me.

There is an intake of breath. 'I'm sorry to hear that. Have you involved the police?'

'No,' I say.

She doesn't ask any more. 'I have an appointment at 11.45 this morning. Will that suit?'

'Yes,' I say gratefully.

As soon as I walk through the estate agency's door, Jenny accosts me.

'Did you get my email yesterday afternoon?'

I shake my head. I haven't looked at my emails since I left the office before lunch.

'Sorry, I...'

I can't think what to say, how to cover up my absence yesterday, how to explain why I didn't return to work after my supposed doctor's appointment. But Jenny doesn't appear to notice my hesitation.

'We've won the contract to sell all the homes on that little new housing estate on the way to Crawley. I'd like you to go over there, get a feel for the place. The photographer is going later today. We need to get the brochures done as quickly as possible.' She looks at me expectantly. I don't answer fast enough.

'That's great news,' I say, but I can hear the flatness in my voice. I don't care. They'll be ugly new builds, created with little imagination, constructed poorly, one on top of the other. Jenny must sense my lack of engagement.

'Bigger bonuses.' She winks.

My mobile phone trills. I ignore it.

'I hope it's okay, but I've got a doctor's appointment at 11.45 a.m.,' I say deferentially. She may be my friend, but she is a director of the business, a partner to Peter, and I am only a lowly employee who can't afford to lose her job.

'Is everything all right?' she asks. 'You had a doctor's appointment yesterday as well, didn't you?'

'Yes, fine, nothing major. Can I go to the new builds later on?'

'Of course.'

I am lucky. If I was having the same conversation with Peter, I expect he would have said no.

Sitting at my desk, I pluck up the courage to look at my phone. There are two text messages. The first one is from Anna asking how I am feeling. The second one is from Ben. I hesitate. Should I read it? My hand is shaking. I don't want to. I know they are only words, but any communication with him feels wrong, dangerous. The trouble is, I can't stop myself from looking.

*'I hope you're feeling better this morning. So sorry I had to rush off. Let me know if you're free over the weekend. Ben x'*

I can feel my lips curl back into a snarl. The bastard.

## 16

I achieve little during the morning. Fatigue weighs heavily on my limbs, and my mind is incapable of concentrating on anything to do with work. I see the death notice, the certificate, and I feel repulsed at the thought of what happened last night. The hands of the clock on the wall opposite my desk seem to move slower and slower, but eventually it is 11.30 a.m. and time for me to slip out. The doctor's surgery is just a five-minute walk away in the town centre. I welcome the fresh air.

The waiting room is full. I pick up a well-worn *House and Garden* magazine and flick through the pages; the pictures blur; the words swim across the pages. When my name is called, I jump.

'Laura Swallow to room four.'

Quite why I hadn't thought of this before, I don't know, but I am taken aback. Dr Smithers is a man. I should have asked to see a female doctor, but it didn't cross my mind this morning. How can I let a man, and even worse, a young man like this good-looking chap, examine me? I hesitate in the doorway. He looks up expectantly and smiles.

'Please take a seat. How can I help you?'

I do as I am told.

I don't know what to say. I glance away and fiddle with my scarf. I can feel tears welling up, ridiculous, stupid tears that I want to bat away. He leans forwards and smiles at me.

'What is troubling you?' he says, his gentle eyes and square jaw making everything so much worse.

'I need a smear test,' I say hurriedly.

'Any particular reason why you need one urgently?'

'I think it is best if I see a nurse.' I get up quickly and make for the door.

'Wait!' he says, rising out of his chair. 'Mrs Swallow, Laura, if I may. I can sense something is wrong. Please share it with me.'

I pause, my hand on the door handle. It is easier if I have my back to him. Maybe I can let the words fall from my lips if he doesn't see me.

'I think I was raped.' I say it so quietly I wonder if he can hear.

'Please, sit down again.' He is behind me now, his hand on my arm. I flinch and step away, moving quickly back to the chair. He returns to his swivel chair, leaning forwards with his elbows on his knees. I wonder when it was that doctors started dressing so casually. Dr Woolley, who Mum took Donny, Becky and me to see at the slightest hint of a sniffle, always wore a suit and a tie, which he tucked into his shirt when examining his patients.

'Have you been to the police?' Dr Smithers asks.

'No,' I screech. 'Everyone wants me to go to the police, but I don't want to. Not yet anyway.' The everyone bit is nonsense, of course, as the only two people who know about my ordeal are Anna and this young doctor.

'You said that you think you have been raped. So I assume you're not sure? Do you think you were given a date-rape drug?'

I nod my head but keep my eyes averted from him.

'Would you like me to do an examination, to take a swab? We can check your blood and urine.'

I nod my head again and then speak. 'But not by you. No offence. Can a nurse do it? A woman?'

'Yes, of course.'

He tells me to wait in his room, and he disappears out into the corridor, the door shutting gently behind him. When he returns, he asks me to go back to the waiting room, where I sit trembling, and then some long minutes later a nurse with a deeply lined face and short, cropped white hair comes over to me. She bends down into her knees and says, 'Come with me, dear.'

I follow her meekly. She is tender with me, apologising when I bite my lip in pain, murmuring comforting words. And then when she is done and I am dressed and sitting waiting expectantly for her feedback, she says, 'I can't see any evidence of assault, my dear, or obvious evidence of penetration. You're as good as new down there. I've taken a swab and we'll send it away, but everything looks fine. That doesn't mean you haven't been attacked, of course.'

'What should I do now?' I whisper. I suppose in my heart of hearts, I know I haven't been subjected to intercourse. Nothing is sore, nothing hurts except my pride and my head. Whatever happened last night has seriously messed with my head even if my body is intact.

'Have you been to the police?'

I sigh and, once again, shake my head. I stand up and thank her for her time. She looks at me, a sadness glazing her eyes.

'We'll call you. You take care,' she says.

I am not sure what to do now. Why did I awake almost naked but with no obvious signs of assault? Did Ben strip off my clothes and then decide that I was too repulsive to touch? Is he a pervert? I shudder as my mind veers off into places of such horror I know it is imperative that I blank out my thoughts.

'Hello, Laura!'

I jump.

It takes me a long moment to place her. It is the distended stomach that jogs my memory.

'Oh. Hello, Charlene. Are you seeing the doctor?'

Her laugh is shrill. 'No! I work here. At least I did.' She leans against the wall, one hand cupping her enormous belly. She pauses expectantly. I don't speak. I have forgotten that she works at a doctor's practice. And for some reason it never crossed my mind that she might be working at my surgery, although given that there are now only three practices in town, it shouldn't be any surprise.

'It's my last day of work.' Her lips pull back across her large sparkling teeth, exposing bright pink gums.

'Until your maternity leave is over.' I finish the sentence for her. 'What do you do here?' I ask before noticing the badge.

'I am a medical administration manager.'

'It says medical administration assistant on your name badge,' I say bitchily, staring at her large, unnaturally pert breasts. Charlene really brings out the worst in me.

'My role is managerial. But as of two hours' time, that will no longer be the case. I'm quitting. Forever!' Her grin is smug.

I stare at her. Is Ian earning enough money to support his new family? Has he totally forgotten about Mel, or me for that matter?

'Good for you,' I say and walk away with a new sense of urgency. Thank goodness Charlene is leaving the surgery today. The thought of her noseying through my medical notes sends a new shudder through me. And damn Ian. I wonder if I should return to the courts after all; go for more money now that his earnings have increased.

What a horrid, horrid week this has been.

As I am leaving the surgery, I reach into my bag for my phone, but then my fingers unfurl from its edges. I switched it onto silent before seeing the doctor and am now about to turn the ringer back on. But my love affair with my phone has ended as abruptly as my feelings for Ben have been extinguished. Your phone can't hurt you, you idiot, I think to myself. Besides it could be Mel; you haven't spoken to her all week. I fish it out and look at it. I have two missed calls and a text, all from Anna. As I debate whether to call her back, she calls me again.

'Laura, how are you? I've been worried about you.'

'Sorry, I've been busy.'

'Are you at work?' She sounds horrified.

'I went to work this morning and have just left the doctor's.'

'Oh. Are you all right?'

'Yes.' I look around me to check no one is listening and whisper into the phone, my hand cupped around my mouth. 'The nurse couldn't see any evidence of rape, but she's done a swab,' I whisper.

'When will you get the results?'

'I don't know. Monday maybe. She said she'll call me.'

'I'm in town. I'll take you out for lunch and then we can watch a film at mine.'

'No, Anna. I've got to work.'

'You've been severely traumatised. I'm sure your doctor would be appalled if he knew you were going to work this afternoon.'

I sigh. 'I've got no choice.'

She is quiet for a moment.

'Do you want Brad to take you to the police?'

'No. I can't face it. I'll have it out with Ben myself when I'm feeling stronger.'

'That's a terrible idea,' Anna squeals. 'What if he hurts you properly or... goodness knows what could happen.'

'I've got to go now, but thanks for your help last night.'

'But, Laura—'

'I'll call you, Anna.' I hang up. She means well, but right now I need to clear my head and get back to work. At least work, however boring it might be, distracts me from the horrors of my personal life. As I'm walking back, I wonder whether Anna will change consultants, whether she will say something to Ben. She is more ballsy than I am; it wouldn't surprise me one little bit if she made a complaint on my behalf. The more that idea takes hold, the more I don't want that to happen. I decide to text her when I'm back in the office.

## 17

I manage a yoghurt and two cups of strong coffee for lunch. The coffee helps a little by making me feel more awake, in a jerky, panicked type of way. My heart feels as if it is lurching around in my chest; breathing is tight and erratic. When Jenny hands me the address of the housing development I'm meant to be visiting, it's a relief to know I can get out of the office, that I can yawn as much as I like in the privacy of my car.

I stride to the car park, shivering in the cold but relishing it at the same time. It helps me shrug off the fatigue. Everything seems out of kilter; I am out of kilter. I glance over my shoulder whenever I hear footsteps behind me, and when I am in the car park, I walk faster still, enveloped by a sense of unease in the gloomy, underground parking lot. Despite its familiarity, I am wary now of every shadow, every nook and cranny behind which there might be... I am not sure what might be lurking. I don't know whether I should be fearful, whether I *am* fearful. I take stock. Yes, I am fearful, of Ben for sure, but of what or whom else, I don't know.

My little silver Renault is snug in its space two-thirds along the second row, positioned exactly where it should be, where I last left it. The car park is empty of people but full of cars, as it normally is in the middle of the day, but nevertheless, I look around furtively before unlocking my car and jumping into the driver's seat as quickly as possible. Immediately, I press the lock button on the doors. I know I am being silly, but knowing and feeling are two very different things. As I start the ignition, I remember fragments of a film I watched where the assassin lay on the back seat and jumped up when the victim was driving. I turn to look, but there is nobody there. And then, as I am pulling out of my space, I wonder if someone is stowed in the boot of the car. If my feet were not otherwise engaged on the pedals, I would kick myself. Bloody stupid woman, I say out loud. I wonder if I should be driving, whether the drugs are fully out of my system. I will drive extra carefully.

As I steer the car out of Horsham and onto the A264 towards Crawley, I begin to relax. But relaxing isn't good. It allows my mind to wander and it swirls up the fear, the confusion, the sheer incomprehension as to why Ben is messing with my life in this way. What have I done to him? As a doctor, it would have been easy for him to get hold of the death certificate, for the newspaper to believe him when he placed the death notice, but why? Why is he doing this? It just doesn't make any sense.

I pull up into the new development, a small cul-de-sac of six executive homes. They are all large, five or six bedrooms, with zero privacy and gardens the size of postage stamps. With a sign proudly announcing 'Show Home', it is obvious where I am expected. There are a couple of cars parked outside and a few builders' vans parked further up the road. The door is slightly ajar.

'Hello,' I shout.

'Up here!' I recognise the voice. Phil and I have worked

together on numerous occasions. Although he isn't employed by our firm, he is our preferred photographer. He is efficient and always manages to make a property look more attractive, more spacious, lighter than it really is. These days his remit extends to a camera drone, which he uses to capture the exterior of the properties. I'm rather hoping he doesn't use it today, or at least if he does, restricts it to only capturing the front of the houses. I can't imagine the proximity to the neighbours will do much to promote sales.

I enter the show home. The house has been decorated and furnished in greys and taupes, with the exception of the living room, which has dark aubergine curtains and silver accessories. 'Adventurous,' I mutter sarcastically. Phil is in the kitchen, his camera bag perched on the large dark brown island unit, whilst he is on his haunches photographing a wall of shining white cupboards, behind which, I assume, the kitchen appliances are hidden. I wait for him to finish. Click, flash, and then he stands up and turns towards me.

'Shit, Laura, you look dreadful!'

'Thanks,' I mutter.

'Sorry. Didn't mean to be rude, but are you okay? You look ill.'

'It's been an awful week.'

'Why don't we pop the kettle on and you can tell me all about it!' He smirks and pauses for effect. 'Oh, now I know why we can't! This house is too modern for an ordinary appliance like a kettle.'

'Ha,' I say. 'Have you done upstairs yet?'

'No.'

'I'll start up there. I'm exhausted so would like to get this done as quickly as possible.'

'Sure thing,' Phil says and returns to his camera. 'I've got a flask in the car if you'd like a cuppa.'

'Thanks.'

Measuring up, writing notes, and concentrating on the house details provide a welcome distraction. I am in the last of the four bedrooms when I hear voices downstairs. I ignore them and concentrate on finishing.

I open the built-in wardrobe to assess the dimensions. There is a mirror on the inside of the door, and as I'm about to close it, I see the reflection of someone standing right behind me, and I feel the whoosh of breath on my neck.

I scream. In an instant, I career into the bathroom and am about to bolt the door when I take stock. It was a woman. My nerves are so frayed, my body so tense, my reaction is to flee. I inhale very deeply and turn around. Jenny is standing in the doorway to the bathroom, a look of deep concern on her pale face.

'Bloody hell, Laura. What was all that about?'

'I'm sorry,' I mutter and burst into tears.

'What's happened?' She puts her arms around me, and I let her hold my trembling body, relief coursing through my veins. Her short, ash blonde hair smells of coconut. I pull away as relief shifts to mortification. That was quite possibly the biggest overreaction I have ever experienced.

'Sit down,' Jenny instructs.

I glance at the room: the perfectly made bed with its shiny silver bedspread and plumped-up green cushions; the cream covered upright chair in the corner near the window. I catch sight of myself in the mirror; my face is white, my eyes set deep. I look away. Jenny points at the bed. I raise my eyebrows and hesitate.

'For heaven's sake, I'll straighten it when we're done.'

The mattress is hard. She sits down next to me.

'Are you going to tell me what's going on?'

I hesitate but then tell her everything. I need to trust someone, and Jenny is a key member of my cabal of close girlfriends.

She is quiet for a long time.

'I can't believe you came to work after being drugged, being raped.'

'Distraction,' I say.

'And you're sure you don't want to go to the police?'

'No, yes,' I say too loudly, too quickly, confused. 'I don't want to go to the police. Swear you won't tell anyone. Not a soul?' I beg as if I am a young girl extracting a promise from a flighty best friend. Jenny doesn't appear to mind. She takes my hand and squeezes it.

'I swear I will not tell anyone, ever. You can trust me, Laura.'

I nod. I know I can trust her.

She stands up. 'Let's get out of here. You look totally exhausted. I'll cook you supper at your house.'

I sniff loudly. Jenny is being so kind and understanding. As I stand, I feel dizzy; my head is pulsating. I grab the side of the bed.

'You're not well. Why don't you leave your car here and I'll drive you home? We can come and collect your car in the morning. You're working this weekend, aren't you?'

I nod.

The sense of relief that someone is looking out for me is utterly overwhelming. Phil has finished taking photographs; his camera bag is packed and slung over his shoulder.

'You take care.' He raises an eyebrow at me. 'Have a good weekend.'

'We'll lock up,' Jenny says. I watch Phil get into his car and drive away. The builders' vans have gone. The other houses are dark, yet to be lived in, and there is something desolate about this empty little cul-de-sac that is crying out for life and laughter. Jenny and I are alone now, her car parked in front of mine. I pull on my coat and stand in the doorway as she switches off the lights and sets the alarm. The light is fading fast, the blue sky has long gone, and the cold air is heavy with the promise of rain. As I am climbing into Jenny's small navy BMW, I notice a dark car parked at the top of the cul-de-sac, partially hidden in the shade of the single tree. I can't see if anyone is in it, but I do wonder. And then Jenny switches on the radio and starts chattering about her day.

## 18

Not for the first time in the past week, I am embarrassed about the lack of provisions in my kitchen.

'Impressive on the wine front.' Jenny laughs as she inspects my fridge. 'Thoroughly unimpressive on the food selection. I'll nip down to M&S and get us something.'

'Really, you don't have to,' I say unconvincingly.

'Take a paracetamol, pour yourself a glass of wine, and switch on the telly,' she instructs me.

'You're an amazing boss,' I say.

She scowls at me and disappears out of my front door.

About ten minutes later, the doorbell rings. Surprised that Jenny has shopped so quickly, I scuttle off the sofa. I am about to press the intercom to let her in when I do a double take. It's a female, but it isn't Jenny. I press the buzzer to talk.

'Hello, what are you doing here?'

'Come to check up on you and bring you food,' Anna says.

I pause. This is awkward. Jenny and Anna haven't met, and as they are from disparate parts of my life, it hasn't crossed my mind to introduce them. Clearly now I will have no choice. I am tempted to tell her I have a headache, to promise to see her tomorrow, but I have never been very good at lying, and I owe it to Anna to let her in. She has been a wonderful friend and, during the past few years, has scooped me up time and time again. Perhaps Anna and Jenny will get on like a house on fire. I hope so.

'Come up,' I say.

Despite the damp, cold evening, Anna is dressed in a short red skirt and long over-the-knee suede boots. She removes her shearling coat to reveal a glittery black jumper.

'Are you going out?' I ask.

'I am out!' She grins as she twirls around. 'I've got us a Chinese takeaway and a bottle of Dom Perignon and...'

The doorbell buzzes again as I wonder what on earth Anna thinks we're celebrating.

'Don't answer it!' Anna yelps.

I frown. 'It'll just be Jenny,' I say, striding towards the intercom again.

'What if it's HIM!' she says.

'It isn't. It's Jenny.' I can see Jenny on the small screen.

'Who's Jenny?' There's an edge to her voice.

'She's a colleague from work. I've told you about her lots of times!'

Anna shakes her head, her long, dark coiffured hair flicking back and forth across her shoulders. 'I don't think you should be letting anyone in,' she says melodramatically.

'Jenny isn't anyone. I've spent the last couple of hours with her. We work together. Anyway, I've told her what happened last night.'

'You've told her?' Anna looks shocked and sounds incredulous.

'Jenny is a good friend. You'll like her. She's as trustworthy as you are. Well, perhaps not quite as trustworthy, but I've sworn her to secrecy. She's a good person.'

A shadow passes over Anna's face, but as soon as Jenny is at the door, she is back to her normal, confident self.

'I've got us some comfort food,' Jenny says as she takes her coat off and places the M&S bag on the floor. 'Chicken, rice and veg will do wonders to soak up any nasties left in your system, followed by bread and butter pudding. I'll go and put the kettle on and warm these up.'

I am slow. My brain doesn't translate my thoughts into words fast enough, and my body is heavy with fatigue. Jenny strides across the living room into the kitchen, where Anna has already ensconced herself.

'Oh, hello!' Jenny says while I stand back and let them introduce themselves.

'I'm Anna. Laura's best friend. And you are?' she asks expectantly.

I sigh.

'Jenny Rowarth. I work with Laura.' She extends her hand, but Anna doesn't take it; instead she turns her back on Jenny and continues decanting the acrid, vinegary-smelling food onto as many plates as she can find in my cupboard. 'Looks like we'll be having quite a feast here tonight.' Jenny laughs.

'Oh. Are you staying?' Anna still doesn't turn around.

I find my voice. 'Yes, she's staying, and we'll have a lovely evening. I've been wanting to introduce you two.'

'I don't remember you mentioning a Jenny!' Anna says lightly. She turns around unexpectedly and hopefully after I have rearranged my face from the grimace I pull at Jenny. 'But it's a pleasure to meet you anyway.'

'I'm going to leave you both to sort out the food. I'm afraid I'm not very hungry and could do with sitting down.' I feel a wave of nausea again and stumble back to the sofa.

'I'm all done,' Anna says, flouncing out of the kitchen with a bottle of champagne. My stomach does another somersault at the thought of consuming it.

Jenny brings the mounds of food into the living room and places them on the table. Anna lets the cork out of the bottle and it pops out with a bang, causing me to tremble. She pours me a glass.

'Thanks, but I'll stick to my one glass of wine,' I say. She frowns.

We sit down. There is an awkward silence. Anna and Jenny start talking at the same time and then both stop. It's Anna who is acting weirdly, I decide, but I can't fathom what to say, how to put them both at ease.

'How can we bring this Ben to justice?' Jenny asks eventually.

'Do you want to talk about it?' Anna peers at me, her face creased with concern.

'Yes. Yes, I do want to talk about it,' I say. 'You two are the only people I can discuss it with. I'm scared. I don't know what happened, but it's pretty obvious Ben wants to do me harm, and I don't know why. I thought we were getting on so well.' I swallow a sob.

'He's not my doctor anymore,' Anna states.

'I didn't know he was your doctor,' Jenny says.

Anna ignores her. 'I've moved consultants. The thought of sitting in his room, him laying his filthy fingers on me...' Her voice trails off.

'Is that how you met him?' Jenny asks.

Neither of us answer.

'But there's a lot of other bizarre stuff going on. The obituary, Facebook. Obviously she won't have told you about that,' Anna flicks her hair towards Jenny and then takes a large gulp of champagne. She turns her body completely towards me. 'I wonder if that bloke you knew from school has something to do with it all.'

'What bloke?' Jenny asks.

'Eddy Drover,' I say.

'Oh goodness. The client. The one who reported you to Peter,' Jenny exclaims.

'You know about it?' I shake my head. Of course Jenny knows. Peter and she are co-directors.

Anna starts humming a song. It takes me a few moments to work out what the tune is, but then I recognise 'Gimme Luv Bruv'.

'Shut up, Anna,' I say.

She responds by singing louder, more in tune now.

'Don't tell me Eddy Drover is something to do with Lolly Luke Drover,' Jenny exclaims, eyes wide.

'Luke Lolly Drover,' I say. 'Eddy is, or rather was, his son.'

Anna smirks.

'He died of a heroin overdose, didn't he?' Jenny asks.

'Drink,' I say.

'I guess you know these things, as an obituary writer?'

I don't reply. Anna stops singing.

'I think it's bloody stupid allowing women estate agents to do viewings by themselves,' Anna states. It is such a non sequitur, it stuns both Jenny and me into silence. I sigh. Sometimes I wish Anna wouldn't expound her views on matters she knows little about. Jenny reacts faster than me.

'You're right, Anna,' Jenny says. 'Peter and I have put in place a new procedure. We'll be getting all potential buyers, and sellers for that matter, checked out before sending agents out on viewings. Otherwise we'll be sending a senior agent and a junior one out together. It's going to cost the firm more, but we can't take any risks.'

'That's a good thing,' I say. 'But possibly an overreaction.'

'Possibly, but actually it was Peter's idea.'

'I'm surprised.'

Anna breaks the silence. 'The thought of reporting to anyone...' She lets her voice trail away.

'What do you do?' Jenny asks her.

'Oh, I don't work.'

'Anna is involved in some great fundraising work,' I say.

'I don't work,' she repeats. 'I don't have to. I'm very lucky. When Laura goes back to court to increase her settlement from Ian – her ex – she'll be able to stop work too. Won't you?'

'That's exactly what I have suggested to her!' Jenny quips. I wonder why my friends are ganging up against me.

'I'm not going back to court,' I say.

'Surely you'd like to give up this little job of yours?' Anna waves her hand patronisingly.

'It isn't a "little" job!' I exclaim. 'And actually, I rather enjoy working.'

'She's a very good estate agent,' Jenny pipes in. 'She's likely to be promoted to director in the next year or so.'

'Really?' I say, my chest puffing out, pride easing away any misery.

'I was going to tell you when we go out for dinner next week, but you need a bit of cheering up now. You've been nominated for the Realtor of the Year award for the whole firm.'

'Who proposed me?' I ask, flabbergasted.

'Me and seconded by Peter. The copy you write for the advertisements is amazing. And the speed you produce those brochures... it's seriously impressive. On top of that we've had great feedback from clients, and in case you haven't noticed, you've sold more properties in the past three months than anyone else in the firm. I think you'll be rather pleased with your end-of-year bonus!'

I have a wide grin plastered on my face. Anna yawns. I am annoyed with her. Why is she behaving like a spoilt child this evening? Why isn't she happy for me? Proud that I am successful in my second career?

'What dinner?' Anna asks.

'Sorry?' I say.

'Jenny said you're going out for dinner next week.'

'We go out for dinner once a month.'

'I thought we could go to Noche's,' Jenny says. 'What do you reckon?' She stands up and starts clearing away some of the plates. There is a shameful amount of food left behind, but I am not hungry, and despite bringing most of it, Anna has only pecked at the fare.

'Donna Carrington got food poisoning after eating at Noche's,' Anna says, tipping the last of the champagne into her glass. She has drunk the majority of the bottle. I don't know who Donna Carrington is.

'Did you want any more champagne?' she asks Jenny, waving the empty bottle in front of Jenny's face. I am struggling with Anna's behaviour. She is normally a pleasure to be around: attentive, interested in others.

'I'm driving.' Jenny shrugs, leaning backwards. 'So how long have you two known each other?' Jenny asks, adeptly changing the focus of the conversation.

I hesitate.

'Nearly four years,' Anna says. 'I was Becky's friend first.'

'Becky's friend?' Jenny looks at us both quizzically.

'Laura's sister. She died. I was Becky's friend first.'

'Oh, yes, sorry. I met Becky a couple of times at Laura's do's over the years,' Jenny says.

'It's the four-year anniversary of her death next Friday. Laura and I go to her grave together and spend the day reminiscing. This year, I thought—'

'Please, Anna, not now.' I cut through her.

'Has Laura told you that she wants to get the police to relook at the events surrounding Becky's death? I've told her that all it will do is bring her more pain and heartache. Sadly, it can't bring Becky back.'

'Cut it out, Anna,' I say. I can't go there. I can't talk about Becky tonight, or even think about her. Not with everything else that's going on. I know I have been rude to Anna, but she deserves it.

'Do you mind if we call it a day?' I ask. 'I've got a thumping headache and would like to go to bed. Leave the washing up; I'll do it in the morning.'

'Ok,' Anna says.

Jenny pushes her chair back and starts piling up the dishes.

'Leave it,' I say limply.

'It'll take me ten minutes to sort this lot out. You go get ready for bed. You need to be with it for the meeting tomorrow morning.'

'What meeting?' Anna asks as she fiddles with her mobile phone.

'Our bimonthly office meeting. It's compulsory for everyone to be there,' I say wearily.

'On a Saturday?' Anna raises her neat eyebrows.

Anna is ignoring Jenny, who bustles from the table to the kitchen. I am so exhausted I can barely keep my eyes open. I sigh. I recall that I promised to have the brochures ready for two large new homes to present at the meeting, and now I can't remember whether I have actually done them.

'That's quick,' Anna mutters, as if to herself. 'Sorry I can't help clear up, Jenny, but my taxi's here already.' She doesn't sound sorry.

The tap is running in the kitchen.

'Let's talk tomorrow, when we're alone,' Anna whispers. 'I'm determined to help you sort this mess, work out what's going on. And let's plot to take down Ben together. The bastard cannot be allowed to get away with this.'

'Please, Anna, don't do anything without discussing it with me first. And don't discuss it with your solicitor friend. I need time to think.' I am so drained, but I can see that Anna has the bit between her teeth, and I need to stop her.

'Stop worrying.' She puts her hand on my shoulder then

removes it quickly, as if she has been burned. 'I'm your friend, Laura. You can rely on me.'

'Thank you,' I say, leaning back in my chair and yawning. I am forever relying on Anna.

I am still in my chair when Jenny emerges from the kitchen a few minutes later.

'You are meant to be in bed,' she chastises.

'I know, but I'm almost too tired to get up.'

She extends a hand. 'Let me help you!'

I smile and slowly get up. 'I'm sorry about Anna. She was quite rude this evening.'

'It's fine,' Jenny says. 'I guess she was a bit put out to find me here.'

I nod. 'I'll get a taxi to my car in the morning,' I say. 'No need for you to have your morning interrupted.'

'If you're sure?' Jenny is hesitant.

'Yes,' I say.

As I bolt the front door, I pick up my bag and glance at the phone. I have had two missed calls from Ben. And there's another text message. My hand is shaking as I open it.

'Hi, Laura, *really worried that you haven't answered your phone. Are you ok? Please let me know. Love, Ben x*'

How could he write something like that? He used the word *love*! He put a little *x* after his name. Is he a psychopath? Does he take his cheap thrills and then carry on as if nothing has happened? Does he have a split personality and can't remember what he did? I am sickened and have no idea what to do. Should I text him back and tell him that it's over? Our relationship that never really was a relationship? I wish Anna was still here so that I could ask her opinion. She's good at things like this. And so is Jenny for that matter. She has had to give the brush-off to quite a few unsuitable men during the short time she has been actively back on the dating scene. I turn my mobile off and get ready for bed.

# 19

Unsurprisingly, sleep doesn't come. My body is exhausted, aching, whilst my mind is sprinting through a maze of ifs and who's. Just as I doze off, my heart starts racing, causing palpitations to jolt me awake. I can't stop thinking of Ben, wondering what happened, what did he do? At 3.30 a.m. I give up trying to sleep, and get up to dig out my laptop, happy to have it back. It appears to be fixed, albeit working much slower than it did before. I bring it back to bed, pulling the duvet up under my chin to keep myself warm.

I Google Dr Ben Logan. If he did that to me, the chances are he's done similar things to other women. I wonder if someone might have exposed him online. My reasoning is that, as he is still practising as a doctor, he has not been convicted of anything. But online, it's anonymous. Safe even. Perhaps someone might have hinted at a misdemeanour. I search through to page twenty on Google, but I can't find anything. He's listed on a website that allows patients to rate their doctors. Kind, considerate, insightful, clever, brilliant: those are all the words used to describe him by his legion of fawning patients. No one has written *stay away, Ben Logan is a rapist.* I will have to be the first. In the middle of the night, I am resolved. I will report him, if not to the police, then to his hospital. It's my duty to stop him from harming other women. He is seriously unhinged, and it is terrifying to think that he is treating vulnerable women, no doubt spending time alone with them in his consulting room, perhaps even doing home visits. He has so many opportunities to take advantage of women.

I slip into sleep eventually. My dreams are lurid, confused, scary, and when the alarm goes off at 7 a.m., I am jolted from a deep slumber, convinced that someone is battering down my front door. Sitting bolt upright in bed, my heart racing so hard it feels as if it will jump out of my chest, I listen. There are the familiar gurgles from the radiator, the faint pattering of feet from downstairs, the dustbin lorry rattling on the street outside. But nothing else.

I must hurry if I am to get a taxi to collect my car and be back in the office for the meeting. With no time for a shower, I wipe a flannel over myself, throw on my make-up and grab a cup of coffee. And then the doorbell is ringing and the taxi driver is waiting for me. It's pouring rain; a dark, dank, miserable Saturday to match my mood. He has music blaring, much too loud for my fogged-up brain.

When we arrive in the new cul-de-sac, it feels more like 5 p.m. on a winter's afternoon than 8.15 a.m. in the morning. I pay the taxi driver. The rain is almost horizontal, driving into my face, so I pull my hood over my head to protect myself, just able to see my feet and run over to my car, quickly climbing in. I shiver from the cold and the wet. I wonder whether these houses will feel more welcoming when they are lived in, or whether the fact they have been built in a dip has given them a chilly, inhospitable feel despite their plushness. As I switch on my engine and the lights come on automatically, I decide it must be me and my mood. I don't have to worry; I won't be living here. I just need to write up the particulars.

I am glad I only need to venture five miles down the dual carriageway. It's exactly the sort of weather I hate driving in, bringing to mind the conditions Becky was in on that late November evening nearly four years ago. I think of the death notice that promises I will die in a car accident. My heart is pounding and my eyes are sore and grimy from staring too hard. A lorry drives into the left lane from a slip road and I'm forced to pull over into the fast lane. A loud horn. A red saloon is right behind me, flashing its lights. Where did he come from? I pull back into the slow lane, and he gesticulates at me as he drives past, water sloshing up onto my windscreen. My wipers are moving so fast, I wonder if they will fly off.

I am going slowly now. A woman with a Volvo load of children passes me, the kids pointing at my Renault. And then a white van roars past, lights flashing, horn hooting. With a thumping heart, I realise something must be wrong with my car. I slow down further and look in the rear mirror, sitting up tall in my seat, peering to check if there is smoke coming out of the exhaust, but with the heavy spray from the rain, I can't see anything. No lights are showing up on the dashboard, and the car isn't making any strange noises. In fact, it feels perfectly normal. I keep my eyes firmly on the road in front of me, driving carefully, slowly, my fingers gripped so tightly around the steering wheel, I can feel them numbing. I try to ignore the burning gazes of occupants in passing cars. I can't stop. It is too dangerous. Only a mile or so more to go until I reach the roundabout, until I can pull over and find out what the hell is the matter with the car.

A large SUV slips in behind me, its lights shining brightly into my rear mirror despite the daylight. I sense it is too close. I put my foot down on the accelerator; I need to put more space between the car behind and myself. If I brake, he will rear-end me, an inevitability in these wet, slippery conditions. But then another car slides in front of me, a silver estate car. It brakes suddenly. Are we at the roundabout already? In that instant, I know what is going to happen. In that instant, I think of Becky and wonder whether she knew that she was about to die, as I know right now. I think of Mel, my darling girl. I think of how I am going to be crushed between these two cars: the silver one at the front, the dark, larger one behind me that is going to mow me down and smash me up. Will it hurt? I brace myself for the bang, the screeching of metal, the pain. They've won, I think. Whoever wrote that in the newspaper, they've won.

But it doesn't happen like that.

## 20

T he dark SUV pulls out from behind me suddenly, with the audible roar of an expensive, powerful engine. Water surges up to the side of my little car, splashing over my windscreen, and despite the rapid tick, tock of my windscreen wipers going fast, faster, the very fastest they can manage, for that split moment, I can see nothing. I shut my eyes and brace my body, slamming my foot onto the brake pedal. I am thrown forwards as I stop, but I can sense the car sliding headlong, and I know it is going to hit the rear of the silver car in front. And I pray that there is nothing behind me; otherwise I will be crushed.

The jarring of my car slipping into the estate car in front throws me forwards and hurls me backwards, my seatbelt cutting into my neck. I expect to be engulfed in an airbag. But I'm not. There are horns blaring, the sound of water cascading on metal. But I am still. I open my eyes and look down at my body, expecting to see seeping redness. I look up, assuming I will see shattered glass. But the windscreen is intact and the wipers are still swiping from side to side, tick, tock, backwards and forwards. I am still. Despite the noise outside, I can hear my ragged breath. And then there is a rapping on my passenger window.

'What the fuck?'

'I'm sorry,' I say before realising that the red-faced man dressed in a tracksuit can't hear a word that I am saying. I switch on my car's hazard lights and take stock. I'm alive! My car isn't crumpled around me. My neck is sore, but that's ok. I flex my arms and my legs, and nothing else hurts. Slowly, I turn and wind down the passenger window. The rain is almost horizontal now and comes slanting into the car. The man in the tracksuit is sopping wet, his brown hair stuck to his forehead.

'You've bashed my fucking car!' he yells, gesticulating at his rear bumper. 'Can't you watch where you're going?'

'I'm sorry,' I say. And then I burst out laughing. It is so funny, so amazing that I am still alive. I know this is an inappropriate reaction, but it's better than crying, isn't it? I just can't help myself as my body buckles over the steering wheel and I let the rain mingle with my tears of laughter, my torso convulsing into hysterics. I wish Anna were here. She would think it funny too.

'You're a fucking madwoman! What with the sicko words written across your car. I'm calling the police. You must be on something.'

He turns away. I pull up the window and watch him as he removes his phone from his pocket and hurries back into his car. A moment later he comes back out again and gesticulates wildly, waving his arm towards the hard shoulder. He wants me to move the car over: the thought forms slowly in my dulled brain. I can do that. My car must be ok if he thinks I can move it. I watch as his rear lights come on and he indicates to the left. He pulls over and then gets out of the car again. His clothes are like a second skin now, an unattractive blue nylon second skin plastered to his fat stomach and thick thighs.

Gingerly, I turn on my engine. When did I turn it off, or did it stall? It starts immediately. I glance to my right. There is a row of cars backed up. I look in the mirror. The cars are queuing as far as I can see. Shit, that's because of me, I think. The laughter stops. I indicate to the left and move the car forwards. There is the sound of scraping metal, but the car moves, and three seconds later I am also parked up on the hard shoulder. As I look out of the window to get out of the car, I see strangers rubbernecking, staring at me, pointing at the car. They're gruesome, enjoying other people's misery, I think.

I pull the hood of my coat over my head, partly to protect myself from the rain, partly as a mask to protect myself from the stares of strangers. I climb out quickly, a pain in my neck causing me to reach up and rub it. And then, as I shut the car door, I notice it. The wording. The black, scrawled writing all over the car. How the hell did I miss that when I got in? I walk around the car, horror increasing. The words are on every side. *Slate Wilders Fucking Useless Estate Agency. Fuck Slate Wilders. Slate Wilders – rip-off merchants.* They are big, black and easy to read. I haven't got a clue how they got there, who graffitied them all over my car.

I run my finger over the words on the rear, hoping that the paint or ink will come off on my hand, but it doesn't. Of course it doesn't. The rain would have washed it off if it had been erasable. The man I rear-ended is standing there, oblivious to the weather, his hands on his hips, rain dripping off the end of his bulbous nose, staring at me aggressively.

'The police are on their way, so don't think about doing a runner,' he barks, hands on his hips.

'I have no intention of doing a runner,' I say. 'I'm the victim here as much as you. In fact, if you hadn't braked so suddenly, it wouldn't have happened.'

'Is that so?' he sneers and takes a step towards me. I move sideways, ostensibly to look at the damage to the front of my car and his rear bumper. Mine is quite crumpled. The bumper is partly hanging off, and wisps of steam rise out of the bonnet. I blink tears away. I can't afford to be carless. I can't afford the inevitable insurance hike that will result from this accident, especially as, on the face of it, it looks like it was my fault. I bend down to look at his rear bumper. There is a small indentation in the centre, but other than that, I can't see any damage. I wonder why he's making such a fuss. We could just swap insurance details, couldn't we?

'Who the fuck drives around with words like that on their car?' His upper lip curls as he strides towards me. Hypocrite, I think. It's all right for him to use filthy language, but he objects to the wording all over my car. He thinks I'm a deranged revenge woman, I assume. That's why he's called the police. And on cue, the blue flashing lights arrive. A police car pulls up behind us.

A policeman and a woman climb out. Angry tracksuit man pounces on them.

'She's a liability, and look at the car she's driving around in! Thank goodness my other half has got the kids this morning. You don't want young ones reading stuff like that!'

'Good morning, sir, madam.' The policeman glances from him to me. 'I'm Constable Patrick Walker and this is Constable Allen.'

'She drove into the back of me. Didn't look where she was going. You need to breathalyse her, test her for drugs or something.'

'It wasn't my fault,' I say and immediately think how lame that sounds.

'Of course it was your bloody fault!'

'Thank you, sir. Why don't you hop back into your car, and Constable Allen here will take your details.' The young policewoman looks far from thrilled to be on the receiving end of tracksuit man's rant. She steps forwards and indicates for him to open his car door for her. Huffing and puffing, he does as instructed. Just a little boy underneath all of that adult flab and nylon; scared of the rozzers, I think.

I stand immobile watching them, watching the people staring at me from the warm comfort of their cars. Shit, I think. I'm going to be late for the bimonthly meeting. I glance at my watch. I am late. It will already have begun. What will Peter say?

'I need to...'

'Follow me into my car, please, madam,' Constable Walker says.

I do as instructed, trying to shake some of the rain off my coat before clambering into the passenger seat of the police car. 'Ouch,' I say as I wince with pain from my neck.

'You all right, madam?'

I nod, which is a silly motion because it hurts all over again. I look around the interior of the car. It's the first time I have sat inside a police car, and other than a screen that is larger than a typical satnav, it looks surprisingly ordinary.

He asks me to explain what happened, why I didn't think it was my fault. I tell him about the threatening black SUV, how tracksuit man pulled in front of me and braked suddenly, and then he asks me about the writing all over my car and I burst into tears. I so nearly tell him everything. So nearly. But I look at him, and he is young enough to be my son, and I think, you won't understand.

'I'm sorry,' I hiccup. 'A grown woman sobbing like a baby. It's not very dignified.'

'Crying is good,' he says. 'Do you have your driving licence, your insurance details?'

I fumble in my bag and find my driving licence. 'My insurance details are at home, but I am fully insured. And taxed,' I add.

He is scribbling things down and takes a while to look up again. I lick away the taste of blood from my lower lip.

'So, Mrs Swallow, can you explain the obscene wording on your car?'

'No,' I say lamely.

'Did you write it?'

'Of course not!'

'Have you reported it?'

'To the police, you mean?'

He nods.

'No. I only just noticed it. Now, when I got out of the car. After the accident.'

He raises his eyebrows. If you had as much on your mind as I have, you would understand, I think.

'I was in a hurry to collect my car and get to work. It was raining. I didn't see it.'

'Where were you collecting your car from?'

'A new development of houses towards Crawley.'

'Were you staying there?'

'No. I'm an estate agent. I left my car there last night because I wasn't feeling well. A colleague drove me home, and I took a taxi there this morning to collect it.'

He is silent again, his pen poised above a pad of paper. 'Do you know who might have done this?'

I shake my head and look away from him. Would Ben do something like this? It seems unlikely. Then again, what do I know about the man? And who knew that I had dumped my car in a deserted cul-de-sac overnight? I remember then, the dark vehicle I had seen as I left yesterday evening with Jenny. Had someone been lying in wait for me? Or maybe it wasn't me at all. The graffiti is targeted towards Slate Wilders. A disgruntled ex-employee? Someone who has been gazumped? Perhaps they assumed that I was driving a company car. That is a much more pleasant thought. It's not me who is being targeted.

And if I was targeted, then why and who? Of course, if I am the target and the police can work out who vandalised my car, they'll work out who wrote the obituary, who raped me. It all points back to Ben. Or Eddy. Or perhaps even Ian. I rub the base of my hands into my eyes and sigh.

'Does anyone hold a grudge against you, Mrs Swallow?'

'No. I don't think so. Could it be someone who wants to harm the firm? Slate Wilders?' I ask.

'That is a possibility. I would like you to come down to the station, and I'll take a full statement and issue you a crime number.'

'What, now?' Panic edges my voice. I am already over thirty minutes late for the meeting. I'll need to text Jenny.

'Yes, now.' His fine sandy eyebrows edge up his forehead.

'I'll just...' I hold up my phone. He nods. The back door of the car opens and the young female constable slips in.

'All done,' she says to her colleague. Tracksuit man starts up his car and roars away. I didn't even get his name and address, but assume the police did. I assume he'll make a claim against me. Constable Walker starts the police car.

'Is it all right if I call the office to tell them I'm going to be late?' I ask. The timidity I suffer around people of authority, particularly people in uniforms in authority, is evident in my voice.

'Of course,' he says as he indicates and carefully pulls out of the lay-by. I glance around and see that a notice has been placed on the windscreen of my car. 'Police Aware'. I shudder as I call the office.

## 21

'Good morning, Slate Wilders. How can I help you?'

'Can I speak to Jenny, please. It's Laura and it's urgent.'

'She's in a meeting.'

'I know. Please disturb her.'

I can sense a heavy doubt in Corinne's voice. She is young, new and beautiful. I can see why Peter put her front of house. And she will have been given strict instructions not to disturb the bimonthly meeting on any account. I am put on hold. I had forgotten how frustrating the music is; around and around it goes, *Eine kleine Nachtmusik.* So unoriginal. I am vaguely disappointed the policeman hasn't put the blue light on the car. I watch as we go back around the roundabout, towards Crawley rather than towards Horsham.

Where are we going? Why aren't we going to Horsham? The roads are so busy despite the lousy weather. Christmas shopping come early, I assume. Why am I still on hold? And what the hell am I doing in a police car?

'I'm sorry, Laura, but they can't be disturbed.'

'I know it's the bimonthly meeting, but I need to speak to Jenny. It's urgent.'

'Hold on.' The music comes on again, and if I weren't sitting in a police car next to two police constables dressed in full uniform, I would have screamed.

Corinne comes back on the line. 'I'm really sorry, but she says she can't be disturbed.'

'Wait… please tell Peter and Jenny I've had a car accident. I'll be there as soon as I can.'

I don't know if she hears me because mid-sentence there is the long beep of a dead telephone line.

'Why are we going to Crawley?' I ask.

'We are going to need to file a report and interview you, and that's done at Crawley these days, not at Horsham.'

'I haven't done anything wrong!' I say. I get no response.

AT THE POLICE station I'm whisked into a small airless room, and Constable Walker fills in some forms. He asks me lots of questions and then, eventually, gives me a crime number and tells me I need to contact my insurance company and organise for my car to be towed away as a matter of urgency. He stands up.

'We'll be in touch,' he says.

I am escorted to the front of the building, and then I am outside in the pouring rain, wondering what the hell has just happened. I stand there motionless. Should I go back in and tell them everything that has happened to me during the past week? Have I just missed a perfect opportunity, or should I go with my gut feeling and get the hell away from the police station and carry on with my ordinary life? How am I meant to get home from Crawley when I'm carless?

I stumble out onto the pavement and find myself walking,

almost running, not knowing if I am even going in the right direction. I need to get to the station, take a train back to Horsham. I clutch my handbag to my chest, my hood far down over my eyes, my feet sopping wet and freezing cold from carelessly walking through puddles. I am shivering now. A car drives a little too close to the pavement and I jump away; my nerves are firing, my heart thumping against my chest wall, my neck tender.

There is a road sign to the railway station, so I follow it. I run now, weaving in between dawdling Saturday shoppers. And then I have a bit of luck. A train to Horsham pulls onto the platform just as I arrive. It is only an eight-minute journey, but I am late, late, late. I need to hurry to work. Jenny told me I'm in line for a directorship, so I need to show my commitment. I assume I'll get a healthy pay rise, which I need desperately. If I could stop Mel from having to take on waitressing to pay her way at university, it'll make life so much better for her. And perhaps we could have a holiday, overseas even. The first since the divorce. That would be amazing. We could visit Anna and Jim in one of their holiday houses.

I jiggle my foot up and down and stare out of the window, the droplets masking the houses, the vegetation, creating an ombre of greys and browns. As soon as the train slows down into the station, I am up and the first out of the carriage, racing up the station steps, hurtling back down the other side, running along the pavement.

And before I know it, I am standing in front of Slate Wilders. I catch sight of myself in the large estate agency window. I look a wreck: sopping wet, make-up smeared across my face, my hair plastered flat. Hardly the professional image of an estate agent. I pause for a moment. Should I go home? But then I glance up and I see a flash of movement at the upstairs window. Peter's office. He's seen me, so I can't go home now.

Shivering, I stamp my feet up and down to try to get warm,

shaking off some of the excess water on my coat, in my shoes, and then I push the door open. Corinne is the only person sitting downstairs. She looks up with alarm as I walk in, quickly picks up the telephone and says, 'Now.'

I stride towards the stairs at the back of the room, but she stops me.

'Um... can you wait down here a moment. Jenny is on her way.'

'Why?' I ask.

Corinne reddens. 'Um... I don't know.' She turns away.

I hear heavy footsteps on the landing above, and Jenny is coming down the stairs.

'Hi, Jen. What a helluva morning,' I say. But then I notice her face. There is something amiss. Very amiss.

'Can you come in here?' Jenny points to the cupboard-sized kitchenette at the back of the office, where there is barely enough space for two people.

'Why?'

But she ignores me and squeezes herself into the room. I look at her quizzically.

'I'm sorry, Laura. You're going to have to go home. I'm really sorry.'

'What?'

'I'll call you later, okay?' She edges out of the narrow space, past me.

'No!' I say, putting my hand across the doorway to try to stop her from walking past me. 'What's going on? I've had a car accident; someone has graffitied all over my car. It feels like my life is collapsing around me.'

'Please, Laura, don't make a scene. I'll call you, I promise.'

This isn't like Jenny. This isn't my warm friend from last night, the person who has collapsed in ridiculous giggles with me when we have had too much to drink; my comrade in arms with whom I have pored over inappropriate dating sites and shared our mutual hopes and dreams.

Her face is expressionless and she is avoiding looking at my eyes. Reluctantly, I pull my hand away, my eyes imploring. What is going on? Why am I being left out? As she walks away, she turns briefly, and her eyes meet mine as if she is trying to tell me something that I don't understand. Then she hurries upstairs.

I run out of the estate agency, pushing past a couple who are on their way in, rushing outside, where my stinging tears mingle with the sharp sheets of rain. I stifle a sob and run back past the shops, dodging in between the recalcitrant Saturday shoppers, hurrying until I reach the front door of my apartment block. I fumble with the keys, and as soon as I am inside the lobby, I shrug off my coat and my shoes and run, in stockinged feet, up the communal staircase. By the time I am at my own front door, out of breath, I am crying, fat globules running down my face. I open the front door and sink onto my carpet in the hallway. Nothing makes sense. Absolutely nothing makes any sense whatsoever.

I have rarely, if ever, felt so alone. Who can I turn to? Who will pick me up and give me a hug and make things better? I have nobody. Now Jenny has turned her back on me, my only real friend is Anna. What would I do without Anna? I try to recall the name of her solicitor friend. I definitely need a lawyer. But first I need a hot bath. My limbs ache and my head is pounding.

I count in my head: one, two, three. But I don't have the energy to get up. I try again. One, two, three, four, five. I heave myself up and drag my feet to the bathroom, turning on the bath taps. The water comes out quickly and is scalding hot. I drop my clothes onto the floor, put my phone next to the bath, and sink into the comforting water, feeling, for the first time today, a sense of great relief. Holding my breath, I shut my eyes and sink my head down under the water, enjoying the sensation of my hair floating around my shoulders, the tension in my neck easing. As I come up for air, gasping, my phone is ringing. Once my friend, now it makes me nervous. But I can't forego it. What if Mel needs me? I lean to the side of the bath and look at the screen.

I'm relieved that it's Anna. Wiping my hand on the bath towel, I accept her call and put her on loudspeaker.

'How are you this morning?'

'Terrible. You can't imagine what has happened to me.' I tell her about the accident, the graffiti, Jenny's strange reaction, and not being allowed back into the office.

'I know you won't like me for saying this, but there's something about Jenny that makes me uncomfortable.'

'Oh, come on,' I say. 'You were just put out because you weren't expecting her to be here.'

'Maybe,' Anna admits. 'But she's hiding something. I don't know what. I just sense she's hiding something. Remember I can tell these things. I'm a highly sensitive person.'

I laugh. It probably isn't the reaction Anna wants, but so be it.

'I've known Jenny for fifteen years. You've met her for five minutes.'

'You were married to Ian for, what was it, ten years?' Her voice is icy.

'Sixteen, actually,' I admit reluctantly.

'Quite. And you didn't know he was a cheating bastard. Sometimes it's easier for an outsider to view things objectively.'

I fall silent for a moment, listening to the drips of my wet hair falling into the bathwater. Perhaps Anna is right. But how devastating it would be if Jenny turns out not to be the friend I think she is.

I change the subject. 'I think I should speak to that solicitor friend of yours.'

'Sure. I'll give him a call. Let me know if you need anything.'

I spend the next couple of hours sorting out the car: speaking to my insurance company and telling them about the accident and the graffiti (it was difficult to explain that one, the man didn't believe me – thought I had decorated my car myself); arranging for it to be towed to a garage; and realising that my insurance cover does not entitle me to a rental car whilst mine is being mended.

I wait all weekend, but I hear from no one. Jenny doesn't call. Anna doesn't call back, and annoyed that she may be right about Jenny, I don't contact her. I try ringing Mel, but even my daughter doesn't pick up or return my calls. I can't work out whether the silence is a relief or a concern.

I spend the thirty-six hours watching episode after episode of *The Good Wife*, grateful that I can lose myself in a drama that is so far removed from my own life, it enables me to forget everything. By Sunday evening, I decide that a bit of Alicia from *The Good Wife* needs to rub off on me. I am not going to stand for any nonsense. I am not going to be scared. I will get a good night's sleep, and then I will go into work and find out what Jenny's problem is. In the evening, I will go to the hospital and confront Dr Ben Logan. Perhaps I'll even track down Eddy Drover. Just as I am drifting off to sleep, I remember. I don't have a car. Shit. I can't do anything without a car. On the other hand, if I don't have a car, I can't be killed in a car accident. There is a silver lining after all.

## 22

I am feeling much better on Monday morning and stride into the office with a confident smile on my face, wearing my highest heels. But I know straight away that something is wrong. The atmosphere is taut, no one looks at me, and despite the fact that I am early for work, it seems like everyone else has already got there before me. I walk up the stairs towards my desk. Jenny blocks my path. She is wearing a black suit, funereal.

'Can you come with me into Peter's office,' she says, unsmiling.

'You could at least let me dump my things.' I smirk, but she doesn't smile back.

'It would be best if you come straight in.' I have never experienced this Jenny before, and I know then that I am in serious trouble.

Peter is standing behind his desk. There are two chairs. Jenny sits on the taller one; I'm left to sit in the lower chair. Neither has suggested I remove my coat. I place my handbag on my lap, as if it is a protective device to halt the wounds that I know are about to be inflicted upon me. My breathing is shallow and my knees are shaking.

Peter sighs dramatically and sits down.

'What's going on?' I look at Jenny and Peter, one to the other. Neither of them appear to be willing to meet my eyes.

'It is with sadness that we will be letting you go for gross misconduct,' Peter says, fiddling with a file on his desk. It is my file. Laura Swallow is written in large capital letters across the front.

'What?'

'You have brought the firm into disrepute, and we have no option but to let you go.'

'For what?'

Peter clears his throat and throws a strangely desperate glance at Jenny. She sighs and takes over.

'As you know, your car was graffitied with words that have caused great embarrassment to Slate Wilders—'

'That's not my fault!' I interrupt.

'We are not of the same opinion,' Peter says.

'But—'

Jenny interrupts. 'We received an email with a pornographic photograph. It was sent from your work email and would have gone to all of our clients, but fortunately it was picked up by our firewall. It went to all the staff though.'

'What? That doesn't make any sense. I haven't even used my work email this weekend!'

'The photo was sent to Eddy Drover, copied to everyone else. It was of you.' Jenny looks at the floor.

'What do you mean, it was of me?'

'It was of you in a compromising position and appears to be a revenge pornographic photo, perhaps because you were so angry about Edward Drover's letter to Peter.'

I drop my bag onto the floor and stand up. I don't know whether to laugh or cry. Sex photos are something for Mel's generation, and as I've had sort-of sex just once in the past six years, it most certainly is not of me. My sex life with Ian was so vanilla cameras never appeared in our bedroom. The very thought makes me shudder. I can't stop myself from shouting.

'For God's sake, Jenny! You've known me for fifteen years. You know I would never do anything like that! It's ridiculous. You know I've been attacked, targeted, threatened. There's shit going on in my life, and I don't know why or who is behind it. I thought you were supportive of me?'

My fury is directed at Jenny. Jenny, who is meant to be my friend but right now appears to have turned into my enemy. She tugs at the sleeve of her black jacket. I am glad that she is looking uncomfortable.

'Don't yell at Jenny,' Peter says; his eyes are narrowed. 'We believe you may have brought the firm into disrepute, so we have no option but to let you go.'

'On full pay whilst you investigate, I assume,' I spit.

'Um, no. We have spoken to our insurers, and we believe we have sufficient evidence to warrant instant dismissal,' he replies.

'But I didn't do this! I didn't graffiti the car. I didn't send any email to Eddy Drover or to anyone. I haven't seen the email that you're referring to! It's obvious that my email account has been hacked, and the photo can't possibly be of me.'

'I'm sorry, Laura,' Jenny says, softening.

'Show me the photo,' I demand. They glance at each other. Peter pales; Jenny reddens. I brace myself. Peter hesitates and then flips his computer screen towards me and presses a few buttons on his keyboard. They both look away, out of the window, anywhere but at me or the computer screen.

I look.

I feel sick.

I yelp quietly. It is horrible, disgusting, repulsive. The only person who has that view is the nurse who does my biannual smear, and if it wasn't for my hand resting on my thigh, with my distinctive small sapphire ring that belonged to my mother and the small scar on my thumb both in clear focus, I wouldn't have even known for sure it was me.

'Oh God.' I sink back into the chair. 'I didn't take that.'

'It's a selfie,' Peter says blandly, switching off the screen and turning it back to face him.

'You know about these things, do you?' I spit.

Peter reddens and purses his lips.

I break the silence. 'Did Eddy Drover see it?'

Peter narrows his eyes. Shit, I think. I've just given him more evidence that it was me by showing an interest in Eddy.

'I don't know.'

'What are you going to do with it?' I am trembling.

'Delete it from the server, of course.'

'I think you should keep it. As evidence. We need to find who is doing this. I'm going to tell the police.' I start pacing up and down the room, tugging at my hair, chewing the side of my mouth.

'We need to find who is doing what?' Peter narrows his eyes at me.

'There is someone out to get me. The obituary, the death certificate, the graffiti. For God's sake, I was date raped on Thursday night!' I screech. And then it clicks in my head as if the pieces of a jigsaw have all aligned. 'The person who raped me obviously took the photograph and broke into my email account. You'll need to give the evidence to the police!'

'Laura, you need to see a doctor,' Peter says. Jenny is looking at her feet and picking at her fingernails.

'Why? I've already seen a doctor.'

'For your mental health,' Peter interjects.

'There's nothing wrong with my mental health!' I am screaming again.

'Keep your voice down,' he instructs. He stands up and

walks towards the window, looking out, his back to us. His grey jacket is shiny at the back where he leans against his chair.

'We think that the death notice in the newspaper has triggered something in you. Obviously it was another Laura Swallow, and we are wondering whether everything else that has happened is a figment of your imagination. We wonder whether the stress has snapped you and you did the car graffiti yourself.'

'What!' I yell, unable to keep control of my fury. 'There is nothing wrong with me! How dare you insinuate that! I'm going to the police.' I grab my bag.

'That isn't a good idea,' Peter says, turning around to face me. 'We think you should keep the police out of it.'

'Why?'

'Don't do anything for a couple of days, Laura.' Jenny puts her hand on my arm. I shrug it off. 'Go and see your doctor. Tell him everything, and then if you're still convinced that all of this is real, only then go to the police.'

'I need to know who sent the email! Who took that photograph!' I can feel any sense of self-control dissipating into desperation. Tears start welling up, but I am not going to shed them in front of Peter and Jenny. I dig my nails deep into the palm of my hand and bite the inside of my mouth. The metallic taste of blood is perversely satisfying. I look around the room, taking it all in, aware that this will likely be the last time I stand in Peter's office. I note the slanting floor, the bookcase devoid of books, the fluorescent strip light in the centre of the dark oak-beamed ceiling. I will be glad to never see Peter again, but Jenny... Is this the end of our long-standing friendship? I take several deep breaths and try to regain some control.

'Will you be paying me my notice?'

'Yes,' Jenny says at the identical time Peter says, 'No.'

'For God's sake!' I yell again. 'This is shambolic. I'll see you in an industrial tribunal!' I wave my arms around as I wonder whether I have just issued an empty threat. I have no idea what happens in an industrial tribunal, but from somewhere deep within the recesses of my memory, I recall Ian talking about it many years ago; how his company hadn't followed precise procedures over someone's dismissal and they ended up at an industrial tribunal. The lack of a letter or something quite administrative had resulted in the company paying the aggrieved employee thousands of pounds. Thank you, Ian, I think to myself. I wonder whether this knowledge will help me.

Jenny stares at Peter, a beseeching look in her eyes. They've argued over this, I surmise. The silence is long and heavily laden with emotion. I am glad Jenny still has a heart. Peter reddens and scowls.

'You will be on full pay for a further week whilst we investigate the matter further,' he says grudgingly.

I hesitate for a moment and then turn to walk out of the room.

'Laura!' Jenny says. I turn, but the look on Peter's face is one of such fury that I ignore them both and walk out of the room, past my desk that is no longer my desk, and back down the stairs. I keep my eyes to the ground and don't look up until I am out of the front door and back on the street.

I have one week. One week of pay and then what? No job, I assume, no money, no reference. I stop walking. Oh shit! I forgot to ask if they would write me a reference. Will Jenny? I pray she will. At least then I might stand a chance of getting another job. If she doesn't, then what? And there I was thinking about holidays and easing the financial pressure on Mel.

'Rob!' I see him hurrying towards Slate Wilders, his hands in his pockets, trousers just a little too skinny to be smart. He looks around, and when his eyes settle on me, I can see that moment of indecision, the thought process that runs through his young brain: can I disappear without her realising, or do I need to face the music?

'Rob!' I holler again. He can't ignore me now.

'Hiya, Laura.' His face is the colour of ripe tomatoes. Poor Rob. He doesn't deserve the embarrassment. He shuffles from foot to foot.

'I know this is awkward, but could you do me a favour?'

'Okay,' he says, not looking at me.

'That email. Can you forward it to me? It's just I haven't seen it and I need to find out who has hacked into my account.'

He looks up, surprised. 'Sure. I knew it couldn't have been you. No disrespect or anything, but you're old and you're classy.' If the situation weren't so perverse, I might have chuckled. As it is, worry eliminates humour. He whips his mobile phone out of his coat pocket, and with a few jabs of the finger, the email is on its way to me. I feel heavy with relief. At least now I might have the chance of tracking down where it comes from, although I have no idea how.

'Thanks, Rob. I would never, ever do something like that. I hope you know?'

'Yeah,' he says. Poor lad. I expect the disparity between my middle-aged private parts and the virile porn he and his generation watch will be deeply shocking. I let him go and he almost trips up in his hurry to get away from me.

## 23

I walk home slowly, too numb to think. On automatic pilot, I collect my post from the little grey box in the communal downstairs hall and traipse up the stairs. There are three envelopes: a brown one, probably a bill; a white envelope with my name and address typed on it; and a handwritten envelope, which looks like a greetings card. I walk into the living room. The answer machine is flashing. With trepidation, I press the play button and exhale with a loud sigh of relief when I hear Ian's voice. Who would have thought that a message from Ian would be welcome!

'Hi, Laura. Just to let you know that Charlene went into early labour yesterday and gave birth to a beautiful baby boy called Rory. Mel knows and she wants to come down this week. I've tried to dissuade her, as it's the middle of term, but she says it doesn't matter, as it's reading week. Not sure what that means. But just to warn you she might show up. Mother and baby are both doing fine, by the way. If you'd like to see them, which you probably won't, they're at home. Bye.'

I'm not surprised that Mel wants to come home to see her new half-brother. She may have been distressed and confused about his existence only a few days ago, but now that he is a reality, nothing will keep her away. The problem is, as much as I want to see my daughter, I don't want her to know about all the dreadful things that have been happening to me. Life has just got even more complicated. I sink onto the sofa. It's strange being at home on a Monday morning with nothing to do. I know someone who will be pleased: Anna. She's been moaning about me working; well, now I can spend time with her. Go to the gym, or perhaps not. Stupid idea. I'll make the most of Mel arriving.

But first I open the letters, the brown envelope first, which is, as expected, a utility bill, twice as much as I had anticipated. How could electricity have gone up so much in three months? Sighing, I drop it onto the sofa. I open the greetings card next. It is a rather charming painting of a theatre auditorium, a woman in a box, another woman about to be seated in a front-row seat, and a debonair gentleman clothed in an evening suit, shrugging off his coat. I turn the card around. The artist is Edward Hopper and the painting is entitled *Two on the Aisle*, painted in 1927. I have never heard of him, but then I am ignorant of art. It shows how slow I am this morning, as it takes me a good five seconds to realise who the card must be from. Ben Logan. I drop it onto the floor as if it is a hot poker. The picture may be attractive, innocuous, but it has been in his hands and he has written inside it. I can't look. I scrunch up my eyes whilst I decide what to do and tear open the other envelope. It's from the doctor's surgery and is a typed letter. The words swim as I read it.

*Dear Mrs Swallow,*

*We have received the results of your smear test and blood test. As the results show some major abnormalities, we request that you make an appointment to see your doctor as soon as possible.*

*Yours sincerely,*
*Drs Drake, Smithers, Chandara and Patel*


'Fuck,' I say out loud. What the hell is the matter with me? What abnormalities have they found? My first thought is cancer. It's everyone's first thought, isn't it? A problem with a smear, issues in the blood. It must be cancer. But then I wonder. Has my rape given me some horrible STD? Would something show up that quickly? But the nurse said she hadn't seen any evidence of injury, and I don't feel sore, so how likely is that? It must be cancer.

My hand is shaking as I dial the surgery's number.

'I've received a letter asking me to make an urgent appointment,' I say. I can hear the quiver in my voice. Everything else that has happened is a might-be, a scare, but this: this is a reality. They got it wrong. I'm not going to die in a car accident, I'm going to die of a horrible disease.

'I can't see anything on the system,' the receptionist says. I can hear the clicking of her typing in the background. 'When did you come for your tests?'

'On Friday.'

'Might be too soon to be uploaded onto the system,' she mutters. 'I'm afraid we don't have any appointments today. The next bookable appointment is on Thursday at 11.45 a.m.'

'Thursday!' I screech. 'I can't wait until Thursday!' What a terrible system to have the sword of Damocles hanging over me for four days.

'You can call in at 8 a.m. in the morning as part of the triage system' – she speaks coolly – 'but that is for urgent, same-day appointments.'

'But this is urgent. The letter says I need to make an appointment as soon as possible.'

'Mmm,' she murmurs. 'It doesn't say urgent though. Anyway, would you like to take the appointment on Thursday?'

'Yes. Yes, I'll take it.' I slam the phone down and tug at my hair.

As I'm going to die anyway, whatever further miseries Ben has in store for me seem rather less potent now. I pick the card off the floor and open it up. His writing is scrawling, spikey, and I have to squint to decipher it.

*DEAREST LAURA,*

*I thoroughly enjoyed our lunch on Friday and just so sorry you didn't feel well afterwards. I hope it wasn't food poisoning! I've tried calling a couple of times and I would have popped by, but I had a clinic on Saturday and then had to rush down to Devon, as my mum was taken to hospital whilst on a bridge-playing holiday. I'm down here now, missing you. Mum's on the mend and I hope to come home tomorrow, so may be back by the time you receive this. Are you free for dinner on Thursday or Friday this week? Text me when you have a moment.*

*Much love, Ben*

Wow. Is he delusional? This is a missive from someone who is at worst a psychopath or at best in deep denial. How could he write that? Chatty, as if nothing had happened? And then I pause and for the first time really contemplate the possibility. Maybe nothing did happen? Maybe Ben had nothing to do with my state of undress on Friday. Could I have drunk so much that I undressed myself? The thought appals me. But even if I undressed myself, I would never have taken a porno-graphic selfie. Of that I am utterly convinced. How can I find out if Ben has done this? If I ask him, of course he's going to deny it. Besides, I am too scared to see him. There is just too much going on, and my head feels as if it will explode.

I wish I smoked. It would be the perfect time to roll a joint or even grab a packet of Marlboros. But I hate smoking. It makes me gag. And at 11.15 a.m. on a Monday, it really is too early to have a drink. Instead, I grab a notepad and a pencil and start writing a list of everything that has happened to me in the past fortnight.

- Facebook announcement saying I'm dead
- Obituary in local paper
- Date rape?
- Car graffiti
- Car accident
- Letter from Eddy
- Porno email to Eddy
- Suspended from work – probably sacked

That's one hell of a scary list. At best, someone wants to scare me; somewhere in the middle they want to destroy my life; at worst they want me dead. But who? And why? I just can't think what I have done to warrant this.

I write another list of all the people who have featured prominently in my life during the past month. Maybe this will help me.

- Ben
- Eddy
- Ian
- Peter
- Rob
- Jenny
- Anna
- Charlene

- Mel

I discount Mel immediately and then strike a line through Rob. He's twenty-two years old and a lovely lad. I put a question mark after Ian's name. We've had our ups and downs, but he was my husband for sixteen years. It can't be Ian. Peter is a jerk, but despite being my boss, he is really on the periphery of my life. He has all the power over me he needs, and I can't begin to fathom what motive he would have for any of the things on my list. If it's not Ben, then it must be Eddy. Perhaps he's been festering resentment towards me all of these years, for rejecting him at school and for the obituary I wrote on his father. Perhaps he tracked me down at Slate Wilders and has been planning his revenge ever since. And so I decide. He will be my first focus. With a clear week ahead of me, I will track down Eddy.

I make myself a cup of coffee and fire up my laptop. First, I find him on Facebook. It's easy enough, as he's now one of my friends. The trouble is, he posts even less than I do. I scroll down his posts and they're all anodyne: repostings of anti-Trump videos, a couple of cute puppy videos, details of a fundraising event for a local school, and that's it. I click on the 'about me' section and it's blank.

I then try his friends and have a bit more luck. He doesn't have many – twenty or so, but he is linked to his wife, or ex-wife now, I assume. Annabel Drover. I click on her name and she is a prolific Facebook user, helpfully providing a photographic documentation of the minutiae of her children's lives. Poor kids, I think. Every cute little sentence that has ever spurted forth from their lips is out there for all to read. Their first steps, potty-training pictures, the all-important childhood milestones are listed for the world to mock. Whilst it shows that her children are her world, it doesn't give much information about her.

I can't tell if she works. She doesn't post photographs of herself or Eddy. It's frustrating.

I try to recall what he said he did. He has his own company, but what is it? Property? No, IT. That sends a shiver through me. If Eddy is an IT expert, he would have the ability to hack into my email, to make it look as if I sent the pornographic image to him rather than the other way around. The more I think about it, the more likely it's Eddy.

I stand up and stretch before sitting down again and Googling Edward Drover. It's an annoyingly common name, but there he is, listed as a director under company check. And then it's easy. He is the managing director of Loll Systems. Cute. He named his company after his dead dad. I click onto the company website. It's dull, talking about offering comprehensive IT outsourcing to medium-sized businesses in the southeast of England. It's when I go to the contact page that I get lucky. Loll Systems is located right here, in a trading estate on the outskirts of Horsham.

I stand up again and roll my head from side to side. I will stalk him. If I can't find out where he lives, I can follow him from work. I'll confront him. And then I remember. I don't have my car. I will have to rent a car. And that will be a good thing, because Eddy won't recognise it. I rub my hands and feel a frisson of excitement and an absurd feeling of gratitude towards Peter for firing me. I have time on my hands, even if I don't have the money to be doing anything as frivolous as renting a car that I don't really need.

I finish off the cold cup of coffee, freshen up my face with a dab of foundation and a quick swipe of lipstick, and pull on my coat. And then I pause. Perhaps it's not such a good idea to go alone. I am not some super-brave detective off a television show. This is my life, and despite everything that's happening, I want to preserve it. The only person I know who doesn't work is Anna, and as she knows everything that has been going on, she's the obvious person to recruit as my accomplice. I know she'll want to help; she's spunkier than me, brave and resourceful. I call her.

'Are you busy?'

'Yes and no,' she says hesitantly. 'Are you at work?'

'No. Long story. Do you fancy having a bit of an adventure with me this afternoon?'

'Sure. But I need to be back for seven. Jim's home at the moment.'

So that is why I haven't heard from Anna over the weekend. I thought she was annoyed with me for questioning her views about Jenny.

'I'll collect you at 3.30 p.m.,' I promise.

## 24

The car rental depot is behind the station and it's quite a long walk from my flat. Not that I mind. The cold, damp air clears my mind and helps me focus. I am tempted to call Ben, to ask him to come over as soon as he is back in Sussex, but I hold back. I need to be sure Eddy is the perpetrator, and then I can allow myself to believe in Ben. I march quickly, my hands deep in my coat pockets, a big checked scarf around my neck, my navy leather cross-body bag bumping up and down as I walk. The orange sign makes it easy to find the car rental office. A young man with impressive facial hair is sitting behind the counter, huddled up, a beanie hat on his head and gloves on his hands. It's not that cold, is it?

'Please can I rent a car?'

He looks up in surprise. 'Have you booked one?'

'No.'

He huffs and puffs and eventually takes his gloves off to enable him to type properly. 'What are you looking for?'

'As cheap as possible.'

He turns the computer screen to face me. I have no idea

what it is, but the picture of the car he shows me is very small. 'We haven't got much and it's the cheapest we have.'

'I'll take it.'

After much form filling and inspection of my driving licence and photocopying of this and that, he walks into a back room and returns with a paper wallet and a set of car keys dangling from his index finger.

'Follow me.'

This is not the car warehouse of Geneva Airport or the parking lot of Tampa Airport. This is small-town Horsham and there are five cars lined up in the backyard. He presses the button on the set of car keys, and the locks pop up on the smallest car, a little white Toyota barely bigger than a Smart car. It's perfect. And then I freeze. It's very small, and if it's very small, I assume it's not that safe. How do I know if it's been serviced properly? What if it has been in an accident and the rental company don't know that the chassis has a crack right the way through it?

'Is everything all right?' He tugs at his beard as he looks at me.

I hesitate. I can't afford a bigger car. Besides, I'm barely going to be driving it, just around Horsham. I won't have the chance to go faster than thirty miles an hour. Nothing much can happen.

I shake myself into the moment. 'Yes, it's fine. Thanks.'

I take the keys from him and slip into the driver's seat. It feels cramped and slightly claustrophobic. It would be awful for a six-foot man. The pedals are light and I nearly shoot straight forwards into a removals van. Slamming my foot on the brake, the car jolts to a stop, and because I'm not used to driving a manual, clutched car, I manage to stall it. Great start. I'm glad no one is watching. I drive at a snail's pace to Anna's house, glancing from time to time at the queue of cars building up behind me. Don't look, I tell myself. It doesn't matter what the people behind think. I need to be strong and calm. If I crash this car, I am in serious trouble. So I carry on driving slowly. Oh, Becky! I never used to be like this.

Anna lives in a beautiful period house with slanting roofs and darkened beams and an Aga in the kitchen. She also has a state-of-the-art steamer oven and all sorts of other culinary gadgets that I have never seen her use. Her house is immaculate, every cushion is plumped up, and the air smells of pine and furniture polish. There is a small lawn to the front of the house that looks like a bowling green most of the year. Once I joked that the grass looked fake, it was so immaculate. Anna gave me such a filthy look, I wondered for a moment if I had stumbled across one of her little secrets. Later I had knelt down and tugged a blade of grass. It came away in my fingers; it was real.

The first time I visited, I decided it looked like a show house but couldn't work out quite why, because with its period features there was nothing obviously show home about it. And then it hit me. There is little personal in Anna's house. No photos, no knick-knacks. Perhaps it's not surprising given that Jim is away so much of the year. I haven't been upstairs, so perhaps the bedrooms are different; perhaps he has a study up there; perhaps they display their wedding photos in their bedroom. I hope I don't ever have to go into their bedroom, as I have no desire to see the hideous picture she bought.

I pull up alongside the kerb outside her house and am about to get out of the car when a knocking sound startles me. It is Anna rapping on the passenger window. I can't work out how to lower the window, so I gesticulate for her to get in.

'What's with the car?' she sneers.

'I've rented it whilst mine is being repaired.'

Her expression is disapproving.

'Have you been waiting for me?'

'Yes.' She frowns. 'You said you were coming to get me, remember?'

'I didn't think you'd be waiting out here. I thought I'd have to ring on the doorbell.' Actually, I had hoped I might get the chance to meet the elusive Jim.

It is as if she was reading my mind. 'Jim is working from home today, so I don't want him to be disturbed.'

'What's the adventure, then?' she asks, tapping her painted fingernails on the door handle.

'Fancy being Cagney and Lacey or Scott and Bailey for the afternoon?'

She raises her eyebrows.

'I got fired this morning for something I didn't do. Obviously. And I'm ninety-nine percent sure it's Eddy Drover who is out to get me, not Ben. I want to follow him.'

'That's a crap idea,' Anna says. The tone of her voice is surprisingly chilly.

'Why?' I am indignant.

'If it is Eddy, then it's dangerous. But the evidence points to Ben, so all you'll be doing is antagonising an innocent man. You could be sued for harassment.'

I am silent. I don't agree with her. I look out of the driver's window and watch the passing cars. I am disappointed; I thought Anna would be up for some sleuthing.

'All I want to do is check out where he works and perhaps follow him home. I'm not going to confront him,' I say. The last sentence isn't strictly true. I have every intention of confronting him if I get half the opportunity. 'Besides, he won't recognise this car.'

Anna sighs. 'Ok, I suppose.'

'You don't have to come with me,' I snap churlishly.

'I'll come with you.'

The engine splutters to life and I pull the car out onto the street.

'Where are we going?'

'Good point,' I murmur, feeling foolish. I have typed his office address into my mobile phone, but I haven't looked on maps to work out where we are going. This little car doesn't have anything as fancy as a satnav.

'On my phone,' I say.

Anna huffs and digs my phone out of my bag.

'Under notes,' I say.

'Got it. Go straight, then take the second left, then first right. Over the roundabout and third on the right.'

'I can't follow instructions that far ahead. Just one step at a time, please.'

She sighs again.

Eddy's office is in a small industrial estate comprising three large, low-slung metal constructed warehouses and two brick buildings with rows of darkened windows. There is a substantial sign at the entrance listing the names of the businesses. Loll Systems Ltd is in unit six. My heart is pounding hard as we creep along slowly, trying to work out exactly where unit six is.

'There!' I say. Eddy's black Range Rover is parked outside.

'And now what?' Anna sighs.

'We'll park up and follow him home.'

'If you think I'm going to sit here for the next two hours, until the end of the working day, you've got another think coming.'

I look at my watch. It's just before 4 p.m.

'It could be fun?' I say unconvincingly.

I tuck the car into an empty space in a parking lot on the other side of the road right opposite unit six. We have a good view of the glass front door.

Anna zips up her coat and opens the passenger door.

'Where are you going?'

'I'm not sitting here for two hours. I'm going to enquire about Loll's services.'

'But what do you know about computer systems?' I ask, an edge of panic in my voice. Anna could severely damage my cover.

'Plenty. I'm going to pretend I have a small relocation business and I need to upgrade my database and CRM.'

'What's CRM?'

'Customer relationship management software application.' She rolls her eyes at me.

'How do you know that?' I ask. I am the one who is in business and Anna seems to have more knowledge than me.

'I worked, once upon a time,' she says, one high-heeled boot now out of the car.

'I want to work in relocation.' I sigh.

'I know,' Anna says.

I wonder how Anna knows. Did I tell her? Or perhaps Becky talked about me.

'Wait here,' Anna instructs me. I watch her stride purposefully across the road, dart in between the parked cars and into the office block. I can't decide if I'm relieved that Anna is taking control or annoyed that she is being so proactive. I pick at my nails nervously, wondering what she's saying, wondering if she'll be introduced to Eddy and, if so, what she will say to him.

As I'm contemplating what might happen, a Volvo estate pulls up outside unit six, gliding into a reserved space next to Eddy's Range Rover. A woman with a lion's mane of blonde hair slips out of the car. She's wearing a sheepskin gilet, skinny jeans and Ugg boots. She leans into the rear of the car, and out tumble three children ranging in age, I'm guessing, from ten to fifteen-ish. The eldest is carrying a guitar. With those looks, there is little doubt these are Eddy's children. I slide down the driver's seat. What are they doing here? Is that Annabel, the soon-to-be ex-wife? The youngest girl, with pigtails and in school uniform, runs ahead into the office, and before the woman has time to lock her car, there is Eddy, his arm around the girl. His face lights up when he looks at the woman.

She walks towards him and lifts her face. Briefly, he kisses her on the lips and they talk. I wind down the window, hoping to hear what they are saying, but their voices are inaudible. There is little doubt that the conversation is amiable. He strokes her hair; she places her left hand, with a large diamond engagement ring sparkling under the artificial lights, on his arm. They smile at each other.

This is not a broken relationship.

He lied to me, that he and Annabel were splitting up.

And then Anna emerges from the door, blithely walking past Eddy and Annabel. Doesn't she realise who they are? Of course not. She has never met Eddy. I hold my breath and only release it when she opens my passenger door.

'Why are you practically on the floor?' Anna asks, looking at me slumped in the driver's seat, my head level with the steering wheel, quite a feat considering the small space.

'That's Eddy and his wife.' I tilt my head towards them.

Anna dismisses what I said. 'I've got an appointment with the sales manager.'

'What for?' I screech.

'To find out more about Eddy Drover. That is what you wanted, isn't it?' Anna sits very still and stares straight ahead. Her voice is cold. 'I am trying to help you, Laura. You asked for help.'

'Yes, I did. But this isn't going to work.'

'Take me home now, please.'

'What?' I ask with dismay. I don't want to go home. I want to follow Eddy or Annabel.

'This is a waste of my time... and yours. Kindly take me home.' Anna is frosty and I'm annoyed.

'Oh, come on, Anna.' I hear the whine in my voice. She doesn't answer. Her face is tilted completely away from me, but

I can see a nerve pulsating in her neck. I've only ever seen that in angry men. I sigh and start up the car. This time I drive faster. We don't talk until we're in sight of Anna's house, and I'm relieved she instigates the conversation.

'It's Ben you should be going after,' she says.

'I think you're wrong.'

'I am not. And you will find out soon enough. I have known Ben much longer than you. He is not who he seems.' I pull up outside Anna's house.

'How can you say that?! And how can you really know him? He's only your doctor.'

By the time I have uttered that final phrase, Anna has opened the car door, slipped out of it and slammed it behind her. She strides up her garden path, not once looking back.

'Shit,' I mutter. I need Anna. We have never argued before. She's normally so supportive. Perhaps it's because Jim is back home and it makes her more on edge. I wish I knew more about her, more about the unusual relationship she has with her husband, whom she rarely talks about. I hesitate briefly and then turn the car around. I'll do this alone. I'm going back to the trading estate.

It's fully dark by the time I'm back there. The Volvo has gone, but Eddy's car is there. I slip my car back into the still-empty space that I vacated only a few minutes ago. I am ready for a long wait, but to my surprise, I don't have one. Just ten minutes later, Eddy emerges accompanied by his three children dancing around him as if he is the Pied Piper. Perfect Eddy with his flawless wife and delightful children and successful business and big fancy car. I start my engine and reverse out of the space. I hope he doesn't drive too fast.

I'm glad he's in a tall car because it makes it easier to track him as he drives ahead of me. I have to drive faster than I'm comfortable with and hope that the amber light I race through doesn't have a speed camera attached to it. The next thing I know, he's pulling into a Beefeater restaurant car park. I follow, parking two spaces away. The children tumble out of his giant motor, followed closely by Eddy, who is laughing about something. They disappear inside.

What should I do? Is it right to follow him when he's with his family? I hesitate and am just getting out of the car when I spot him walking back out of the restaurant. He's on the phone. Should I? Now is my chance to confront him. I'm in a public space, so it'll be safe. I stumble as I turn to close the car door and twist my ankle. 'Ouch!' I yelp. I hold on to the roof of my little rental car, shake my foot out and take a moment, waiting for some of the pain to dissipate. Then I limp over to where Eddy is standing. He is talking animatedly and doesn't see me. The excitement of the chase gives way to fear. What am I about to do? This is a really bad idea. I am about to turn back, but it is too late. He sees me. He smiles warmly and then glances away, as if embarrassed.

'Mike, can I call you back later?' he says to the person on the phone and slides the phone into his trouser pocket.

'What a nice surprise to see you here!' He leans down to kiss me on the cheek. I step back and wince as I put weight on my sore ankle. 'I've been meaning to contact you to apologise for not showing up to that viewing.'

'What?' I can't process what he's saying.

'The viewing a couple of weeks ago. I meant to cancel, but things got so busy, I totally forgot. I hope you weren't waiting around for me?'

'I want to talk to you about the letter you sent to Peter Fielding.' I stand up straight, ignoring the pain. People are milling around in the car park. I am safe here, I reassure myself.

He frowns. 'I'm sorry, but I don't know anyone called Peter Fielding.'

'You wrote my boss a letter saying that I attacked you and then there was the photo...' My voice wavers.

He shakes his head. 'I'm sorry, but I don't know what you're talking about.' He looks at me as if I am deranged. For a moment, I wonder if I am.

'Who's the woman in the Volvo? Is she your wife, and are those your children?'

Eddy narrows his eyes. 'Have you been following me? What's this all about, Laura?'

'I've received a letter and an... email. I need to know what your involvement is?'

He stamps his feet a bit. I can sense the annoyance.

'I've already said I don't know what you're talking about.' He scowls.

'You told me you were looking for a house because you and your wife were splitting up. You don't look like you've split up.'

He looks coy now. 'We've made up,' he says, eyes darting around. 'My marital affairs are none of your business, and I'm very sorry I made that inappropriate pass at you, but I have no idea what you're talking about.'

'You've made up?' I repeat.

'Look, it's none of your business, but I was convinced Annabel was having an affair. I thought she was leaving me, so I took steps to get things in order; get a house so I could move out as soon as I had confronted her. It turns out she wasn't having an affair. She was organising a surprise party for our twentieth wedding anniversary.'

You smug sod, I think. And then I wonder if it's true.

'I kind of wanted to get my own back,' he mutters. The light is bad, but it looks distinctly like Eddy is blushing. 'My behaviour towards you was inappropriate, unfair, and I'm sorry.'

I sigh.

He continues. 'Annabel is inside with the kids. It's my daughter, Matilda's birthday. I'll introduce you if you like. To all of them. We're not looking for a new house anymore. We're quite happy where we are.'

It all sounds so plausible. I squeeze my eyes shut and suck in my breath. 'There has clearly been a major misunderstanding,' I admit. Now it's my turn to say sorry. Neither of us know what to say, where to look. Eventually he takes the lead.

'See you around,' Eddy says before disappearing back inside the restaurant.

I doubt it, I think.

## 25

I sit in the car for a long time, running back through my conversation with Eddy. He seemed so genuine, but then I didn't have the chance to ask him about his father's obituary, to probe as to whether he had any motive for wanting me to come to harm. I am annoyed with myself for not thinking more clearly in the heat of the moment. I try to process his reactions, mull over everything he said, and the more I think about him being the culprit, the less likely it seems. Anna must be right after all. I'm annoyed with myself now; I've squandered a day focusing on the wrong person. I try calling her, but her mobile goes to voicemail and her home phone goes to an answering machine. I leave a message, apologising for wasting her time, telling her she was right.

But if Eddy didn't send the letter and the email, how am I going to prove my innocence? I need Eddy to tell Peter that I am not to blame, that I have been wrongly accused, and that I deserve my job back. And the only way I can do that is by asking Eddy to help me. I'm not sure what to do now. I cannot disturb his family supper, but I will need to arrange to see or speak to him again.

I drive home. The pain in my ankle has eased a little, but I still limp back after parking the midget rental car in the underground car park. Everything is catching up with me, and my bones feel heavy and aching. I put my key in the lock to the communal door and nearly trip over a pair of legs stretching across the hallway.

'What the...?' I exclaim. And then I see who it is.

'Mel! My darling, what on earth are you doing here?'

'Dad said he'd told you I was coming home.'

'Yes, well, sort of.' I can't remember now. Did Ian say that Mel was definitely coming home or that she might be coming to see the baby? Mel clambers to her feet, picking up a rucksack with books poking out of the top.

'But why aren't you in the flat?'

She looks coy. 'I left my keys in Manchester. One of the guys from downstairs let me in here.'

'You could have gone to Dad's,' I say.

'Nah. I didn't have enough money for a taxi, and he's busy with the baby. It's okay. I haven't been waiting that long.'

'Are you hungry?'

'Chill, Mum! I'm fine.'

I squeeze her in a hug so tight, she squeals, 'You're hurting me, Mum,' and wriggles out of my grasp. But I need to enfold her tightly, to give me strength, for me to feel her vitality when mine could be eked out of me either through the hands of someone else or from the illness that my body is harbouring. How am I going to keep my visceral fear from Mel, whose radar is finely tuned?

We walk upstairs with my arm around Mel's shoulders. She dumps her bag in the living room and rushes into her bedroom.

'Oh, it's so good to be home,' she shouts. 'I've missed my comfy bed!'

'And I've missed you,' I say, smiling as she lies spread-eagled across her made-up bed.

'Don't smother me, Mother.' She levers herself up. 'Can I have a bath?'

'You don't need to ask,' I say, amused.

'I haven't had a bath all term.'

'So that's what the stench is.'

'Ha ha. Showers only in halls.'

THE NEXT MORNING, I lie. I tell Mel that I have the rest of the week off work so I can be with her. There is no way that I am admitting I have been fired. She needs to be protected from worries. I had hoped that Jenny might have contacted me, but there has been silence. I suppose it would put her in too much of an invidious position, but Jenny and I go back a long way. One of the many idioms my dad taught me rings in my ears: don't mix business and pleasure. Of course Jenny is going to put business first. It affects her livelihood and her future. I wonder if I would do the same if the boot was on the other foot? Nevertheless, it is a disappointment. And I'm annoyed with Anna for being annoyed with me and not returning my call.

We polish off a late breakfast: eggs, bacon and plenty of toast, a special treat to mark Mel's return home.

'We'll need to go to Dad's today because I won't have a car tomorrow.'

'Why?' Mel asks.

'There's something wrong with the car, so it's in the garage and I have a rental car.' I busy myself clearing the table.

She wrinkles her forehead. Unlike her peers, Mel has been in no hurry to learn to drive. Becky's death put paid to that. Although she won't admit it, I know Mel is scared of driving and doubly scared of anything happening to me. Losing her aunt when Mel was such a tender age has forced her to consider the fragility of life much sooner than she should have, and although I haven't said anything, it won't have escaped her notice that she will be home for the anniversary of Becky's death. Surprisingly, I am grateful for Ian's new baby. Whilst I do not want to coo over my ex-husband's new child, at least it takes my mind off my own problems and is a good distraction for Mel.

BECKY DIED ON 28 NOVEMBER. The police never found out why her car was parked up on the hard shoulder of the A272. They examined it forensically, but could find nothing wrong with it, nothing to suggest a malfunction of the car that would have given her reason to pull over. They checked her mobile phone records, and the only call she had made earlier that day was to me. She got out of the car and was mown down by an articulated lorry. She didn't stand a chance, they said. She would have felt nothing, they reassured me. The lorry driver was treated for shock and later treated for post-traumatic shock. Anna tells me that he hasn't worked since. I'm not sure how she knows.

Becky and I were close but not that close. We didn't share the same group of friends and led disparate lives. Mine was one of homemaking and cosy domesticity up until the year before Becky died, of course, when Ian left me. Becky was a nurse and she gave everything to her job, quickly rising through the ranks. After her marriage failed, she became single-minded about her career. I doubt she would have had time to pursue a relationship even if someone suitable had come along.

When Mel was small, Becky was around our house all the time. In those days, she worked in a hospital in Guildford and lived near us. As the years went on and Mel showed less inclination to spend time with her maiden aunt, our lives deviated. After Mum died, and we both came into a bit of money, Becky moved jobs: a promotion to matron at St Richard's Hospital in Chichester. She bought a small house in Pulborough and commuted every day. We spoke weekly, on a Sunday evening, and were always together for Christmas and birthdays, but I can't say I knew what was happening in her life on a day-to-day basis. I had always assumed that Becky would still get married, still fulfil her dream of having children. I hope she had a lover, but I never felt able to ask her. Despite the ridiculously long hours that she worked, after Ian left, she bent over backwards to be there for me, ringing in between shifts, sending me texts full of emojis. I was so self-absorbed during that last year of her life, I rarely enquired after her. And I regret that deeply. I can't even remember if I told her that I loved her. I hope I did.

On 28 November, I was still in our family home although it was up for sale. Ian was renting a one-bedroom apartment in the centre of Cranleigh, and our divorce was approaching its final stages. It was a Friday evening and I had just dropped Mel off at Sasha's house. Mel had been ridiculously excited at the prospect of spending the night with her childhood best friend. They'd been apart for the previous eighteen months, as Sasha had been sent to a fancy private girls' school whilst Mel went to the local state school. Sasha's mum, Emily, and I had exchanged some pleasantries, but I hadn't felt inclined to linger, wanting to avoid the pain of explaining the breakdown of my marriage.

As I got back in the car, I remember feeling a chasm of loneliness at the prospect of facing forty-eight hours of silence and solitude. It was a cold, dark night and my car struggled to expel enough heat to warm up my bones. When I arrived home, I registered the police car parked up on the other side of the road, but I didn't pay it much notice. That was until I got out of the car, the lights at the front of the house went on, and I was unlocking the front door. I heard footsteps behind me and the clearing of a man's throat.

'Are you Mrs Laura Swallow?'

I turned. There were two of them. He was in uniform and had bitten nails. The woman was wearing a navy trouser suit and ugly stainless-steel-rimmed glasses.

'Yes. Why?'

'Please, can we come in?'

I don't remember walking through the front door into the hallway, but somehow the three of us were standing in the living room.

'My name is Sergeant Jason Ball, and this is Constable Sarah Jones. Please, can you sit down.'

My knees were already shaking when I dropped onto the edge of the sofa.

'Mel,' I whispered. 'I've only just left her.'

'It's not Mel.'

I remember thanking God, breathing out with a loud puff. I almost didn't hear the next sentence.

'I'm very sorry, but your sister, Becky, has died in a road traffic accident.'

I think I screamed. My throat felt abrasive and I was icy cold. Sarah Jones kneeled down on the floor and held my hands, tried to still my quivering body. She was the family liaison officer – a lovely girl, a lousy job.

'Is there anyone we can call to be with you?' she asked in a gentle voice.

'Mum and Dad are dead. Donny, he's our brother. He's in Australia.'

'Is there anyone else who lives nearby who can come over?'

'Ian,' I said. 'My husband.'

In that moment, I forgot that Ian would very shortly no longer be my husband. They called Ian then, and sometime later he came striding into the house, and the anguish of our broken relationship gave way to a deep and shocking bereavement, inexplicable to anyone who hasn't experienced it. When Sarah Jones left, Ian wrapped me in his arms, and later, he got into our bed and held me throughout the night.

## 26

I haven't been into a shop to buy baby clothes for over a decade, and I have forgotten how adorable the little baby-grows and miniature dresses can be. I spend too long trying to select suitable presents, but eventually decide on a pale blue cotton baby-grow with a tiny rabbit poking its head out of a pocket, which I decide will be a gift from me, and an overpriced but traditional teddy bear that Mel can give. I hope the bear will sit in baby Rory's cot and be his constant companion in the way that Bunbun, Mel's battered soft-toy rabbit, has been a comforter to Mel. When she packed up her belongings to take to university, I noticed her slip Bunbun into her suitcase. I wonder whether we ever grow out of our favourite childhood toy?

Mel is silent during the journey to Ian's house, and when I ask her the occasional question, she snaps at me. But when we arrive, everything changes. She flings her arms around Ian, as if she is a young child, hugging him so tightly, I wonder whether she is subconsciously trying to reclaim him as her father, and her father alone.

'Come and meet your new brother,' he says, taking her by

the hand. I shudder. Feeling like a spare part, I follow them into the living room, bracing myself for seeing 'my' wallpaper again and the saccharine Charlene. As expected, it is a scene of domestic bliss. Charlene is lying on the sofa, dressed in pale grey velour tracksuit bottoms and a white T-shirt, her little toenails are painted baby pink, and there, suckling at her breast, is the newborn.

'He's just about finished,' she says. Mel looks away, flushing. Charlene removes the baby, wipes his face gently with a muslin cloth, and tugs down her T-shirt. She shifts up the sofa so she is sitting up, and then she holds the baby out towards Mel.

'Here. Hold your baby brother,' she says.

Mel shivers, lets go of Ian's hand and steps back behind me.

'I couldn't,' she says dramatically.

'No problem,' Charlene says generously, placing the baby over her shoulder and gently rubbing his back. 'I don't expect I'd have wanted to hold a baby at your age. How's college?'

'It's good, thanks. We've got some presents for Rory,' Mel says, nipping back out into the hall to get the hastily wrapped gifts. She hands them to Ian, who puts them on the sofa next to Charlene. She places the baby down and eagerly unwraps them.

'Ooo, they're gorgeous! Thank you!' she exclaims. 'I'm starving, Ian love. Any chance you could finish off lunch?'

'Of course.' He turns towards Mel. 'Want to help me?' They scuttle out of the room.

Feeling awkward, I glance at Charlene.

'Would you like to hold him?' she asks, smiling kindly. I wonder if I would be so happy handing over my newborn to the wife who came before me. When I am settled in an armchair, I look down at baby Rory in the crook of my arm, at his long dark lashes and tiny button nose and miniature fingers that wrap around my index finger, and I smell that baby scent and feel the peachy softness of his cheeks, and I burst into tears.

'What's the matter?' Charlene says, jumping up, alarm crossing her face.

'I'm so sorry,' I say, trying to stifle my sobs, not wanting to alarm Rory. Gently, I rock him backwards and forwards, but it's fine: he is fast asleep. I guess what she's thinking. That I'm jealous of her baby and angry at her for stealing my husband; that I'm mourning the loss of my own fertility and that I will never have another baby of my own. But it isn't that at all, and I'm not sure why, but I let the truth tumble from my lips.

'I'm never going to hold my grandchild; I'm not going to be there for Mel when she's a new mother, and I don't expect I'll even see her graduate. You will look after her for me, won't you?' I sniff. 'You and Ian? I know Ian will, but you've got the baby now and she's all grown up, so you might forget about Mel?'

'What are you talking about?' Charlene is kneeling on the floor in front of me, holding out her arms for me to hand her the baby. Reluctantly, I give him back. 'Is it that death certificate thing?' she asks, her eyes bright.

'No.' I sniff. 'I think I'm dying.'

Charlene pulls her head back.

'Of what?' she asks. I notice that Charlene is wearing very little make-up. She's fresh faced and pretty. At least she'll live long enough to care for my family.

'I don't know. But I went into the surgery for—' I pause '—for some routine blood tests, and then I got a letter asking me to come back in urgently. They wouldn't do that if there wasn't something seriously wrong, would they? And now I can't get an appointment until Thursday, so my mind is working overtime.'

'It doesn't work like that,' Charlene says, carefully standing up, rocking the baby protectively in her arms. 'We don't send out letters unless we can't reach the patient by telephone. Did you get any messages on your phone from the surgery?'

I frown. 'No.'

'Well, it doesn't make sense.'

'Are you sure?' I ask. 'Maybe things are different since you left.'

Charlene's forehead creases. 'I only left a week ago. Rory came early. I doubt they would have changed their administration practices since I left.'

'I guess you're right,' I concede.

Charlene is pacing slowly up and down the room, her bare feet leaving little imprints on the long-tufted carpet. 'Have you got the letter with you?'

'I don't think so.' But I get up anyway and find my handbag and rifle inside it. And to my surprise, I do have the letter, crumpled and dirtied. I smooth it out and hand it to Charlene, who takes the piece of paper, already adept at holding a baby in her left arm and carrying on as normal with her right arm.

'It's fake.'

'What?' I exclaim.

'It's fake. Like the death certificate. I asked one of the doctors about the real death certificates, and he showed me the pad. I'm pretty sure that the watermark on the one you got isn't the real deal.'

'Obviously it's not the real deal,' I snap. 'I'm alive.' And then I regret my harsh tone. Charlene is only trying to help.

'I'm sorry,' I say wanly. 'I'm a bit emotional at the moment.'

'Me too.' She chuckles. 'Have you still got no idea who is out to get you?'

'No.' But Ben's face looms in my mind. 'Can any doctor access anyone's medical records?'

'How do you mean?'

'Could a doctor who isn't my doctor get access to my records?'

Charlene pauses for a moment. 'No, I don't think so. The surgeries' records are on a local database. It's a bit of a fallacy that all NHS data is centrally held. You'd need to check, but I think that another doctor would need to request for your records to be released.'

'Thanks,' I mutter, thinking that perhaps Charlene isn't as dim as I assumed.

'But why would a doctor who isn't your doctor want to access your records?'

'If they're being nosey.' I laugh. But it isn't a laughing matter.

'Honestly, I don't think so. There'd be a trail. I can check for you if you'd like?'

Ian comes back into the room. 'So, ladies, what are you talking about?'

Charlene and I roll our eyes at each other. I chuckle inwardly. Who would have thought that I would be chatting cosily to my ex's new wife, cooing over my ex's new baby? And then I feel a surge of elation. If the letter is fake, I don't have some life-threatening illness. I might live to see Mel graduate, settle down, have babies. I grin inanely, and when Ian asks me if Mel and I would like to stay for lunch, I eagerly accept.

For the first time since Ian and I split up, I feel relaxed in his company. Perhaps it is because Mel is home, but I think it's largely because Charlene is so welcoming and easy-going. I feel guilty about thinking badly about her previously; after all, she is not the reason Ian left me. Charlene is straightforward, a bit naïve, but she is kind and not unintelligent. Reluctantly, I can see why Ian decided to marry her. We chat about the baby, about Mel's university course, and I think how very modern it is that we are sitting around the dining table being more than civil to each other. And then Ian changes the subject.

'Would you like me to come with you to the cemetery on Friday?' he asks.

I look at him blankly. Mel frowns.

'Charlie and I have been talking, and she was wondering whether I should go with you this year, to visit Becky's grave?'

A shiver runs through me. In the false joviality of the lunch, I have forgotten that it is the anniversary of Becky's death.

'I feel bad I haven't been with you the last couple of years.'

'Anna and I have spent the day together. It's become a bit of a tradition, I suppose.'

'But she's not family,' Ian mutters.

'Neither are you,' I say.

'Yes, he is!' Mel exclaims, thumping her fist on the table.

'I mean he's not Aunt Becky's family.'

Silence settles. I wonder whether perhaps I would like Ian to come along after all, and Mel too if she is still staying with me.

'Do you really not mind?' I ask Charlene.

She shakes her head and smiles.

'It was Charlene's idea,' Ian explains. 'I think she'd like me out of the house for a day!'

'Thank you,' I say. I wonder what Anna has got planned and whether she'll mind if I cancel.

After lunch, I start fidgeting, looking at my watch. I have to return the rental car, and although for a while it felt good to be part of an extended happy family, when the baby starts wailing and Charlene takes out one of her plump breasts, I turn to Mel.

'I've got to get back, love.'

'And I've got to study.' She pulls a face.

We say our goodbyes. It is a relief to leave.

## 27

I drop Mel back home and drive the car to the rental depot. After nipping into M&S to pick up a few things for supper, I walk slowly back through town, trying to ignore my aching bones. As I turn the key in the lock to my front door, I can hear voices inside. I pause. For a moment I wonder if Mel has got a friend over. I shut the door behind me quietly.

'Oh, Mum!' Mel sees me. She's carrying two cups of tea. 'You've got a visitor.'

My heart plummets. I do not want a visitor. I am feeling unsettled. My head is spinning. I can't trust anyone and, other than Mel, don't want anyone else sullying my apartment, my only safe place.

'Who is it?'

'Hi, Laura. I hope you don't mind me turning up unannounced.' Jenny stands behind Mel. She looks sheepish, but I am not in the mood for being conciliatory. I don't want her here.

'Actually, I do mind.'

'That's rude,' Mel says, an eyebrow raised.

'Your mum has every right to be rude to me,' Jenny says, taking a mug of tea from Mel. I barge past them into the living room.

'Why? You two have been mates forever.' Mel furrows her brow.

'You remember Grandpa saying never mix friends and business,' I say to Mel. 'Well, it's true. Never do it.'

'I don't remember Gramps much,' Mel says quietly. Of course she doesn't. He died when she was nine.

Jenny shifts from one foot to another. 'I was just asking Mel what she is doing at home. I wasn't expecting her to answer the door. It's a lovely surprise.'

'I thought you knew I was home to see the baby? It's study week. Mum said she's got a few days off work because I'm here.' Mel puts down her favourite red mug with a picture of a cat on it and scratches her head.

Jenny and I glance at each other.

'Yes, of course,' Jenny says, expertly cobbling together a lie. 'I forgot. That's what middle age does to you.'

'Thank you,' I mouth to her from behind Mel. And then I think it would have been better to stick my finger up in the air at her. Jenny has not been my friend. I turn to Mel. 'Love, Jenny and I have got a few work things we need to discuss.'

'Sure,' Mel says, taking the hint. 'I've got a stack of studying to do anyway.' She picks up her mug and turns to Jenny. 'See ya. Say hi to the boys for me.' She disappears into her bedroom and shuts the door behind her.

I sit at the table and motion for Jenny to do the same.

'I had a call from Gordon Farmer.'

'Who?' The name rings a bell, but I can't place him.

'My contact at the *Gazette*. They've received a photograph of your car with the graffiti all over it.'

'And?' I sigh.

'The photo shows you in the driving seat and a police car parked up in front. They're planning on running a headline about a disgruntled employee driving around with offensive advertising on her car and then causing an accident – or something with a punchier headline, obviously. They're going to name you and Slate Wilders.'

'But I didn't do it! I'm the victim here.' I slam my hand on the table. Tea slurps over the side of Jenny's mug. She looks around for something to wipe it with, but I don't move. I don't care if the table is stained.

'Has anyone from the newspaper been in touch to ask you about it?'

'No!'

'The thing is, it's really bad for our reputation.'

'I don't give a sod about the company's reputation! What about mine? My name will be tarnished forever if that article is run in the *Gazette*.' I groan as I think of Mel and my friends reading it.

'I'm going to see what I can do to stop Gordon Farmer from printing it. We hold quite a bit of sway at the *Gazette*, being a major advertiser and all of that. Just make sure you don't speak to any reporters if they contact you.'

'Of course I won't.'

'Have the police come up with anything?'

I shake my head. I've heard nothing from them. I need to chase them. I haven't heard from my insurance company either: no update on whether tracksuit man will be claiming against me, and no update on when my car will be fixed.

She glances around the room, her eyes settling on the card that Ben sent me. I left it on the floor, but Mel must have picked it up and placed it on the mantelpiece.

'Don't you believe me?' I lean forwards, encroaching into her personal space.

'Yes, I do believe you. I don't think you've had anything to do with any of this.' She waves her hands around.

'I'm just the scapegoat.'

'Unfortunately, yes.' She sighs. 'You've had a horrible time and I'd like to help you find out who is after you. But I have to do that as your friend, not your employer.'

'So now what?' Tears smart my eyes. I really have lost my job and it is utterly unfair.

'I suggest you hand in your notice. That way there won't be anything negative on your employment record. I'll give you a month's pay in lieu of notice. Then, when you've cleared your name in a couple of weeks or a month's time, you can reapply and I'll give you your job back.'

'What if I can't clear my name that quickly?' And what if I'm killed in the meantime? Is my life really under threat? Has the time come to involve the police and tell them about Ben?

'I'll keep your job open for a month, but I can't do more than that. We will need to recruit a replacement for you.'

'Does Peter know about this?'

'No.' Jenny looks coy. 'I wanted to discuss it with you first. Peter is incandescent with rage, and it'll take quite a lot of sweet-talking on my behalf to get you reinstated. But let's worry about that when the time comes. You've done well for Slate Wilders. I meant what I said the other evening, Laura. You were in line for a directorship.'

I snort, but am relieved that my friend Jenny has reappeared, as opposed to my harsh boss Jenny.

'By the way, a client came in looking for you this afternoon. A Dr Logan.'

'Oh my God,' I say, my hand rushing towards my mouth.

'He was very polite and quite charming. I can see why you fell for him.'

'I haven't fallen for him. He's a rapist and a liar.' I pause and then say, 'I think he is. Anyway, what did he say?'

'He spoke to Hannah and enquired after you. I'm afraid all the staff know you've been suspended, so she got a bit flustered and rang me. I went downstairs to find out what was going on. He just wanted to know if you were in the office. I said no and asked if anyone else could help.'

'What if he comes here?' I ask, panicked. 'If he's been to the office, he'll come here next.'

'There's nothing he can do,' Jenny says reassuringly. 'Don't let him in, and call the police if you feel scared.'

'I am scared,' I murmur. We are both silent for a while.

'Do you want my resignation letter now?' I ask.

Jenny nods.

I get my laptop, connect it to the printer that I keep stashed behind the sofa, and bash out a one-line resignation letter. I print it out, sign it and hand it to Jenny. She hesitates before accepting it.

'I probably shouldn't be telling you this, but what I'm doing is tantamount to constructive dismissal. If this gets out, then I will likely lose my job too. I'm suggesting you resign as your friend. We have grounds for firing you. Instant dismissal. I don't mean that to sound threatening; it's just how it is. I really want to help you, Laura.'

I exhale loudly. 'I know, Jenny. Stop worrying. I know you're doing this as my friend. It's our secret to add to our long list of secrets.'

'What's a secret?' Mel says. I didn't hear her come out of her bedroom. I curse at the memory of squeezing WD-40 onto the hinge of her door at the end of the summer, fed up with the incessant squeak every time she went in and out of her room.

I open and shut my mouth. I hate lying to Mel.

Jenny comes to the rescue. 'Your mum's been offered another job. We're giving her a month to decide whether she's going to take that one or stay with us. You should be very proud of your mother. She's a great estate agent.'

Mel rolls her eyes and retreats into her room. I am impressed with the fluidity of Jenny's untruth. It hits me then that everyone around me is telling fibs, and it makes me feel extremely uncomfortable, caught as I am in a web of lies.

## 28

By the end of Wednesday, I have three missed calls from Ben. One of them I genuinely missed. The other two, I knowingly missed. I watched my phone as the calls came in, bile in my mouth, adrenaline pumping through my veins, not daring to touch the phone in case I accidentally answered it. He left two messages. In the first he asked how I was and wanted to know if we could meet. In the second he sounded worried, perhaps even slightly desperate. He was concerned for me but also wondering whether I was avoiding him. Bingo, I think. Will I ever have to face up to this man, or will he just go away?

Mel is out shopping. I have given her thirty pounds to buy herself a treat. Meanwhile, I am enjoying my newfound freedom, luxuriating in doing nothing. The trouble is, doing nothing makes my imagination run wild, and I am indulging in horror movies in my mind, all of which end in my painful demise. When the doorbell rings, I jump up. I am surprised to see Mel on the little screen.

I press the button to let her in, slightly annoyed that she has forgotten her key again. She now has the only spare set and it's complicated ordering new ones. As I'm walking away, the buzzer goes again.

'Mum,' she says, 'there's someone here who wants to see you. Ben Logan?' She utters his name with a rising intonation at the end of his surname.

'No!' I scream as I slam the receiver down. He's got my daughter! I run out of the flat, bare-footed, down the stairs and come face-to-face with Ben, who is chatting to Mel in the corridor near the front door.

'Get up to the flat, now!' I yell at Mel, who looks at me in horror.

'What the...?' she asks.

I try to quell my shaking body. 'Please,' I say, grabbing her arm. 'Just go up to the flat and lock yourself in. If I'm not back up there in ten minutes, call the police.'

'Mum, you're scaring me!' She looks from me to Ben and back again, but she doesn't question further, and she runs up the stairs with nimble athleticism.

'What's going on?' Ben asks. His amber eyes are dark, and his face is contorted with confusion.

'Just go away and then I won't call the police. Just go!' I am screeching now.

'Laura, please. I don't understand. What have I done? What's happened?' He strides towards me, and I step backwards, stumbling on the bottom rung of the stairs. He reaches out to help me, but I push him away.

'We had such a lovely time. I thought we had a great connection. I wanted to be with you to support you on the anniversary of your sister's death.'

'How do you know about Becky's death?' I ask, alarm choking my throat.

'You told me.' He is looking at me as if I am deranged.

'I don't discuss it with anyone, least of all you!' I spit.

'We talked about it in bed,' he says gently. 'I told you about

Sadie. The anniversary of her death is 28 January, and you told me that your sister died on 28 November. At least I think you did?' He looks confused now.

'If I didn't tell you, who did?'

'Maybe—'

I interrupt him. 'Just go away. I don't want you anywhere near me!'

'Laura, I really don't know what you think I have done, but please tell me.' His eyes are imploring.

'I refuse to get into a dialogue with a rapist!' I spit.

'What?' It is his turn to raise his voice.

I move around, as if to go up the stairs, but he grabs my arm. I push him with all my strength, but he is too strong and too quick for me. He reaches for my shoulders and pulls me towards him, the scent of his aftershave evoking memories of him naked in my bed. I am shaking, but my brain is fogging over. I don't know what to say, what to do. I think of fight, flight and freeze, and somewhere it crosses my mind that I have lost the fight, am incapable of flight, and now I am in the freeze.

He releases his grip on my shoulders and takes my hand. I try to tug it away, but he won't let go.

'Sit down,' he says, pulling me down to sit next to him on the bottom step of the stairs. I shift as far away from him as I can. I clutch my arms around my knees, partly as protection, partly to still my legs, which are shaking like jelly.

'You need to tell me what's going on. At least be fair to me.'

'Fair! I don't owe you anything. It's you who owes me for not reporting you to the police, for not...' I burst into tears, all-consuming, body-heaving sobs. I sense him deciding whether to comfort me or not. He stays away from me, glancing at me with an expression of alarm.

'Laura, what do you think I did?'

'You drugged me,' I whisper. 'Then you raped me, or perhaps you didn't. And then you took revolting photos of me and hacked into my email account, and...' I can't get any more words out.

Ben stares at me. His mouth is slightly parted, his eyes wide. They look almost bruised, they are so sunken. Tired, I think. He looks exhausted.

'I did not! How can you possibly accuse me of that? It's horrific.' He stands up now, leaving me sitting on the stairs. He paces backwards and forwards quickly.

'Mum! Do you want me to call the police now?' Mel shouts down the stairs.

Then another quivering voice says, 'Is everything all right down there?' It's my elderly neighbour, Mrs Steel, who turns her television up to maximum volume, but due to her docility and kindness, I have never complained. She looks out for me and I look out for her.

'I'm fine. Everything is fine,' I say, getting up, wiping my wet face on my sleeve. 'I'll be up soon, Mel,' I say. 'Sorry to have disturbed you, Mrs Steel.' I wait for a moment, listening to the doors shut.

'Something has happened to you, hasn't it?' Ben asks, standing still now, his hands in his trouser pockets. I don't answer. 'What do you think happened after our lunch last week?'

'You know perfectly well, and I am damned if I am going to spell it out to you.' I also stand up. 'I would like you to go now.'

Ben nods at me. His eyes are downcast, his lips sealed tightly together. He takes a step towards the door and then falters, turning to look at me. I stand resolute, glad that I have found some inner strength from somewhere.

'Just before we got back to your apartment after lunch, I was bleeped by the hospital. You weren't feeling well, and I didn't want to leave you, but I had no choice. One of my patients had been admitted as an emergency and I had to go to the hospital. I didn't know what to do, so I accompanied you upstairs to your living room. You can check with the hospital, Laura. Call me any time if you want to talk. You know where I am.'

And then he opens the door and leaves. As the security lock slips into place with a crunch, I collapse onto the floor like a puppet without strings.

MEL ISN'T EASILY APPEASED EVEN though it is far from the first time she has seen me in a state. When Ian left, I was furious and screamed and shouted, although I tried to let rip when she was at school or after she had gone to bed. When Becky died, she experienced my raw grief, the relentless tears, the wailing about the injustice and fragility of life. But she has never seen me scream at a stranger; she has never seen me utterly terrified. I have always known that fear is contagious and that one of the greatest gifts we can give to our children is to conceal our fear. When Mel was a toddler, I pretended to like spiders just so she wouldn't develop an irrational phobia. When she was at primary school, Mel and Sasha were due to perform a singing duet at the Christmas concert. Sasha was a far better singer than Mel, holding her pitch perfectly. I recall Emily telling Sasha, 'Don't be scared, darling,' before pushing her onto the stage. 'Enjoy it, Mel,' I said. Little Sasha stood there, frozen with terror, whilst Mel led the way, belting out the tune with her inferior voice. If you plant the seed that your child might be scared of doing something, then chances are they will be. I got a lot wrong on the parenting front, but not that one.

I take several deep breaths before walking back into the flat. Mel is at the door the second I rap on the knocker.

'What the hell was all that about? And who is that man?'

I give her an abbreviated version; an all-out lie requires too much brain capacity. 'We had a date and he tried to attack me.'

Mel lets out a long whoosh of breath. 'He doesn't look the

type.'

'You can't tell,' I mutter. 'Learn that lesson from me. You can never tell what someone is really like.'

And then the phone rings.

'Don't answer—' But I am too late.

'Mel speaking. Yes, she's here.' She hands me the phone.

'Just checking in to see how you are,' Anna says. I am so relieved to hear her voice. Mel disappears back into her room, and I take the phone into my bedroom, shutting the door behind me. I don't want Mel to listen to all the gory details of my involvement with Ben.

'God, Laura, that's awful,' Anna says when I eventually pause for breath. 'Are you going to tell the police?'

'Maybe, probably. I don't know. I've got to sort out Eddy first. I have to prove that I didn't send the pornographic photo, and that Eddy didn't make a complaint about me. My priority is my job. I think I'll have to meet Eddy again.'

'Forget about Eddy and let's concentrate on Ben, the real culprit. If you don't report him to the police, then I'll do it.'

'Please don't make things worse than they already are.' I sigh. I know Anna means well, but I need to take control of things myself.

'All I want to do is help you, Laura. Anyway, we can discuss it on Friday. I'll collect you at 9 a.m. I've booked a taxi to take us to the graveyard.'

'About Friday. Would you mind if we take a rain check and commemorate Becky together another day? As Mel is down from Manchester, Charlene thought it would be nice if we did something as a family: Mel, Ian and me.'

I wait for a reply, but there is silence.

'Anna?' I say. No answer. I press the end call button and try dialling her back, but her phone goes straight to voicemail. She must have run out of battery. I send her a quick text.

*'Sorry about bailing out on Friday. See you next week? Lx'*

## 29

Despite Charlene's reassurance that the letter from the surgery is suspicious, I still have a knot of fear in my sternum as I sit in the doctor's waiting room. When I made the appointment on Monday, the receptionist hadn't asked me which doctor I wanted to see, and in my desperation for the earliest possible appointment, it hadn't crossed my mind to ask.

'I have an appointment with Dr Smithers,' I say as I arrive at the reception desk.

'Mrs Swallow. Yes. But your appointment is with Dr Chandara, not Dr Smithers.'

I cannot stop the look of dismay on my face.

'Please, can I swap and see Dr Smithers?' I beg.

'I'm sorry. Dr Smithers is fully booked. That won't be possible.' She carries on typing. I am dismissed.

Dr Chandara is my age, with thick hair that has faded to a dark grey.

'How can I help you?' she asks wearily, in an Indian accent.

'I've been told to come in because of some test results.'

She types something and peers at her screen. Her smooth

face wrinkles into a frown. 'I can see that you have had a swab and a blood test, but everything has come back as normal. Why did you say that you were asked to come in?'

'Um, I received a letter saying that my test results were abnormal.'

'No.' She shakes her head, peering even closer at the screen. 'Everything is perfectly normal. There must have been a mistake.'

'Is it possible to check with Dr Smithers? I saw him last week.'

She hesitates but then gets up, smoothing down a beautiful pale grey silk skirt, much too lightweight for the miserable autumnal weather. 'Please wait here.'

She returns surprisingly quickly. 'Dr Smithers doesn't know anything further. As far as we are concerned, there is no evidence of sexual intercourse, no STDs and your bloods are perfectly normal.'

I wince. 'I'm very sorry to have bothered you. There must have been a mistake.'

'Do you have the letter?'

'Yes.' I fumble in my bag, take it out and hand it to her.

'It's fake. And we never send out letters unsigned. I will need to report this to our practice manager and carry out investigations.'

So Charlene was right. The letter is fake and designed to make me paranoid. It certainly is achieving that.

'Can you leave this with me?' Dr Chandara stands up. She pats my shoulder and throws me a sympathetic glance as I leave. 'This is a serious matter, Mrs Swallow, and we will investigate accordingly.'

I am a great deal more frightened leaving the surgery than I was entering it. Although the doctors have given me a clean bill of health, and Dr Chandara has promised to investigate, I know for sure that someone is trying to do their damnedest to terrify me. And they're succeeding. I mentally take stock of everything that has happened. The false allegations that I am dead, the supposed rape, the car graffiti, the fake email, the horrible photo. I am almost sure it isn't Eddy, but then again, he is the one with the greatest motive. I was sure it was Ben, but now I have a lingering doubt. Why would he want to hurt me? The trouble is, I just can't work out why anyone would want to harm me. I have crossed people over the years, and I know not everybody likes me, but that is normal. I just can't work out what I have done to provoke someone to target me.

When I return to the flat, Mel appears, but I can sense she is uneasy.

'Dad rang,' she says, hopping from one foot to another, then turning her back on me.

'What is it?'

'Will you be annoyed if I don't come with you tomorrow?'

'What do you mean?'

'If I don't come to the graveyard? It's not just that I've got so much work to do; really, it kind of freaks me out going to graveyards and...' Mel looks pained. 'Sorry.'

'It's fine, darling.' I give her a hug. 'Just the fact you're thinking about Aunt Becky is enough. I don't expect you to come with me.'

'Dad wanted to know if we'd like to go out for lunch afterwards. Can you call him?'

'Why don't you stay here in the morning, and then we'll come back and collect you for lunch?'

Mel grins. 'Thanks, Mum. Will you take some flowers for me?'

'Of course.'

~

A COUPLE of days after Becky died, Sarah Jones, the family liaison officer, came to see me.

'There's going to be an inquest into Becky's death,' she said after accepting a cup of sugary tea from me. I wondered whether it was obligatory for family liaison officers to like tea.

'Why? She was knocked down by a lorry.'

'Unnatural deaths are referred to the coroner. It's normal procedure,' she explained. But nothing was normal in those days. The future I had planned out for my family had disintegrated. Firstly by divorce, secondly by death.

'Was she murdered?' I began shaking again.

'No. But we need to know why she got out of her car. Did something happen to force her to be in harm's way? Or did she choose to step out in front of the lorry? We need to check if there were any substances in her bloodstream that might have affected her judgement. There are quite a few unanswered questions.'

'You think she might have committed suicide?' I screeched. 'No, no.'

'We're not suggesting that, but we need to rule it out.'

'So you're suggesting it might have been deliberate, that someone murdered her!'

'I'm not saying that either, Laura,' Sarah said gently, balancing her cup of tea on her knee and leaning forwards. 'Please don't worry about it. It's standard practice. We just have to try our best to establish why she died, and the police must decide whether to press charges against the lorry driver.'

'I thought it was an accident,' I whispered, wiping the tears from my cheeks.

'And it probably was,' Sarah reassured me. 'But it will mean that you won't be able to organise the funeral until the coroner has authorised the release of Becky's body.'

'Is she going to be cut up?' My voice quivered. The thought

of her being laid out on a stainless-steel bed in a mortuary and dissected with a knife by a stranger was too much to bear.

Sarah shook her head. 'Why don't we talk about what you'd like to do for her funeral?'

I don't want her to have a funeral at all, I thought. She should be here, sitting next to me, vibrant and alive.

It was only with hindsight that I came to realise that the sole advantage of the inquest was it gave me nearly three weeks to plan my sister's funeral. I visited every church and graveyard within a twenty-mile radius. She hadn't been a believer and nor am I, but I wanted her to be buried somewhere beautiful.

The church I chose is in a hamlet on the edge of the South Downs. Built in the eleventh and twelfth centuries, it is Saxo-Norman, with mighty thick walls constructed out of large higgledy-piggledy flint stones and substantial grey slates on the roof. It is a small church, but it looks imposing, solid and grounded, having been there for so many centuries. I wanted that for Becky. Long-lasting. The interior is simple and of little relevance to me. It was the graveyard that mattered most. It is small – perhaps only fifty or so graves, high up on a hill with far-reaching views, protected by beautiful oak trees and a magnificent yew tree with a gnarled trunk so large it would take four men to put their arms around its girth. There is history in that graveyard. I have been meaning to research into it, find out who Becky's companions are, the ghosts that, in more fanciful moments, I imagine rising out of the earth for a middle-of-the-night get-together.

To begin with, Ian didn't understand why I was so insistent Becky be buried there.

'Don't you want her to be with your parents?' he asked.

I shook my head. I wanted Becky to be close by. Selfish perhaps, but somewhere I could visit her, not up in Leeds over two hundred miles away. Besides, our parents had chosen to be cremated. Our brother, Donny, would have understood, but he was on the other side of the world, and I didn't involve him in the decision. It was solely up to me. And then we hit a seemingly impassable boulder. Becky had not been living in the correct parish. Having set my heart on that church, that graveyard, it seemed as if my wishes were to be thwarted.

'I'm sorry, but as she isn't one of our parishioners and you haven't purchased a plot, it won't be possible.' The vicar's administrator was very polite but insistent. My tears, my pleadings met with an intransigence that I thought cruel considering what heartache I had been exposed to. I asked Sarah Jones to intervene. I asked the funeral home, who still had no body or a date for receiving one, to intervene. All to no avail.

And then I met Anna.

I didn't answer the phone in those first couple of weeks, having no desire to speak to anyone, no desire for my grief to be appeased in any way. Ian came over most evenings to cook supper, to make sure Mel was cared for. He had wanted to whisk her away to stay with him, but I had such hysteria at the thought of being left alone, he backed off quickly. Ian had gone home and Mel was in the bath when the phone rang. Alone in the living room of our soon-to-be ex-family home, staring at old photos with unseeing eyes, I let the answering machine kick in and listened to the message in real time. She spoke tentatively.

'Hello, my name is Anna Moretti, and I am, was, a friend of Becky's. I don't know if she mentioned me to you?' She stifled a sob. 'I'm just so sorry. She was such a dear friend to me, and I know your grief is incomparable, but I want to tell you how loved she is and how much I will miss her. If there is anything...'

I grabbed the phone. This was the first of Becky's friends who had reached out directly to me, and I wanted a piece of my sister, however vicarious that might be.

'Yes, Becky did mention you,' I lied. I surprised myself with my question. 'Would you like to meet up?'

Anna came over the next day. We spent hours poring over photo albums while I reminisced about our rather miserable childhood, which somehow I managed to sugarcoat. I shed buckets of tears over my sister while Anna sat opposite me, making countless pots of tea, from time to time wiping away her own tears. She told me how Becky had introduced Anna to her husband, Jim, what a kind, funny friend she had been. It didn't strike me until much later that I did most of the talking, that I never once asked Anna how she and Becky had met. At some point I shared my desperation about wanting Becky to be buried in St Mary's churchyard and bemoaned how the 'wicked' system was rigged against me, and where was the morality and Christianity in that? A little smile played at Anna's lips, the first time I had seen her beautiful face light up.

'I might be able to help,' she said. 'Can you leave it with me?'

It was the first time in that desperate fortnight that I felt a ray of hope.

Two days later, the doorbell rang. It was early afternoon, Mel was at school, and I was still in my pyjamas. I ignored it. But whoever was there was insistent. Eventually I hauled myself up from the sofa and peeked out from behind the curtains. Anna was standing outside, her dark hair flowing from underneath a bobble hat, dressed in an olive-green anorak with an indulgent real fur collar.

'I'm looking like shit,' I said through the letterbox. 'Can you wait whilst I put some clothes on?'

'I couldn't care less what you look like,' she said. 'I've got some good news for you.'

I let her in. She grinned at me as she peeled off her winter clothes.

'Becky is going to be buried in St Mary's churchyard, and when the time comes, you'll have the funeral there too. Reverend Sumner will do it.'

'Oh my goodness, thank you!' I moved as if to fling my arms around Anna. She stepped backwards away from me, so I stumbled like a drunkard, and embarrassed, I asked her if she would like to go into the kitchen, make herself a drink whilst I got dressed. Anna stayed the rest of that afternoon and into the evening. She helped me make supper and even charmed Mel into completing her homework without fuss. The next afternoon she came around again, and over the next few days we planned Becky's funeral with military precision. I don't know what I would have done without Anna.

'How did you do it?' I asked the day before the funeral. 'How did you get Becky a burial plot at St Mary's?'

'I have my ways and means.' She tapped the side of her nose.

'Money talks,' Ian said when he came around after work to cook supper for Mel and me. 'Probably paid for a new roof.'

'Oh, come on! Why would she do something like that for a friend, however good a friend they might have been? It's a ridiculous suggestion!' I rebuffed. 'Besides, I know nothing about her personal circumstances.'

'She obviously doesn't work,' Ian said. 'Otherwise she wouldn't be free to spend all this time with you.'

'Maybe she slept with the vicar!' Mel smirked.

Ian and I shouted at her simultaneously. Mel just flicked her hair and rolled her eyes. I assumed that Anna had links with the church, knew someone on a committee, but I never found out. She always changed the subject, told me it was a gift to our family, that it was nothing, easy to arrange.

The coroner released Becky's body twenty days after she died. There was to be no inquest. And then there was the funeral. I don't remember much of it. The church was so full, people were left standing outside in the cold. That's what happens when someone dies too young. Anna held court, shaking mourners' hands, supporting me on one side whilst

Ian supported me on the other. Donny talked about coming back from Australia, but I told him that was ridiculous; he would only be doing it for me and that wasn't necessary. Come next year, I said; but he didn't. The reception was in a local pub. I felt like a voyeur. There was a feeling of hysteria, false joviality, as everyone shared their stories of Becky. I knew so few people at the funeral, I might have been grieving for a stranger.

## 30

The following year was in some ways even harder. Ian was fully out of my life. I had started working, and the anniversary of Becky's death loomed, bringing palpitations and terror. My grief got in the way of everything. Anna came to the rescue again. She told me to ask for compassionate leave for the day. Peter agreed, probably at the dictate of Jenny.

'We're going to make a day of it,' Anna announced. 'Firstly, we'll lay some flowers by the side of the road; then we'll take some more flowers and put them on her grave. We'll go into the church and light some candles. Then we'll go to the pub and have a big hearty lunch and a bottle of wine and share stories about Becky. Afterwards, we'll come home and watch a rom-com.'

'I don't want to drive,' I murmured.

'You won't have to. I've ordered a car.'

Anna rang my doorbell at precisely 9 a.m. I had dressed casually in black jeans, a black polo neck and my navy anorak, while Anna looked as if she was going to a business meeting in a sharp woollen black suit and a long cashmere coat. A large black Mercedes hummed outside, and when Anna and I appeared, a driver in uniform jumped out of the car and opened the back door. It reminded me a little of being in the hearse when we were taken to Becky's funeral, but I didn't say anything. I placed the two small bouquets of roses next to me on the back seat. They were pale pink: Becky's favourite colour and hard to come by in late November.

I was shaking by the time the driver pulled on to the A272.

'I don't know if I want to do this, to stop at the place where she died,' I said.

Anna turned to me, an earnest expression on her face. 'You do, Laura. It's very cathartic. Believe me, I know.'

'How do you know?' I asked. She didn't answer.

My fear of standing in the spot where Becky died grew by the moment, so much so that by the time the driver parked up in the lay-by, I was in danger of having a full-blown panic attack.

'Breathe,' Anna instructed. 'In and out, in and out.' She guided my breath and held my gaze until my body began to relax. I glanced up at the driver, who was staring at me in the rear mirror, his heavy brow wrinkled, eyes narrowed with concern.

'If you don't want to do this, we won't,' she said. 'I'll put flowers down by myself.'

But I'm her sister, I thought to myself. I picked up one of the bouquets and was about to open the rear door when I screeched.

'I'm sitting on the wrong side!' My door opened onto the road; if I got out, I would have been standing in the exact spot where she died. Would there still be specks of blood on the ground, I wondered.

Anna opened her car door. 'Slide along,' she instructed. I followed her instructions.

She walked around to the boot of the car, which magically

swung up. Inside were two extravagant wreaths made from orange lilies, gypsophila and carnations. Becky hates those flowers, I thought to myself. Really hates them. Garage forecourt flowers, she used to describe carnations and gypsophila. And orange was her least favourite colour, a hangover from the orange and brown curtains that hung in our parents' front room. But then again, how would a friend know all of that? I'll tell Anna another time, I decided, so she won't make the same mistake again next year.

As I clutched my bouquet of roses, which looked measly and insignificant next to Anna's prolific wreath, I felt nothing. Absolutely nothing. And later, when we stood at Becky's grave in the shadow of St Mary's church, I tried not to think about her body rotten now in the earth below me. Although the tears flowed, I couldn't get a sense of her there, either. And inside the church, all I could recall was from the year before at her funeral, when the vicar said anodyne things about Becky, my sister, whom he never met.

'She's gone,' I said when we were seated at our table in the pub.

Anna looked at me strangely, as if to say, well, of course she's gone. And then she asked me something about how Becky got into nursing, and my mood lifted a little.

For the past three years, the routine has been the same. A chauffeured car, roadside, church, graveyard, pub. I have never been brave enough to tell Anna that Becky didn't like orange flowers. On the second year we watched a rom-com at Anna's house afterwards, but last year I didn't feel like it and excused myself with a headache. And this year, year four, I am changing things altogether and won't be going with Anna at all. I feel bad. After all, it is thanks to Anna that Becky is buried in such a beautiful location; it is thanks to Anna that I got through my grief and faced up to some of my fears. I send her a quick text apologising again for going to the graveyard with Ian this year. I have a lot to thank her for and just hope that she understands.

Ian is late. I decide to wait downstairs so the intercom bell doesn't wake Mel, who is still fast asleep. It is a cold but clear day, the sky a pale silvery blue, weak rays of sunshine just beginning to slant in between the rooftops. I pace up and down the pavement in front of the block, clutching my bouquets of flowers: three this time, one from Mel, one from Ian (as I assume he won't remember to bring his own) and one from me. I don't intend to visit the roadside today.

A car screeches to a halt next to the kerb, level with me.

I get into the passenger seat. Ian is all flustered, darkened rings around his eyes, looking every one of his fifty-four years. That's what happens when you have a newborn and you're old enough to be a grandfather, I think nastily.

'Sorry I'm late. Rory was up all night and so were we. I wish I hadn't taken paternity leave!' he jests.

I don't laugh.

'Is everything all right? Any more death notices?'

'He denies it, but I think my creepy ex might be behind everything that's happened to me: the obituary, the death certificate, etcetera.'

'Really?' Ian frowns. He has the good grace not to look surprised that I have, or rather had, a boyfriend. A ridiculous term for someone my age.

'Not everything,' I say. 'I don't think he's responsible for everything, but...' I let the sentence peter out. I have no intention of discussing the possible rape and pornographic email with my ex-husband. 'It's complicated. Let's go, shall we?'

I push aside the baby dummies, muslin squares, a car mobile and a fabric ABC book.

'Have you had any more threats?' Ian asks.

'It hasn't been a great fortnight.'

'Charlie mentioned the fake doctor's letter. Isn't it time for you to go to the police?'

I nearly tell Ian about my car, about the email, about the fact I may or may not have lost my job, and that the police are already sort of involved, but something holds me back. If I permanently lose my job, I may need to return to this man and beg him for money. It's possible that I might, as Jenny suggested, need to face him again in the courts. But I don't want to. Ian and I are getting on better than at any time over the past few years. It would be a shame to destroy that. He deserves to bring up his new family in peace, and I will just have to sort out my own life. I exhale and give myself a virtual pat on the back for my magnanimous thoughts. I'm doing it for Mel, if not for myself, I think.

Ian parks the car at the bottom of the little path that leads up to the church. I have been focusing so hard on myself, my problems and fears, I haven't given any consideration to why we are here. I conjure up memories of Becky and can feel my eyes welling up with tears. Ian walks alongside me and gives my shoulder a squeeze. I would have liked him to put his arm around me, but he's someone else's husband now. The large wooden door to the church is ajar.

'I'm surprised the vicar is here, early on a Friday morning,' Ian comments.

'Could be anyone,' I say. 'Shall we light a candle? I normally do that with Anna.'

We push the church door fully open and step inside. It is as cold inside as it is out. I shiver. There doesn't appear to be anyone here. A solitary candle burns near the altar. It must have been lit recently because it has barely burned down.

'I had forgotten how lovely this church is,' Ian whispers. 'Pass me the flowers so you can light a candle.'

I stuff a five-pound note into the collection box and try to light a match. My hand is shaking. Ian doesn't say anything. It takes me a couple of attempts to light the candle. I walk towards the altar, slip into a pew, bend down and say a silent prayer. In previous years, my mind was blank. I had glanced over to Anna, who was mouthing words, her head bent earnestly. All I could think of was, why am I here? Why was Becky taken from us so cruelly? But today, my thoughts are lucid and they flow. I remember to thank God and I remember to ask him to look after Mel and Ian and Charlene and the baby, and I ask him to look out for me because I am not ready to die yet.

When I stand up, Ian is still clasping the bouquets of flowers and reading through some notices at the back of the church.

'Ok?' He tilts his head, and a little nerve quivers to the edge of his right eye, a mannerism that is so familiar and that, once upon a time, sent my stomach into flutters. I nod.

'Let's go.'

We walk out of the church and Ian carefully closes the door behind us. We saunter down the path, past the oldest grave-stones covered in moss and algae, wording barely legible, and then towards the newer ones, a few of which look startlingly new, shiny with every letter standing out in proud relief. We approach Becky's grave from behind, and as Ian is walking slightly ahead of me, he sees it first.

'Oh my God!' His hand rushes up to his mouth. 'Laura, don't look!'

But it's too late. I see how Becky's grave has been defiled. I read the word scrawled in heavy black marker across her head-stone. *Bitch*, it says. And I see the extravagant orange flower wreath laid out in front of the headstone, the same one that Anna puts there every year, looking a little less pristine than normal.

'How could anyone do that?' Ian says, clutching me,

crushing the bouquets of pale pink roses that I am still holding. 'Laura, I'm so sorry.'

He releases me and then strides away.

'Don't go,' I say. My voice sounds strangled.

'I'm not going anywhere. I need to see if any other graves have been vandalised.' He paces up and down the rows of graves. I watch him because I cannot bear to rest my eyes on Becky's headstone. It is so cold in that graveyard. Despite my three sweaters, thick scarf, hat, gloves and down-filled coat, I am trembling.

'This one has some black marker across it, and this one,' Ian yells. And then he walks back to me, his shoulders curved, his face white, no doubt mimicking my own expression. 'But no words, just marks. I wonder if someone got disturbed and ran off?'

'Why would Becky's grave be targeted first?' My brain feels mangled. For a few long moments, I can't think straight, and then I am hit by a moment of clarity. 'I think it's whoever is out to get me.'

'That's fanciful,' Ian says, sounding unconvinced. 'Who would have left that wreath?'

'Anna,' I whisper. 'She leaves the same one every year. And Becky didn't even like orange flowers,' I cry.

'She must have got here early. What's Anna's number?'

I hand my mobile to Ian, who, remembering my pin code, quickly dials Anna's mobile.

'It's not Laura, it's Ian,' he says, not waiting for any niceties. 'What time did you lay the wreath on Becky's grave?' He pauses as he listens to the answer. 'That's early,' he says. 'Was the gravestone vandalised?'

I wish I could hear what she's saying.

'You would have seen this fucking mess even if it was pitch dark!' he yells. 'No, I'm sorry. Yes, of course.' Pause. 'Yes, we most certainly will be ringing the police. Desecrating sacred ground is a very serious crime.'

He hands me back my phone. I am on my hands and knees, trying to wipe the letters off the headstone, but they have been written in indelible ink. Ian pulls me up.

'It'll need to be cleaned by a specialist,' he says softly.

'What did Anna say?' Tears are flowing down my cheeks, but Ian has seen me looking much worse, and I don't care.

'She was here about 4 p.m. yesterday, and the headstone was untouched. Or so she says.'

'What was she doing here then? I would have expected her to visit today.'

'Apparently her driver was busy today, so she came yesterday instead. Why does she have a driver?'

'She can't drive. She has epilepsy and uses a driver or taxis.'

'I've never liked her,' Ian says.

'You don't know her,' I say, thinking that Ian could only have met her a couple of times, because Anna only came into my life after Ian and I had divorced.

'We'll need to let the vicar know and find out what the protocol is,' Ian says.

I don't respond. It crosses my mind that if I notify the police of a further graffiti incident, they may start looking much closer, and probably much closer at me. They will ask me why I didn't tell them about the rape, the fake death notice and everything else. They will think that it is me who is the liar, and then my life really will unravel. I leave our bouquets of flowers on Becky's grave, whispering, 'I'm sorry, darling,' to her, just in case she can hear me. Then I follow Ian back up the path to the church. There is a phone number on a noticeboard for the vicar. He calls it, pacing up and down, waiting for a reply.

'Shit. There's no answer,' Ian says. 'Let's try again a bit later. I don't want to leave a message.'

Ian puts his arm around my shoulders now, but it does little to quell my shaking. I hope Charlene doesn't mind.

'Let's get you a brandy,' he says. 'It doesn't matter that it's only noon.'

Ian knows me well.

'I think we should stay around here though,' he continues. 'Maybe have lunch here rather than in Horsham, and then we can pop back up to the church when we get hold of the vicar.'

'But we were going to go back and collect Mel, have lunch the three of us.'

'Call Mel and tell her we'll have an early supper instead.'

'Won't Charlene mind?'

'I expect she'll be relieved to have me out of the house all day. She says I'm stifling her, getting in the way. I'll ring her to check.'

'Are you changing nappies?' I ask, surprised.

'Of course.'

'Wow! You never did that for Mel. Things have changed over the last eighteen years.'

'Indeed they have,' he muses. 'Where's the nearest pub?'

'It's the Rose and Crown, where Anna and I have had lunch on 28 November for the past three years.'

'You okay to go there?' he asks.

I nod.

## 31

I call Mel as Ian drives. There is no answer on her mobile, so I try our landline, but just get my voice on the answering machine. I leave a message on both and send her a text message as well. She will be expecting us back any time now, so I assume she is in the bathroom getting ready. With the promise of dinner instead of lunch, hopefully she won't mind having a few hours to herself.

The pub is comprised of three rooms: the smarter dining room where Anna and I usually sit for our annual 28 November lunch; the bar area, assigned predominantly for drinkers; and a more casual room, frequented by families with children and the eye-rolling latecomers who can't get into the dining room. Whilst Ian goes to the bar to collect a brandy for me and a half pint of beer for himself, I make my way into the casual room, where the beams are slightly higher and the room not quite as cosy, with a log-burning stove as opposed to an open fireplace. As we're so early, I place my coat over a chair at a table nearest to the stove and stand in front of it, rubbing my hands. The scent of well-cured burning logs is soothing.

'Drink this. It'll warm you up body and soul,' Ian says,

handing me my brandy in its bulbous glass. 'You must miss Becky terribly.'

I blink at my ex-husband. That was not an Ian sentence. He was never emotionally sensitive during our marriage, so I wonder if Charlene has unleashed his feminine side.

'Yes, I miss her every single day.'

I clench and unclench my fists a few times, debating whether or not to tell Ian. But if I can't say anything to him, who can I share this with? 'I've tried to get the inquest reopened.'

'You what?' He wipes his nose with the back of his hand, an unhygienic gesture that used to annoy me.

'It's never made sense to me as to why Becky was in the road. Why did she stop her car at that lay-by? Where was she going? Surely someone must have seen her?'

'Oh, Laura,' Ian says, disappointment heavy in his voice. 'I thought you let those questions go when the coroner decided it was an accidental death?'

'I tried to, and for a couple of years I managed. But the more I think about all the circumstances, the more it doesn't stack up.'

'Are you sure this is nothing to do with the death threats and stuff that's been happening to you? It would be enough to make anyone paranoid.'

'I'm not paranoid, Ian.' I bat away the memory of Jenny and Peter's suggestion that my mental health is impaired. 'Besides,' I continue, 'I came to this conclusion six months ago. It's nothing new. In fact, I contacted Sarah Jones, my family liaison officer, back in the summer, and she put me in touch with Detective Inspector Colin Evans, who was what they call the road policing lead investigator. I asked him if we could get the coroner to reopen the inquest.'

'Bloody hell, Laura. What did he say?'

I stare into the flickering orange flames in the log-burning stove. 'The short answer is no. Apparently, of all the thousands of inquests coroners hear every year in the UK, only about twenty-five are reopened. And they only reopen cases when they can prove that there is an overwhelming public interest to do so.'

'I assume they need new evidence as well,' Ian says.

'Exactly.'

'So what now?'

'I have to find new evidence.' I sigh.

'The police won't help you?'

I shake my head. 'DI Evans said suspicion isn't enough. They're overstaffed and under-resourced.'

'He's got a point.'

We are both silent for a while until Ian, somewhat belatedly, raises his glass. 'Here's to Becky.'

'To Becky,' I say, blinking away tears, tears of loss and tears of frustration. 'I've been trying to work through things, trying to find out a bit more about Becky's life just before she died.'

Ian raises his eyebrows. They are good eyebrows, nicely arched and sufficiently full without being bushy. 'I'll order us some food, and then tell me all about it.'

I eavesdrop on other people's conversations whilst I'm waiting for Ian; anything to offer me a distraction from my own life.

And then, when Ian returns, I tell him all about the day I started my search.

I VISITED the lay-by on the A272 back in July. It was a Sunday; one of those perfect summer days that we rarely seem to get anymore, when the sky is pale turquoise, the air is warm enough to wear thin cotton tops but not so hot that it makes one feel sticky and uncomfortable. The sun was high in the sky, and the air smelled of verdant meadows despite the fact the grass was just beginning to brown.

There was one of those retro VW camper-vans taking up most of the lay-by. The vehicle was painted deep red and white with gleaming silver wheel hubs and a pop-up roof in matching red and white candy-stripes. I used to lust after one of those, thinking what fun it would be pitching up for the night wherever you fancy. But latterly those VWs seem to have become the must-have weekend vehicle of choice for trust-fund thirty-somethings who, thanks to daddy's successes, can afford to stay in fancy hotels but choose glamping and seventies throwbacks instead. Personally, I'd choose a hotel, but then I experienced the era the first time around.

Such a vehicle shouldn't have been parked there. It seemed irreverent somehow that a vehicle of fun was desecrating the space where Becky died. When Anna and I had visited the lay-by on the first anniversary of Becky's death, she had suggested we create a little shrine, perhaps with a cross and the planting of some flowers. I don't like seeing those permanent roadside memorials. They seem ghoulish to me. But at that moment I wished we had created one. It might have deterred the week-enders. I had a bunch of flowers with me, natural wild flowers that might have come from my garden if I still had one, but instead came from the little florist's shop in the centre of town.

I had asked DI Colin Evans which way Becky's car had been pointing. Towards Petworth apparently, with the driver's door adjacent to the passing traffic. I parked facing the same way, so that my car was nose to nose with the VW camper-van. The A272 is a narrow, winding road, chock-full of traffic on a summer's Sunday afternoon. I opened my door, just a smidgeon, but a blue estate car came past, just centimetres away, creating a whoosh of air that tugged at the door and billowed up my cotton skirt. It took my breath away and made my heart pump violently. As melodramatic as it sounds, the voice in my head screamed 'you can't die in the same place as your sister'. Inelegantly, I clambered over to the passenger seat and stepped out onto the verge. I stood there for a moment, clutching the flowers, before walking up the bank slightly.

'Hello, lovely day, isn't it?'

I reckoned she was nearing seventy, stick-thin, wearing cropped leggings and a T-shirt, with a face that in both texture and colour looked like a walnut. I nodded at her and attempted a smile.

'Nice bunch of flowers you've got there. From the garden?'

'No. My sister died here and I'm leaving them on the roadside.'

She looked startled. 'We're just leaving.' Then she repeated herself, several decibels louder this time. 'We're just leaving, aren't we, Winnifred?'

I thought Winnifred would have been a good name for the camper-van, but it turned out Winnifred was human.

At least three times the size of stick-woman, she popped her conker-like head out of the window and grinned, exposing a broken front tooth. The camper-van swayed precariously and coughed as she started it up, belching out three puffs of dark grey smoke from its exhaust. I watched with relief as they pulled out and drove away. No problem easing out into the traffic if you're facing the correct way, I thought. And the visibility was just fine without a vehicle parked up in front.

I sat down on the bank, laying the flowers next to me. Becky had been facing towards Petworth. Her car door was unscathed, so she didn't get hit getting out of the car. In fact, the whole car was in perfect condition. Had it started juddering or doing something strange, I wondered. Was that why she pulled up at the first lay-by she could find? Did she get out of the car and wander around it, checking the tyres, sniffing to see if the brakes smelled acrid? But it was dark, so it would have been hard to see anything in the pitch black on a cold, late

November evening, far from any houses or street lamps. But she would have seen the lorry's headlights.

And then it struck me. Perhaps she wasn't checking her car at all; perhaps she had been meeting someone. The more I thought about it, that theory began to make the most sense. If she had stopped to take or make a phone call, that would have shown up on her mobile phone records. So if there was nothing wrong with the car, she wasn't lost and didn't feel ill (which couldn't be ruled out but seemed unlikely, as she had been at work on the early shift, and none of her colleagues suggested she had been feeling unwell), then the only obvious reason she had been there was to meet someone. Quite why she was meeting someone in the middle of nowhere, I needed to fathom out.

I left the flowers, got back into the passenger's seat and shuffled over to the driver's seat. My heart was in my mouth as I pulled out onto the road, putting my foot down as a car rounded the corner in a flash, braked and blared its horn. Strictly speaking, being run over isn't a car accident, but my brain has never quite processed that one. My relationship with cars hasn't been the same since, and no doubt it never will be. Large vehicles bearing down on me give me the worst palpitations.

I carried on towards Petworth, winding down my windows to enjoy the warmth from that July Sunday afternoon, all the while thinking. The 28th of November had been a Monday the year Becky died. Was she on her way to meet someone for dinner? Mondays are bad days for eating out, with many restaurants choosing to close for the night. On the other hand, it was the start of the Christmas party season, so perhaps the establishments that were normally shut on a Monday might have stayed open in the hope of getting more trade.

At the T-junction I turned left into Petworth, following the increasingly narrow road, passing the imposing tall walls encircling Petworth House on my right-hand side, carrying on until the road became a single track and one way. With imposing Georgian townhouses shoulder to shoulder on both sides of the road, the traffic slowed and then stopped. For long minutes, I was at a standstill. I had forgotten how impossible the small town was to navigate at the peak of the tourist season.

Bored and hot, I rang Anna from my mobile phone. I regretted not asking her to join me on my mission. Actually, I was surprised she answered because I was sure she had told me Jim was home for the weekend.

'I'm in Petworth,' I said. 'Stuck in traffic.'

'Beautiful place not designed for cars,' she said. 'Your sister hated Petworth.'

'Really? Why?'

'Same reason as you, I suppose. Lousy traffic and she said the fancy antique shops made the place so upmarket it was out of the reach of the locals.'

'She had a point,' I mused, thinking that sounded just like Becky. 'Do you know why she might have been going to Petworth on the night she died?'

Anna was silent, and for a moment I wondered if she'd heard me.

'Oh, I thought we'd discussed that before,' she said. 'Didn't her boyfriend live in Midhurst? She'd have had to have gone through Petworth to get to Midhurst.'

If the traffic had actually been moving, I might have crashed my car. What boyfriend? Anna hadn't mentioned Becky having a boyfriend before. I tried to cast my mind back.

'Boyfriend?' I screeched. 'In three years, you've never mentioned that Becky had a boyfriend.'

'Oh, just that Joe bloke. It's nothing to get excited about. Don't you remember the guy who made a scene at the funeral, sobbing his pathetic heart out as if it had been torn from his body? I think they slept together once or twice, but he made out as if Becky had been the love of his life. It was definitely not reciprocated.'

And then the traffic started flowing smoothly, as if a cork had been dislodged from a bottle.

'Gotta go,' I said, annoyed with Anna that despite hundreds of hours of conversation reminiscing about Becky, she had never mentioned the boyfriend. Even if he strictly speaking wasn't her boyfriend. 'We're on the move. I'll catch up with you later in the week.'

Most of the funeral and the aftermath was a blur, so perhaps it's not surprising I had forgotten all about Joe. Mid-thirties, he had introduced himself to me at the funeral, tears pouring down his cheeks, telling me he would never get over the pain of his loss. Me too, I remember thinking. It came back to me then, how Anna told me Joe loved Becky a lot more than she cared for him. How he had been her plus one on a couple of occasions but nothing more. As Anna had never mentioned him to me again, I took his grief with a pinch of salt. But if Joe lived in Midhurst, then he should be the person I should be talking to. And if he had cared for her more than she did for him, he was a person of significant interest to me and quite possibly should have been to the police too. The next question was, how to find him?

The traffic eased me into the market square but was still moving at a snail's pace. I glanced at an antiquarian bookshop, and that jogged a memory. The book of condolences. Everyone at the funeral wrote in that book, but I have never had the emotional strength to read it. I had wrapped the black leather-jacketed book carefully in tissue paper and put it in a box in the attic with Becky's things.

I needed to go home and look at it. Rather than carrying on to Midhurst on a wild goose chase, I followed the road back around the town and drove straight home in the hope that Joe had written his full name in the condolence book.

With a bit of help from Anna, I was hopeful I could track him down.

'Did you find Joe?' Ian asks. He has finished his fish and chips while I have barely made an indent into my lasagne.

'No. I went through the condolence book, and his name was there. Joe Smith. So frustrating that he has such a common name!'

'Typical,' Ian agrees, leaning his elbows on the table. 'What was his message?'

'Short and sweet. Something along the lines of "I'll love you until my dying day. We will meet again." It was definitely more emotional than any of the other messages.'

'Couldn't Anna help track him down?'

'She tried. The trouble is she only met him a couple of times. I just wish that I had known Becky's friends, that our lives had intertwined more.'

'Don't beat yourself up for it. She lived a very different life. Younger than you, single, working. We did our bit.'

I look away. I did my bit. I can't say that Ian ever made any effort with my sister.

'What then?' Ian asks.

'Nothing.' I sigh. 'I started looking through Becky's photographs, and I even fired up her mobile phone, but I don't know her pin code, and then it all seemed too intrusive. I had a go with her laptop, but it's so old I couldn't get it to switch on.'

Ian swirls the remaining dregs in his beer glass. I know what he's thinking. Just as well, let sleeping dogs lie, or some other cliché like that.

'Anyway, shouldn't we try the vicar again?' I remind him, glad to be changing the subject.

He takes out his phone and walks to the doorway of the

pub. I watch him. It's a strange feeling watching your ex-husband from a distance. And for the first time, I realise I feel very little. Just an acorn of affection and two decades of memories. The hurt, the anguish, the jealousy, the betrayal: it's all faded as if I'm seeing myself acting out those emotions on a television screen that is playing in someone else's living room. He is speaking, nodding, grimacing, gesticulating.

'The vicar is going to report it to the police,' Ian says, hovering by our table. 'It's not the first time graves have been vandalised, but it hasn't happened for a while. He's given me the name of a stonemason who can clean the stone. He says don't get your hopes up. Apparently, it is way down the police's agenda for investigating. They prefer to help the living over the dead.' Ian grimaces. 'The vicar implied that it's extremely unlikely that Becky's grave was targeted. Probably just youths mucking around last night.'

'How many youths hang around a remote countryside graveyard?' I ask angrily.

Ian shrugs. 'Come on, let's go.' Ian extends his hand and then quickly drops it to his side as he realises that it is his ex whom he is with and not his current wife. I try to conceal my smirk.

As we're leaving the pub, my mobile phone rings. I fumble in my handbag, trying to find it quickly, assuming it is our daughter. But it isn't. It's the garage.

'Your car is ready, Mrs Swallow. Could you come and collect it?'

'Please hold on a moment.' I turn to Ian. 'Any chance you could drop me off at the garage so I can get my car?'

'Of course,' he says.

# 32

Ian takes me to the garage, and we make a provisional arrangement to meet early evening, with Mel, for a Chinese in a very non-authentic Chinese restaurant on the outskirts of Cranleigh. It's a pain for me, as I'll have to drive there and back, but as Ian has been so reasonable, I feel I can't object.

As I'm getting out of his car, Ian says, 'I know it's hard to accept that Becky's death was an accident, but you really need to, Laura, for your own sanity.'

'And what about all the threats to me?' I ask.

'Some horrible pranks by a man whom you've rejected?' he asks, a lame tone to his voice.

I scowl.

'Come on, Laura. You're still an attractive woman,' he says.

'Not attractive enough,' I bite back. 'You left me for someone else.'

'I'm sorry, Laura.'

'Thanks for your help,' I say. 'I'll call you later when I've spoken to Mel.'

BACK IN MY OWN CAR, I feel anything but safe. I can't stop thinking about Becky and the moment she was hit. Did it hurt? Did her life really flash in front of her eyes? And then I think of my own accident only a week ago, and I hear that crunch of metal and the silence immediately afterwards. And terror chokes my throat. I need to get home, have a chat with Mel, make myself a cup of tea, and then I will indulge in memories, perhaps lie on my bed and flick through some of my photo albums and, if I have the strength, some of Becky's too. I need to replace the imaginary images of her death with real memories of her life.

Darkness is falling now, so early at this time of year. I park my car in the underground car park and hurry back to the flat. Keeping my eyes straight ahead, I ignore the shadows thrown by the metal stanchions in the car park; I rush quickly past shop and office doorways and whatever might be lurking in their depths. When I put my key in the communal front door and stand safely inside, I let out a long, audible exhale and wriggle my shoulders to release the aching tension. I walk slowly up the stairs, shaking my legs out on the landings, again to ease the tight muscles. And then at long last, I put the key in my own front door and open it. I stand for a moment, disorientated. Why are the lights off in the hall?

'Mel!' I shout.

There's no answer. I kick off my ankle boots and walk into the living room. The lights are off there too. Has she gone out? Switching all the lights on, I walk down the little corridor. Her bedroom door is closed.

'Mel, are you there?'

There is no answer. I knock, and then I open the door. Mel's duvet is crumpled up at the end of her bed, her pillow slumping off the top of the bed. There is a pile of dirty clothes on the floor, and her books are open on her desk. I sniff the scent left behind from the incense sticks she burns when she is studying. But Mel isn't there.

I go back to the living room, collapse on the sofa and call her mobile. But it goes straight to voicemail. That's strange. Has her phone run out of battery? Or perhaps she is deep in a changing room in the town's small shopping mall. I doubt there's decent mobile reception in there. But it's not like Mel to disappear off without letting me know. She hasn't responded to my texts that I sent earlier today, and as I scroll through them, I notice that she hasn't even read them.

Oh, Mel, I think. Typical teenage girl: she's either lost her phone or has forgotten to charge it. I hope she gets home soon, as it's dark, and whilst I know she's away by herself at university and Manchester is a much larger, grittier town than polite, southern-counties Horsham, I am still worried. It's a mother's job to worry, whatever age her child. And the difference is, in Manchester, I've no idea what she's getting up to, so I can't worry. When she's here with me, I do.

I send Ian a text, asking if he has heard from Mel. I get an instant answer back: no.

Feeling unsettled, I return to Mel's room to see if I can spot her phone. I don't like to go through her things, so I don't touch anything, just scour the mess: the books, the discarded T-shirts, the make-up and the pens overflowing from her turquoise and yellow pencil case, the same one she has had for the past five years. I hesitate at her laptop. The light is on, and it is tempting to fire it up, to see if I can find her social media feeds and probe into her life, but I restrain myself. No. Mel deserves privacy.

Returning to the kitchen, I put on the kettle and make myself a cup of camomile tea. I keep my photo albums in a cupboard underneath the television in the living room. They rarely come out, but this afternoon is a time for indulgence. I balance my cup of tea on top of three large albums and carry them into my bedroom, nudging the door open with my backside. Placing the cup on my bedside table, I drop the albums onto the bed and then step back to the door to switch on the bedroom light. As I turn back to the bed, I see a piece of paper that has fluttered to the floor.

Ah, a note from Mel. She normally leaves me notes on the dining room table or in the kitchen next to the kettle, where she knows I'll see them, but still... I bend down to pick it up and turn it around. The words are typed in a large font. I read them and then the bedroom spins uncontrollably and my world goes black.

When I come to, I am on the carpet, collapsed by the side of my bed. I raise my head carefully and sit up. I am dizzy, but the room quickly rights itself. For a moment, I am confused. Why am I lying on the floor, next to my bed? Then I see the piece of paper, the words facing up, and I have to swallow hard to keep the bile from my mouth.

Dear Mum, I've gone to meet Becky. Love, Mel

What the hell does that mean? Does she mean she has gone to the graveyard? But no. How could she get there? She doesn't drive. She doesn't have enough money for a taxi, and it's just not somewhere she would want to go. And why is it typed out? Mel's notes are always hand scrawled with a biro or pencil on a scrap of paper. As it dawns on me, I clutch the side of my bed, my fingers grabbing, plucking the edge of my duvet, a sound rising from the back of my throat that is totally alien.

Mel didn't write that note! Ben has taken Mel and he's going to kill her. My daughter is going to die, today, on the same day of the year as her aunt! I am shaking so uncontrollably, I slip as I try to stand up, and I am aware that my ankle hurts, but then a second later I am unaware of it. My scream has disintegrated into hiccupping sobs. What should I do? Where should I go? I will have to call the police now. Everything is related. Everything. I stumble back to the living room and find the phone. I ring 999.

'Emergency services. Where should I direct your call?'

'Someone's abducted my daughter! Help me!' I yelp.

'I'll transfer you to the police,' the woman says. The moment seems too long, but then there is another voice, a male this time.

'Police. How can I help you?'

'My daughter. She's been taken and he's going to kill her!' My words jumble altogether, and in the pause before he speaks, I wonder if I'm making any sense. My whole body is shaking, uncontrollable tremors clouding my sight, fogging my mind, and there is a loud buzzing in my ears, coming from somewhere inside my head.

'Where are you, ma'am?'

'At home.'

'And where is home?'

'Flat 6, 14 Castle Street, Horsham.'

'How old is your daughter?'

'Eighteen, nearly nineteen.'

The policeman clears his throat. 'And who is it that you think is going to kill her?'

'Dr Ben Logan. He's been threatening me and now he's taken Mel, my daughter. He's left me a note. It says...' And then I realise the note is next door and I can't remember the precise wording. 'Please hold on a moment.' I hurry back to the bedroom and pick up the piece of paper, holding it in my fingers as if it is dirt. 'It says, "Dear Mum, I've gone to meet Becky. Love Mel."'

'Okaaay.' There is a very lengthy pause. 'And who is Becky?'

'She's my sister. She died four years ago today, so I know that the note is a covert threat. Mel couldn't be going to meet Becky. She's dead!' The pitch of my voice is rising higher and higher.

'Take a deep breath, ma'am,' the policeman says. I dig my fingernails into the palm of my left hand.

'Could it be another Becky, perhaps? A friend of your daughter's?'

Oh God! Have I made an assumption that is totally wrong? Could Mel have a friend I don't know about. No, of course not! I would know.

'No, no,' I say, shouting now. 'And the note was typed out, not handwritten. It hasn't been left by Mel. She's in danger. Terrible danger! And her mobile phone is off; I can't reach her.'

The policeman exhales loudly; I can hear him typing, and then he clears his throat. 'We'll send someone around to see you.'

'How quickly?' I ask.

'Current response time is within four hours,' he says.

'But she could be dead by then!' I screech. 'This is an emergency. That's why you're there, isn't it? The police are there to help in emergencies.'

'Yes, ma'am. But we have to assess the level of threat and prioritise. Your daughter is an adult, and it is extremely unlikely that she will have come to any harm.'

'But Ben Logan tried to attack me. He raped me. He vandalised my car. He sent me death notices.'

'Have you reported any of this?'

'No. Yes. The car. I had a minor car accident and the graffiti was reported.'

There is a very long silence now. It is as if I can hear the cogs going around in this man's head. Got a crazy woman here, he is thinking. If any of this were true, she would have reported it. But she hasn't. Just a car accident, which was her fault.

'I will file a report and send it through to your local team. If someone can get to you sooner, then they will. Please give me your best contact numbers.'

## 33

I feel a wave of desperation. I put my hand to my throat, rubbing it up and down as if it will help unblock the constrictions inside. My stomach is clenching too, and I wonder if I'm going to be sick. I pace up and down the flat, noting but not caring about the throbbing in my ankle. There is no way that I am waiting around for hours in case the police might or might not show up. I will have to confront Ben myself. Ian will help me. I'll call Ian. But as I am about to dial his number, I think of Charlene. Do I fully trust her? I think I do. But even if I do, she has just given birth. It isn't fair of me to involve them. But Ian is Mel's father. He will want to help?

No. I will not call Ian. Ben's appearance in my life is due to me, and I need to confront him. I have to do this alone. My heart is pounding hard now as I wonder if I have the courage to do this. Yes. I must. I will save my daughter. I would give my life willingly to save Mel's. That's what I will do. I will tell Ben to kill me and release Mel.

My hand is shaking so much it is extremely difficult to call Ben on my mobile. I hold my breath as I wait for him to answer. But he doesn't answer. It rings five or six times and then goes to voicemail. Of course he isn't going to answer the phone to me. I wonder if he has a clinic today, whether he is in the hospital. If he has Mel, I assume not, but it might be worth my while contacting his secretary to see if she knows where he is. I search on Google, screaming with frustration; my fingers are shaking so much, it is hard to type. Eventually I find him listed on the hospital's website. He has an NHS secretary and a private secretary. I call the private secretary first.

'Hello, Lisa speaking. How can I help you?'

'I'm trying to get hold of Ben Logan.'

'Are you a patient?' she asks.

'Um, no. It's a personal call. It's urgent.'

'I'm afraid he's in clinic right now and I can't disturb him. I could leave a note for him in between patients. Who should I say is trying to reach him?'

This throws me. He is in the hospital right now. How can that be? Has he holed up Mel somewhere in the hospital?

'Hello?' She speaks again. I cut the line. Is his secretary telling the truth? The only way I will find out for sure is by going there myself. That's what I will do. Go to the hospital right now.

I throw on my coat, ease my feet back into my boots, and grab my handbag. I run like a lunatic, back the way I have just come, sidestepping commuters leaving shops and offices, weaving in and out, ignoring the searing pain in my ankle, taking the stairs two at a time until I'm at my car, panting, my throat burning, my eyes sore. It's school pick-up time, which whilst it's not standstill traffic, is still frustratingly slow. I bang my fist on the steering wheel. 'Come on! Hurry up!' I yell at the unsuspecting drivers around me. Eventually I am out of the town centre and onto the dual carriageway. I drive like an idiot. To hell with being photographed by the speed cameras or even being chased by a police car. In fact, it might help me if I am tracked by the police. Would they blue-light me to the hospital if I explained the urgency? But no: there isn't a police car in sight.

I push my little Renault, knowing I am driving dangerously, too fast around the tricky corners, revving up too close behind slower cars, flashing my lights manically until they pull over to let me pass. When I drive past the signs to the crematorium, I slow down. How will you be able to save Mel if you're dead from crazy driving? Mel needs me; I have to stay safe for her sake. The thought crosses my mind that this is exactly what the author of those notes would want – me crashing on the 28 November. Nevertheless, a journey that would normally take forty-five minutes takes just under half an hour.

I screech around the corner, into the hospital entrance, grab a ticket from the automated machine, and speed into the car park. I get lucky. A car is pulling out of a space, so I hover. 'Go faster, go faster!' I bang my fists on the steering wheel. As soon as it has reversed out, I am driving into the space. It's only then that I notice an elderly couple pulled up ahead, indicating to reverse into the space that I have just bagged. 'I'm sorry!' I mouth at them, throwing my hands up in the air as if that is any consolation, and then I run, ignoring the stares of people coming in and out of the hospital.

'Dr Ben Logan, please, can you tell me where his clinic is?' I pant.

'Second floor, room 2.47,' the receptionist says. 'What's your name, please?'

'I'll register upstairs,' I say. 'I'm really late.' And then I run again. I can feel the receptionist's eyes on my back and wonder if she will call security. But if I'm quick enough, I can dodge them, can't I?

I take the stairs two at a time, my ankle throbbing intensely now. Nearly there. There is another reception area, a smaller one, with a couple sitting reading the papers. I ignore them. A nurse glances up as I stride past. I need to find room 2.47. The consulting rooms are well signed, and then, there it is. Room 2.47, with his name on a sign on the door. *Dr Ben Logan.* Now I'm not sure what to do. Should I knock? Should I go in? But what if he has a patient inside? Or could he have left already? I should have asked the receptionist downstairs what time his clinic finishes.

I glance up and down the long corridor with its mottled blue vinyl floor and grey doors and harsh strip lighting, but no one is there. I tiptoe up to Ben's door and lean in towards it, putting my ear up close. Yes. I can hear voices inside. A man. Two men and now a female voice. Could it be Mel? I listen again. It's hard to tell. I pull back from the door and stand in the corridor. My ankle is pulsating with pain, so I shift my weight onto my other leg and lean against the wall.

Just four or five minutes later, the door opens. A man holds the door, his jacket over his arm, short almost-white hair shimmering in the artificial light.

'Thank you, Dr Logan,' he says. A woman walks past him and he grabs her hand. Her fawn parka is buttoned up wrongly, dangling further down on one side. She appears dazed, weaving slightly as if she is drunk. Perhaps evil Dr Logan has given her some inappropriate drugs. I watch as the man pulls her closer. Her left leg is dragging. Poor things. I hesitate. Should I go in? I stand right in front of the door, my hand raised as if to knock on it. And then the door opens and I practically fall in.

'Laura!' Ben exclaims. 'What are you doing here?' He is holding an empty teacup and saucer, which wobbles precariously.

'How dare you play the innocent with me?' I spit, my hands on my hips. Rage is coursing through me now. I am going to make this bastard pay.

Ben looks from left to right, as if he is nervous as to which of his colleagues might hear us, might see us. I follow his gaze, wanting someone to see us, but the doors remain stubbornly closed and the corridors disappointingly empty.

'You'd better come in,' he says. For a moment, I hesitate. There is an examination bed in there. Will I be safe? Dare I be alone with this man? But I don't have any choice. He stands back, propping the door open, and I barge past him. As soon as the door has closed with a gentle plop, he walks back to his desk, places the empty tea cup and saucer on it and sits down. He waves at me to take the chair recently vacated by his patient, but I need to stand and pace as I speak.

'Where's Mel?'

'I've no idea,' Ben says wearily.

'Don't lie to me.' I place both hands on his desk and lean forwards, staring at him menacingly.

'Laura, I really don't know what you're talking about. I have been in clinic since 9.45 a.m. this morning. Has something happened to your daughter?'

'She's gone missing.'

'What's that got to do with me?'

'I don't know! You tell me!' I cry. 'Where is she?'

'I have no idea where she is.'

'Don't lie to me!' I yell.

'Tell me what's happened,' he says.

'No, because you'll twist it, like you twist everything, you perverted bastard!'

'Okay! That's enough!' Ben stands up and kicks back his chair. My heart hammers as if it is going to burst out of my chest. Do this for Mel, I think to myself. Be strong. It is as if the moment is in slow motion, him walking around his desk, stepping closer and closer. I lift my hand as if to strike him, but I have nothing to strike him with, and then he grabs my wrist and holds my arms away from both of us, snaking his other arm around my waist.

'Laura,' he whispers, 'something has happened to make you

suspicious of me. I don't know what, but you'd better tell me. Sit down.' He releases both my wrists and I sink down onto the chair. And then immediately I think, that was so lame, woman, you need to be stronger for Mel.

I lean forwards, staring at those beautiful amber eyes that I now know are brimming with evil.

'What did you give me? Which date-rape drug was it you gave me before attacking me in my own home?' I spit.

He sighs. 'I took you home because you weren't feeling well. When we were en route, I got paged by the hospital to go in immediately because one of my patients had suffered a subarachnoid haemorrhage. Connor Schofield, the neurosurgeon who was about to operate on the woman, needed to consult with me before surgery. It was a matter of life or death, so I had to go. I supported you upstairs. You lay down on your bed fully clothed and I put a blanket over you. I found a bowl and a couple of towels, as I assumed you would be sick. You told me to go. You said you thought you had food poisoning and would be fine. I would never have left you if I hadn't had an emergency.'

'Prove to me what time you came to the hospital.'

'Fine. Come with me.' He stands up, knocking some files off his desk, which he glances at and leaves on the floor. He walks to the door and holds it open for me. I follow him to the small reception area, where a nurse is seated. He walks behind her and swipes a card over a door.

'Follow me,' he says. The nurse looks up, surprised.

We walk into a small office with two desks facing each other. A young woman with titian hair swept back into a plaited ponytail is typing and simultaneously talking on the telephone through headphones. She glances up at Ben and mouths hello. Her eyebrows rise ever so slightly when she sees me. She finishes the call quickly.

'Hiya.'

'Lisa, can you confirm where I was a week ago Friday.'

'Sure.' I notice the Australian accent now. She must have been in the UK a long time.

'Okay. You were here first thing, then had two cancellations, so you took the rest of the day off. Oh yes! You were called back here mid-afternoon for an emergency consultation with Connor, who needed to operate on Mrs Woods. Subarachnoid haemorrhage. Let me see.' She scrolls through some screens on her computer.

'Yup. She's pulled through nicely. You waited until Connor had operated and then visited her in ICU. Do you want me to print off her notes?'

'No, thanks, Lisa. That won't be necessary.'

So it proves that Ben was here at the hospital, but he could still have done his perverted business before he left me. He could still have Mel holed away somewhere here at the hospital or at his home. This proves nothing.

'I've finished my list, so I'll be off home shortly, Lisa. Have a good weekend, and see you Monday.'

'You too, Ben.'

'Laura, please come with me.'

As I'm limping a few steps behind Ben, it suddenly crosses my mind. 'Has Anna got anything to do with this?'

'Anna Moretti?' Ben says, frowning. 'Is she a good friend of yours?'

'Yes, and she's your patient. She told me what a terrible reputation you have.'

'We need to go somewhere to talk,' he says wearily.

'I'm not going anywhere with you.' But nevertheless I follow him back into the consulting room.

His sigh is loud and heavy. He slumps down into his chair. It's as if all the energy has been extracted out of him.

'Anna was my patient.'

'Yes, I know,' I say irritably. 'She quit being your patient this month and has moved to a colleague.'

'No!' he says, his voice rising at the end. 'Anna hasn't been my patient for about four years. She became fixated with me. Oh God!' He runs his fingers through his hair and squeezes his eyes shut. After a long moment, he looks up. 'Anna. Your friend. She's not a well woman.'

'I know. She has epilepsy.'

'It's not that.' He pauses again. 'I won't deny it, there was a frisson of attraction. Anna's a beautiful woman, but I have never, ever had a relationship with a patient. It was about two years after Sadie had died. Anna invited me to a charity dinner, or at least I thought it was going to be a charity dinner. It turned out to be a dinner for four: her, me, a friend of hers and this woman's boyfriend. It was awkward in the extreme. Anna was flirting with me, placing her hand on my thigh, as if we were an item. After dinner, she tried to kiss me. I stopped her. She slapped me, accused me of leading her on. The harassment was quite severe for several months afterwards. I had to threaten her with a restraining order, and then, suddenly, the harassment stopped. I never heard from her again, that was, until the charity art exhibition where I met you. I had been worried she might be there, but as the funds were being raised for my department, I couldn't get out of it. I'm glad I went though, because I met you.'

I open my mouth to speak but can't articulate words. This doesn't make any sense. Would Anna harass a man? Wouldn't Jim have found out? And why would she tell me Ben was her doctor when he wasn't?

'Why would I want to hurt you, Laura?' Ben places his palms upright on the desk. His eyes are creased. 'I'm falling in love with you. You're the person I want to impress not scare away.'

'Did you hack into my email account and send a porno-graphic photo of me to everyone at Slate Wilders?'

'What? If this wasn't so sick, I'd laugh. I can't even send emails on my own phone let alone hack into anyone's account. I'm barely computer literate.'

'But what about the clinical trial you're running? The one that requires you to be computer savvy and set up databases and pull together information on middle-aged women and the effects some epilepsy drug has on them?'

Ben's brows are knotted together. 'I'm not running any trial,' he says. 'Who told you this?'

'Anna,' I whisper. I am wondering now. Why has Anna told me lies? Or are they lies? Is it Ben who is twisting things? How can I know for sure? Anna has been in my life for four years; she has become a good friend, a great friend, and before that she was Becky's friend. But Ben, I've only known him for a few weeks.

'Does Anna know that you've been seeing me?' Ben asks.

'Yes.' I nod.

'Please don't think this is conceited of me, but I think she might be jealous. I wonder whether she's doing things to scare you off me?'

'Oh, come on!' I snort. 'She wouldn't do that. She wants me to be happy.'

Ben raises one eyebrow.

'But the issue isn't me! I need to find Mel! She's gone miss-ing.' I stand up and wring my hands. I tell Ben about the note, how her phone is off, and how we had agreed to meet her for lunch but wanted to defer it to supper.

'Does Mel know Anna?'

'Yes, of course.'

'Would she go somewhere willingly with her?'

I nod. And Mel would not go anywhere willingly with the man sitting in this room with me because she saw how terrified

I was of him, what a fuss I made, only two days ago. If Ben had taken her anywhere, he would have had to have abducted her. That is a possibility; he has access to drugs.

'How long have you been in the hospital today?' I ask.

'Since 8.45 a.m.' He glances at his watch. 'I was here until 2 a.m. this morning. I then went home to sleep and returned to the hospital in time for my clinic at 9 a.m.'

'You could have gone to my home before 9 a.m. You could have got in and done something to Mel at any time because I was out.'

'Laura, I know a lot of horrible things have happened to you, but your imagination is working overtime.'

'Don't accuse me of lying!' I screech.

He looks at me with an expression of pity that infuriates me even further. I would like to scream until my voice is hoarse.

'You can check I'm telling the truth.' He sighs. 'There is a security system here and it logs us in and out. You can also see my roster of patients. I had a fifteen-minute break for lunch at 2 p.m. Lisa brought me a sandwich and I ate it here, at my desk. She'll confirm it with you if you want to check.'

I turn away from him so he can't see the confusion on my face. What he is saying is so plausible, but I still am unsure if I believe him.

'Could there be a more benign reason for Mel not to be answering your calls?'

'That's what the police suggested,' I say, swivelling around to look at him and flinching as I put weight on my sore ankle.

'It's good that you have involved the police,' he says calmly. 'Have you told them about Anna?'

'Of course not! I've told them about you, though.'

Ben flinches. 'I'd like to prove to you that I've been here all day long, that I couldn't possibly have had anything to do with Mel's disappearance. I can also prove to you that I left your flat immediately after dropping you off there.'

'How?' I ask.

'I'll ring security to show you the records.'

'I mean, how can you prove you left my flat immediately?' I want to shake my head to ease out the confusion.

'Your neighbour. A woman, I'm guessing mid-seventies, thinning grey hair, wearing a tartan mac. I couldn't forget the mac in a hurry. She saw you and me at your front door. She wanted to know what was going on, and I explained that you weren't well. I think she was a bit suspicious, so she walked with me back down the stairs and saw me outside. She said that she worried about you, living on your own and all of that.'

I harrumph. 'Mrs Steel. She also lives alone.'

'She seems a nice lady,' Ben says. 'Do you know her phone number? Perhaps you could call her and see if she remembers that afternoon?'

I extract my mobile phone from my bag and scroll through until I find Mrs Steel's number.

'Hello,' she says very slowly and very loudly.

'Hello, Mrs Steel. It's Laura Swallow from upstairs. How are you?'

'I'm fine, dear. And how are you? I've been worried about you these past two weeks.'

'I'm all right, thanks,' I lie. 'I've got a question. Do you remember a week ago last Friday. It was the afternoon and I came home early with a gentleman friend.' I wince as I say that but am unsure how else to articulate the situation with the proper Mrs Steel.

'Oh yes, dear. You were poorly and he helped you back home. Not long after he left, that pretty friend of yours with the long dark hair, the one who looks like that actress off that American soap, the name quite slips my mind. Anyway, that friend of yours, she came by. I told her that you were poorly and that your gentleman friend had left. She promised she'd look after you. I made quite sure that the gentleman did leave, as I hadn't seen him before and didn't want a strange man loitering around, especially as you looked so sick.'

'You saw me then?'

'Yes, dear. You said hello to me. Don't you remember?'

'No,' I say. 'I wasn't very well.'

'I asked that gentleman friend if I should call a doctor for you, and he said that he was a doctor. Still, you can't trust anyone these days, can you?'

'No,' I agree.

'And as I said, then just a few minutes later your pretty friend arrived. I had to go out for the rest of the afternoon. Betty and I went to the cinema. We saw—'

'Thank you, Mrs Steel,' I interrupt her. 'You've been very helpful.' I hesitate for a moment. 'You haven't seen Mel today, have you?'

'No, love. I'm sorry. I was at the hairdresser's this morning and it's been quiet in the block ever since I got back. How is that lovely daughter of yours?'

'She's fine, thank you.'

'I'll pop around and see you soon,' I say, finishing the call with more haste than is polite.

'Shit,' I whisper, sinking back into the chair.

Ben looks at me quizzically.

'You are right,' I say. 'You left. And Anna was there.' I shake my head. 'But perhaps Mrs Steel got confused. Anna came around later in the evening.'

Ben exhales. 'I don't think Mrs Steel got confused. I think Anna has been playing games. She's very good at playing games.'

I let out a screech of frustration. Surely Anna didn't have anything to do with this? It must be this clever man who is able to twist everything; who, with his silver-quick tongue and brilliant brain, can come up with an excuse or a rebuttal to every theory I put to him.

I glance at him as he is looking away, his face contorted. But is that expression of anguish put on for me, or is it real?

'I think we need to go,' he says suddenly. 'For the first time in my life, I'm going to break my oath of patient confidentiality and I want to call the police.'

'Why? What?' I feel even more panicked now that Ben seems so concerned. I am still not sure if I believe him.

'We need to go to Anna's house. Immediately. I'll tell you about her on the way.' He grabs his briefcase from under his desk and pulls a jacket off the back of the door.

'My car is in the parking lot,' I say.

'Leave it there. Come in mine. We can go faster.'

'I'm not coming with you.' I step backwards.

'Laura, you need to trust me. I care about you deeply. Anna is a sick woman, and I don't want to scare you, but I think she is capable of doing some real harm.'

'What do you mean?'

He sighs. 'She was sectioned five years ago and has some major mental health issues. Please come with me. I can put the emergency siren on the roof of the car so we can speed.'

Still, I hesitate. I haven't noticed anything strange about Anna, and I know her well. Don't I? She has been my constant friend, my confidante. What does it say about me if I have totally misjudged her? She is needy and clingy on occasion, and sometimes that frustrates me, but I just put it down to insecurity, the result of a difficult childhood. And just because she had some mental health issues a few years ago doesn't make her a psychopath.

'Please, let's go!' Ben holds out his hand, but I don't take it. I follow him out of the room and trot after him as he speeds down the corridor. Stumbling slightly as my sore ankle gives way on the stairs, he reaches out for me, and eventually I accept his arm, wondering if I am cavorting with the devil.

## 34

We pass the car parking attendant in his little metal hut.

'Geoff, this lady has a medical emergency and is coming with me. Can you put a free twenty-four hours on her parking ticket?'

'Sure, Doc.' He produces a clipboard and asks me to fill in my car's registration number, make and model.

And then I am sitting in Ben's car, wondering whether he is about to take me to my death, whether he already has Mel somewhere and he will be killing us both. I gasp at the thought. He reaches over and squeezes my hand. I tug it away.

'We'll find her,' he says, as if he is reading my mind.

He starts the siren as soon as we have turned out of the hospital car park.

'I didn't know doctors had sirens.'

'It's a green light and they're only used in emergencies. It's been years since I've used mine; in fact, I'm surprised it still works.'

'Do you have to stick to the speed limit?'

'Yes. I'm not police. Having said that, they'd probably turn a blind eye. But I have no intention of speeding. After what I went through with Sadie and you've been through with your sister...' He lets the words peter out.

'Where are we going?' I ask.

'Your flat first to check Mel's not there and then to Anna's house. I assume you know where she lives?'

'Don't you?'

He grimaces. 'Why would I? I've never been to her home.'

I nod. I try Mel's phone again for the hundredth time and it goes to voicemail.

We don't talk as Ben drives. Occasionally I glance at him and note the taut knuckles clenching the steering wheel, the biting of his cheek, the flicker of a nerve at the side of his eye. I try to keep down my terror, breathing in and out slowly, trying to stop horrific images from tainting my mind. He drives well, weaving in and out of the traffic as cars pull to one side to let us pass, keeping strictly to seventy miles per hour on the dual carriageway, and quickly we are back in Horsham, just a street away from home.

'I'm going to park on the double yellow, put my doctor's badge in the windscreen.'

'I'll go up alone.'

'I don't think that's a good idea. What if Anna is there, waiting for you?'

'If I'm not out in five minutes, call the police.'

We're outside my apartment building now.

'I'm not happy about that,' he says.

'I'm not happy with this whole fucking situation!' I shriek.

Ben flinches. 'I'm coming with you.'

I don't have the energy to fight. I skedaddle out of his car, fling open the front door and run up the stairs, my ankle screaming at me with every step I take. Ben's footsteps are heavy behind me. At the door to my apartment, I pause, putting my ear to the door, trying to hear if there is any noise coming from inside. My heart is thumping so loudly, it feels as if it will explode out of my body.

Be brave. You're doing this for Mel, I think. I turn the key in the lock and open the door quietly, stepping inside into the darkened corridor. I pause again. Silence. Ben puts his hand on my arm.

'Mel?' I say. There is no answer. I switch the light on in the corridor, picking up a long umbrella that I keep behind the door. I realise it won't do much damage, but it's all I've got. I step into the lounge, switching the light on. There is no one there. My little kitchen is equally empty. I switch the umbrella for my large, never-used rolling pin and tiptoe to Mel's bedroom. Gently, Ben takes the rolling pin from me. The flat is exactly how it was a couple of hours ago. Swallowing metallic-tasting blood, I swing open the door to my bedroom. I don't know whether to be relieved or disappointed. My flat is empty and there are no signs that anyone has been in it since I left for the hospital. That simply means I have no idea where my daughter is.

BACK IN THE CAR, I give Ben directions to Anna's house.

'I'm going in alone,' I say. 'If she sees you at the door, she'll know something is up, and that could make things one hundred times worse.'

I can sense Ben's conflict. He wants to come in with me, but he's agreeing with the logic in my statement.

'We need a sign,' he suggests. 'I'll call you on your mobile after two minutes. If you can, answer. Tell me you'll call me back later. If you say anything else, then I'm calling the police immediately and coming in.'

'What if Jim is there?' I say.

'Who's Jim?'

I look at Ben askance. 'Anna's husband.'

'But she's not married!' he exclaims.

'Don't be ridiculous. Of course she is!'

'Do you think I would have had dinner with a married woman?' Ben snarls.

'I've no idea,' I mutter.

'I wouldn't. She always came alone to her consultations, and her medical forms state that she is single. That's unusual in itself. Even people who are single tend to bring a friend or a relative. Most of my patients in relationships come to see me with their partners, at least for the initial diagnosis, if not for the follow-up consultations. Anna was always alone. It is standard practice for me to ask my patients who is around to support them. When I asked Anna, she looked at me coquettishly and said, "No one at the moment." I remember it distinctly because she was so beautiful. It seemed strange that this forty-something-year-old woman was all alone.'

'This is ridiculous!' I screech. 'Jim is her husband. He's extremely good looking, works in Dubai, comes home about once a month.'

'Have you met him?'

'Only briefly. Once when he was hurrying out somewhere, and the second time, I didn't exactly meet him.' I blush as I think of how I stalked Anna and Jim from the grounds of the hotel where Mel was working. And then I remember Anna's frosty reception of me. It was strange and out of character.

'Don't you think it's odd that someone who is such a good friend has only introduced you to her husband once in four years?'

'Are you saying that she's not really married?' I ask in a small voice.

'Maybe.'

'Then who is Jim?'

'I don't know.' Ben shrugs.

'Her house is down this street on the left-hand side.'

'I'll park several doors down.'

As I slip out of the car, Ben turns to me. His eyes look dark and his face tired and grey. 'I'll call you in two minutes.'

I nod.

'Take care, Laura.'

If my heart had been hammering when I entered my own apartment, now it feels as if it has taken over my whole body, pulsating with a life of its own. My mouth is dry and my knees are shaking. I inhale deeply, trying to still my quivering body. Anna's gate squeaks as I open it, so I leave it open and tiptoe down the garden path. I look up at the darkened windows, wondering if my girl is being restrained inside, wondering whether Anna has constructed an imaginary life that has caught me in her web. I put my hand up to the doorbell. It's an old-fashioned gold dome, and I don't want to ring it, but I must. Mel needs me. I take a deep breath and press it. It chimes. I wait. I hear nothing and see no movement. I press it again.

'Hello?'

I jump. I don't recognise the quiet, tentative voice.

A woman appears from the side of the house. She is tiny, barely five feet tall, wearing a beige apron that fully covers her clothes. Her legs are bare despite the cold, and she's wearing cheap white hotel slippers.

'How can I help?' Her accent is strong. I assume she is from the Philippines.

'I was wondering if Anna is at home?'

'No.' She doesn't look at me and I find her subservient manner disconcerting.

'Is Jim at home?'

'Jim?'

'Jim Moretti. Anna's husband?'

At that, the woman glances up warily. She looks at me now,

her small eyes fixed on my face, her petite features creased with confusion. She looks so young, barely older than Mel.

'No husband here.'

I falter. 'Is Jim Moretti in Dubai?'

'I don't know Jim Moretti,' she whispers, shifting from foot to foot. I want to put her out of her discomfort, but at the same time I need to be sure I understand.

'So Anna doesn't have a husband?'

'I'm sorry. I can no talk about my boss. She out now. Please come back next week.' She turns as if to go back inside.

'Please don't go!' I implore.

She looks at me and wraps her arms around herself as if she is protecting herself from me, the crazy woman.

'I just need to know where Anna is. It's a matter of life or death!'

'Sorry. She say she go away for weekend. I don't know where.'

'And to confirm. There is no Jim Moretti. No husband?'

The little shake of her head is the giveaway. Ben must be right. Anna is not married. My stomach feels as if it's curdling.

'Who are you?' she asks. 'I tell Anna you here.'

'I'm just a friend,' I say. 'I'll call her myself. Thank you for your help.'

She nods at me, her wan face impassive, and then turns away.

I call out after her. 'I don't suppose my daughter has been here, has she? She's called Mel and she's twenty. Brown hair tied back in a ponytail?'

The woman turns back towards me. 'No visitors. Mrs Anna has no visitors.' And then she hurries away, leaving me standing on Anna's doorstep with no idea what to do next.

My mobile phone rings. Ben.

'I'm on my way back.'

'I'm calling the police!'

'No, it's all fine. I'm really on my way back to the car!' Now I am on the road, hurrying towards Ben's car, waving my arms at him. His expression when he sees me is one of such relief, his smile so wide, my stomach tingles, and I know now that I was totally wrong to doubt him.

'What happened?'

'She has a Filipino maid – awful word, isn't it? – who said Anna's gone away for the weekend. And I think you're right. There is no husband. How could she have lied to me? How do I know what to believe and what not to believe?' I lean back into the passenger seat. Ben takes my hand and squeezes it. This time I don't pull it away.

'We don't know for sure that Anna has Mel. And we don't know for sure that she was behind everything that has happened to you.'

'But if it's not Anna, the only other person it could be is Eddy, and I'm ninety-nine percent sure it wasn't him.'

'Who is Eddy?' Ben asks.

I explain, reddening as I gloss over the details of my teenage antics and Eddy's inappropriate advances towards me.

'You could have a word with him, but it sounds very unlikely.'

I nod. 'But first I need to ring Ian and tell him we won't be having supper. I need to tell him about Mel too.'

'Why don't we go back to your flat and regroup. Show me the note and the obituary and everything else you've got. I'll have a look at the death certificate too.'

'Okay.'

## 35

I an goes apoplectic when I tell him I think Mel is missing, that she might have been abducted by Anna.

'I think Anna's trying to hurt me. It's something to do with Becky's death, and I'm not sure what it's all about.' I start crying, fat tears rolling down my cheeks as I feel a desperation for the loss of my sister, and the terror envelops me as I consider the horrors that might be befalling my daughter.

'I'm coming over and I'm calling the police,' Ian says.

'I've already notified the police.'

'What did they say?'

'That we have to wait.'

'Bollocks to that,' Ian cusses. 'Leave it with me.' He hangs up.

~

MY APARTMENT FEELS hollow and cold. I need Mel to be there, to fill it up with noise and clutter and youth.

Ben sits down on my sofa and I recall the last time he sat there, when he kissed me and caressed me, and how that seems like a lifetime ago. I hand him the death notice from the paper, a printout of the Facebook post, the death certificate. I can't bring myself to show him the pornographic email.

'Today should be about Becky.' I choke up.

'Show me a photo of her,' Ben says.

I reach down and take out my photo album, flipping it open to near the back, where I have slipped in the latest photos I have of Becky, from Christmas lunch, the year before she died.

Ben stares at her photo; his face pales. 'I know her,' he whispers, 'but where from?'

'She was a nurse. The hospital perhaps? Although she worked at St Richard's, so I don't see how you would have come across her.'

'No. It was social. I'm sure.' He wipes his hand across his brow and then jumps up, letting the album slide onto the sofa.

'She was the double date. She's *that* Becky! I'm so stupid – not putting the two together! She was there that dreadful evening I had dinner with Anna.'

'You mean she was part of the other couple? Oh my God, you met Becky!'

'Yes! And her boyfriend. It's all coming back to me now. He was a genial chap, called Joe something. He's a carpenter based over in Midhurst. He showed me some photos of his work, and I was really impressed. I got him to make me a bookcase. It's in my study at home. Oh goodness! She was your Becky?'

'I'm so happy you met her.' I grin.

'She was lovely. They both were. But they seemed unlikely friends of Anna's, and to be honest, the evening was so dreadful for me, all I recall is Anna fawning all over me, describing me as her boyfriend, her lover. It was excruciating.'

'At least the bit about Anna being Becky's friend is true,' I say.

'Yes.'

I sit down and lean my elbows on the table, placing my head in my hands. Now is the time to tell Ben about my doubts.

'I tried to reopen the inquest into Becky's death. I also tried to find Joe, but with such a common surname as Smith, I failed. I asked Anna if she knew how to track him down, but she said no. She implied that it was a one-way relationship. He was much keener on Becky than she was on him.'

'From what I recall of the evening, it didn't seem that way. But of course things could have changed later on. Why do you want to reopen the inquest?'

I tell Ben about my doubts, my concerns, my hunch. 'I was hoping that Joe might be able to tell me a bit more about Becky's state of mind just before she died. That he might be able to explain why she had pulled over into that lay-by on the A272.'

'I think we should contact him. But first we need to focus on finding Mel. And Anna.'

I let out a little involuntary cry. Ben is right. We need to focus on the here and now.

'Let's be rational about this. We don't know for sure that Mel is missing. We don't know for sure that Anna has Mel. We need to establish those two facts first.'

'And work out if Anna has been behind all the horrors that have happened to me.'

Ben nods, his face grave.

'Try calling Anna,' Ben suggests.

He's right. In our hurry to accuse her, I haven't even tried to speak to her. I pull up her number on my mobile phone and press call. My hands are shaking and my mind is blank. What should I say to her?

I don't need to worry. Her mobile goes straight to voicemail. I hit the end call button.

'No answer. But she can't have gone very far unless she's

taken public transport or a taxi, and then there'll be witnesses. How would you abduct someone without being able to drive?'

'What do you mean?' Ben looks perplexed.

'She hasn't got a car; she hasn't got a driving licence.'

'Why not?' He frowns.

'Because of her epilepsy.'

'But her condition is under control. She takes medication, and as far as I'm aware, she hasn't had a seizure in years. If she had to stop driving, she would have got her licence back by now. You can reapply for your driving licence twelve months after having a seizure. I might be wrong, but I think I wrote a letter to DVLA on her behalf confirming she was fit to drive.'

'She's lied about that too.' I feel as if all the air has been extracted from my body. 'All those times when I had to drive her or when she paid for taxis. It just doesn't make sense.'

'Perhaps she doesn't like driving?' Ben suggests.

'She told me that her epilepsy came about as a result of a car accident. Is that true?'

'Yes, I seem to recall that is the case.'

'She could be anywhere.' I let out a tormented cry.

'May I hug you?' Ben asks, standing up and walking towards me. I fall into his arms and burst into tears.

'The more I think about this, the more I think Anna is behind everything.' I sniff, trying not to get my tears on Ben's shirt. 'She could have easily defaced Becky's grave when she laid her wreath there either last night or early this morning. But why? Why does she want to hurt me so much?'

Ben kisses the top of my head. 'I don't know, but let's contact everyone connected to her. Why don't you try to get hold of Eddy? At best it will eliminate him, and possibly he might be able to shed some light on Anna's skills. I'll call Joe.'

My phone rings before I can call Eddy. It's Ian.

'Any news?'

'I was calling to ask you the same question. I've heard nothing.'

'Me too. We went to Anna's house, but she's not there. I've worked out she has told me a pack of lies.'

'I never liked her,' Ian says unhelpfully. I swallow a groan. He's so good after the event.

'I think she's got Mel.'

'The police are on their way over to your place. I'm coming too.'

'But we need to go out and look for Mel.'

'Who is we?'

'Ben. Ben Logan is here with me.'

'What! That creep? You told me he was a rapist and a total dickhead!' Ian yells.

'I was wrong,' I say quietly.

'For God's sake, be careful,' Ian says. 'I'm on my way.'

'Hold on! I'll leave a key for you with Mrs Steel in case we're not here. Is Charlene okay and Rory?'

'Yes. Why shouldn't they be? I need to go.'

He hangs up on me. Ian is good in a crisis. He'll know how to handle the police, unlike me, who turns into a quivering idiot in the face of an official uniform.

Ben looks at me askance.

'Ian, my ex-husband,' I say. 'He's on his way here to meet the police. I can't believe this is happening. I'm so scared.'

Ben hugs me again, but even his firm grasp and warm breath on my neck doesn't still my quivering limbs. He lets go.

'Come on. We need to make those phone calls. Why don't you call Eddy from the bedroom, and I'll call Joe from here?'

My bedroom, with its pale hues and luxurious bed, which cost me a small fortune, and the chaise longue that curves beautifully, on which I shamefully chuck my clothes, and the pictures of seascapes; it was my haven, my safe place. But now I stand at the doorway and survey it. I sniff the air to assess if it smells different. Anna wears an expensive floral scent, but I get no whiff of it in here. Even so, the room is spoiled, tarnished. I force myself to sit on the edge of the bed and pull up Eddy's number. He is the last person I want to talk to. I wonder if he'll answer.

But he does.

'Hello, Laura. What can I do for you?'

'I'm sorry to disturb you, but I was wondering whether you know a woman called Anna Moretti? I understand that your sales director – I've forgotten his name – had a meeting with her. The thing is, I think she's abducted Mel, my daughter.'

'Wow,' he says. I can hear screaming children in the background. 'Why would she do something like that?'

'It's a long story and I don't understand it yet.'

'The thing is, Laura, I'm wondering if the problem is you. You accused me of writing some letter—'

'I know and I'm sorry. I was wrong.' I take a deep breath. 'Someone sent an email with a pornographic attachment that went to everyone at Slate Wilders. Supposedly the sender was me and the recipient was you.'

'What the hell!' Eddy yells.

'I'm so sorry that I got you caught up in the mess around me.'

'I wish I'd never met you again,' Eddy mutters. I am silent. I don't blame him.

'Forgive me for asking, but I assume you had nothing to do with this?'

'Of course I didn't! Why the hell would I? You're nothing to me. Just an estate agent who was a bitch when she was younger. Maybe you still are.'

'I'm sorry.' I can feel a deep flush scouring down my face, enveloping my neck and chest. I deserve that. 'Anna is behind everything that has happened to me, and I'm dreadfully sorry that you got caught up in this mess.'

I wonder whether to mention the obituary I wrote about his father but decide to let that one go. I am positive that is just a red herring.

'This Anna woman. Is she the one with dark, wavy hair, smartly dressed, talks the talk?'

'Yes, I assume so.'

'She did have a meeting with our sales director. He was impressed with her understanding of computer systems and was hopeful we might get some work from her. From what you're saying, I suppose that meeting was a waste of his time.'

'Yes, I fear so.'

Loud thumping music starts up in the background, and the yells from young voices get louder.

'If you'll excuse me, I need to sort out the children.'

'Yes,' I say. 'I'm sorry to have disturbed you. Again.'

But he's already hung up. I want to scream. That conversation got me precisely nowhere. The only confirmation I have is that Anna is accomplished with IT, not that she ever shared that skill with me. Retrieving a Facebook password is probably within the grasp of most people, except a computer luddite such as me. I wonder if anything Anna ever told me was true. I stumble back into the living room, where Ben is still talking. He holds up his thumb in a gesture that I assume is positive. At least he is having some success. I lean against the table, waiting for him to finish.

'Joe Smith suggested we meet him. He'd be delighted to talk to you about Becky and couldn't stop apologising for not getting in touch with you after her death. It sounds like they really were in love. Says he hasn't dated anyone since. Most interestingly, he claims that Anna repeatedly tried to break up his relationship with Becky.'

'But why?' I say. 'Nothing makes sense. Does he have any idea as to where Anna might have taken Mel? In the note, it says that she's gone to meet Becky. Could that be the graveyard?'

'I don't think so. Did you know that Anna has a house in Petworth? She runs it as a holiday cottage apparently. Joe says Becky took him there once. When Anna found out that Becky had used it to "entertain" Joe, she became enraged.'

'No, I didn't know. She claimed to dislike Petworth; said Becky was disdainful of it too. Full of wealthy London week-enders buying overpriced antiques and jerks in Mercs who can't drive. Do you think she might have taken Mel there?'

'Possibly. Joe said he will meet us in Petworth. I don't want to scare you, but where exactly did Becky die?'

My hand flies to my mouth. 'On the way. On the A272. Do you think she meant that Mel has gone to meet Becky in the same place where Becky died, or was it metaphorical and she means that Mel is going to heaven? My little girl. I need to protect her!' My thoughts are becoming increasingly incoher-ent, and my words tumble out of my mouth as if I am spitting out metal bullets. 'Did Anna kill Becky? Oh my God! We need to go!'

Ben and I race out of the apartment and down the stairs. When we are in the communal hallway, I remember I promised Ian that I would leave my key with Mrs Steel. I race back up again and ring her doorbell, relieved to hear a Beethoven symphony playing loudly from her record player.

'Laura love, is everything all right?' Her hair is tightly permed and she's holding a gingham dishcloth.

'Yes, no. I'll explain later. We think something might have happened to Mel. Can I leave my key with you for Ian, my ex-husband, to collect? And if Mel turns up, please will you call me?' I rifle through my bag to find a business card so she has my mobile number to hand.

'Oh, golly gosh! I do hope you find her soon.'

'The police are on their way, so please let them in.'

Her eyes widen. Probably the most excitement she's had in the past decade, I think as I sprint back down the stairs, welcoming the pain in my ankle. Ben's car is idling outside our block, the flashing green emergency light rotating in sync with the throbbing in my head and my ankle.

'Try Mel's phone again and Anna's,' Ben says as he weaves out of Horsham. We're in the rush hour traffic now, and despite the emergency light, we are moving slowly, too slowly. My foot is jangling up and down, and blood is oozing from the edges of several fingernails where I have torn the skin with my teeth. Yet again, Mel's phone goes straight to voicemail, but I am shocked when Anna's phone rings. My breath is coming out in short pants as I anticipate her answering and wonder what I am going to say. After five rings it also goes to voicemail. I hang up.

We are driving fast now, along the Billingshurst bypass road and turning onto the A272. The road becomes narrower, and with every bend we take, I feel the terror mounting, my breath quickening, bile rising up my throat.

'It's difficult to see where the lay-by is in the dark,' I say. Ben slows right down. There is a queue of cars behind us, and the lights that reflect in the car's mirrors add to my panic.

'It's here!' I say. 'The next bend.' But as Ben indicates to turn off the road, no lay-by appears. The car behind hoots at us.

'Piss off!' I screech.

'We'll crawl along until we see it. Don't worry,' he reassures me. His deep voice exudes calm, but the nerve at the side of his eye and the way he hunches over the steering wheel suggest he is feeling the tension too.

'What if she's there? What will we do?'

'We'll cross that bridge if we have to.'

'There!' I yell.

He indicates to the left and pulls over onto the lay-by.

There is no other vehicle parked there, no person in sight. He turns off the engine and we're plunged into black. As the cars behind us ease away, the inky darkness settles, and it's impossible to make out anything until the next car passes, throwing shadows across the road from the bare branches of the oak trees and spikes from the hawthorn hedge.

'Stay here. I'm getting out to check if anyone is around.'

'No!' I yelp as I reach across to restrain him. 'Don't open your door on the road side.' I am almost hyperventilating. 'I'll get out and you can climb over.'

I open the passenger door and jump out, wondering in that instant whether Anna is crouching down in the shadows and will spring up and hit me over the head. I tell myself not to be so stupid, to stop catastrophising, but it's hard to remain rational. Ben does as I instructed, sliding over the central controls and onto the passenger seat. He squeezes my shoulder as he stands in the cold and the dark next to me.

'Get back in the car and keep the doors locked.' He hands me the car key.

'Don't go far,' I whisper as I get back in the car.

'I won't.' He squeezes my shoulder.

I watch him take his mobile phone out of his pocket. It lights his face up in a ghostly blue, and then he switches on the torch and shines the light slowly around him.

'Oh God!'

I see the flash of orange at the same time as Ben does.

He walks towards it, his body blocking my view. But I know what it is. Ben crouches down and picks something up and then strides back to the car. He stops, looks left and then right, and before I can yell at him to get back in the passenger side, he dances around the car, pulls open the driver's door and slips back inside.

'There was nothing coming.' His smile is gentle. 'I could see and I could hear. No lights. Silence. No traffic.'

'Okay,' I say, my voice small. 'What's that?'

He is holding an envelope.

'It was attached to a circular wreath of orange and white flowers.'

'Anna leaves those flowers every year. I don't know why. Becky hated orange flowers.'

'This was attached to the wreath.'

He hands me a small envelope. My fingers are shaking too much, so he gently removes it from my grasp and extracts a note. 'Do you want me to read it?'

I nod. Ben switches the light on in the car.

He hesitates. 'It's typed. It just says, "For bitch one, shortly to be joined by bitch three. Rot well."'

I feel as if I am going to choke, as if an iron fist is grabbing me around the throat. Now I know for sure. Anna has Mel and she is going to kill her.

'She wrote bitch on Becky's gravestone,' I whisper. 'Should we call the police?'

'Ian is dealing with the police, isn't he?' Ben says, firing up the car engine. 'We still don't have proof that this is Anna's work, or that she has Mel. Forgive me, but I wonder whether the police will just think you are a bit deranged. Let's go and find Joe and see if we can track down Anna's cottage. Petworth is a small place; I doubt it will be that hard to find.'

Ben pulls out of the lay-by slowly and then puts his foot on the accelerator as we speed towards Petworth. He leaves the doctor's light off. As he pulls up Joe's name on his car's touch-screen, I want to tell him to keep his hands on the steering wheel. But Ben lost his wife in a car accident, so surely he will be as wary as me.

'Hello.' The man's voice is curt as it comes out of the car's speakers.

'Hi, Joe, it's Ben Logan. How soon can you get to Petworth?'

'I'm already here,' he says. I pant out with relief. 'Meet me at the Stuffed Boar. Do you know it?'

'Yes,' Ben says. 'See you in five.'

## 36

The road into Petworth is mercifully empty of traffic, so different to the last time I visited in July. Ben pulls into the market square and parks on a double yellow line.

'I've used my position illegally more today than I have in the whole of my career,' he says as he leaps out of the car. I follow suit. It is bitterly cold and just beginning to rain.

'Laura, Ben?' I don't recognise Joe. I had expected him to have a roughness around the edges, to be casually attired, perhaps with flecks of sawdust in his hair, but he is nothing like that. Slender, in a shirt and tie and sporting an abundant beard, there is an empty beer glass on the table in front of him. Neither Ben nor I take off our coats as we slip onto stools opposite Joe.

'We are convinced that Anna has Mel. Could you take us to her house here in Petworth?' Ben says.

'Have you been in touch with the police?' Joe asks.

'Yes, but they weren't very interested. My husband—' I quickly correct myself. It's been a long time since I called him that. 'Ian, my ex, is liaising with them.'

'Anna is a psycho,' Joe says.

Ben opens his mouth as if to say something, but lets it go.

'What did she do?'

'Everything in her power to stop Becky and me being happy together.' He sighs. 'To begin with she seemed fine, but as Becky and I started spending more time together, Anna became increasingly needy. She would ring Becky up all times of the day and night, asking her advice, wanting them to meet up. She would ring and speak for hours, all about herself and never asked after Becky. Then she started threatening Becky. It was emotional blackmail, really. She said she'd come off her medication and it would be Becky's fault if she died from a fit; that she had no one in her life who understood her, and she needed Becky; otherwise she'd slit her wrists. Becky was so torn. It was as if Anna saw Becky as her plaything. I took Becky away for a long weekend in London the week before she died. Anna was apoplectic with rage, telling her that she had bought expensive theatre tickets and how could Becky have forgotten. I asked Becky to marry me when we were on the London Eye.' He smiles at the memory, but the sadness is evident in his eyes. 'I thought our capsule was going to come off the Ferris wheel; Becky couldn't stop jumping up and down with joy.'

'But I didn't know anything about you!' I exclaim. 'Why did Becky keep you secret from me?'

Joe looks away as he gulps down his grief. I wipe tears from my eyes, and Ben reaches out for my hand.

'You had suffered so much through your divorce. She told me all about you, about your heartbreak, and she didn't want to flaunt her happiness when you were feeling such sadness. I told her that was nonsense, that you would be happy for her, for us, but she wouldn't listen. I'll tell Laura when the time is right, she said. And then, when we got engaged, she was so excited about telling you. It was all she could talk about, wanting you to be her chief bridesmaid.' His voice fades into a whisper.

'Oh God.' I push my knuckles into my mouth.

'And then she died.' Joe puts his glass to his lips, but it is already empty. His hand is shaking as he sets it down again.

'Did you ever suspect Anna?' Ben asks.

Joe shakes his head. 'I knew she had a screw loose, but it never crossed my mind that she had something to do with Becky's death. After she died, I assumed Becky was on her way to see me that evening. I wasn't expecting her, but sometimes she came over to see me without telling me. I told the police that. We were so excited. We were planning on moving in together.'

There is a long pause and we look at each other.

Joe speaks first. 'Do you think Anna killed Becky?'

'Possibly,' Ben answers for me.

'I tried to get the inquest reopened,' I say. 'The more time went by, the more suspicious her death appeared to me. Everyone else thinks I'm mad.'

'Did you tell Anna you wanted to reopen the inquest?' Ben sits up straighter and frowns.

'Yes. Yes, I did.'

'We need to go.' Ben stands up suddenly and the table wobbles. 'It's too late for Becky, but it mightn't be too late for Mel. Come on! Do you remember where Anna's cottage is, Joe?'

'I think so. It'll be harder to find it in the dark, but I'm pretty sure.'

We race to Ben's car. Joe gets in the front passenger seat; I throw myself into the back. The wheels screech as we pull out of the market square, driving much too quickly along the narrow streets, and just seconds later we're out of Petworth and hurtling into the dark countryside.

'Left here,' Joe says, 'and then left again and I think it's somewhere on the right.' We're deep into the countryside now, all bare hedgerows and spiny tree branches and narrow potholed roads, deep unexpected holes that Ben tries his best to avoid, but they throw the car, bumping us up and down. Occasionally we pass a house, a light or two illuminating the windows, or a sign to a farmhouse set back deep in fields, invisible from the road. I know we are not far from town, but it feels as if we are in the deep countryside far from humankind. A barn owl flies low over the car; its white heart-shaped face and dark eyes frighten me. I can't decide whether it's a good omen or a presage of something bad. Mel loves owls. She has a long necklace in the shape of an owl made from artificial filigree gold and a peacock feather. It hangs around her neck most days. Come on, I scream inside my head. Hurry up!

'It's here, I think.' Joe peers into the darkness. 'Yes, definitely here. I remember the picket fence and the well in the garden. It's called Orb-weaver's Cottage. She lists it on TripAdvisor. Got quite a few five-star reviews. I find it hard to understand why anyone would choose to stay in a holiday home named after a spider. There's a large ornamental spider on the wall near the front door and—'

I'm not interested in anything except the task in hand, so I cut Joe's musings short. 'I'm going in by myself.'

'No!' Ben exclaims.

'If she sees you here, we won't stand a chance. Ben, you rejected her. She's jealous of me because she knows I'm in a relationship with you.'

Ben's lip curves upwards momentarily. I wonder if I've overstated things by describing myself in a relationship with him, but now isn't the time to ponder semantics.

'Laura's right,' Joe interjects. 'Anna is obviously so irrational, seeing you might totally push her over the edge.'

'That means that neither of us can go in with Laura.' Ben looks grim.

'So be it,' I say. 'She might listen to me and I know her the best.' I feel surprisingly calm now that Mel's safety lies solely upon my shoulders. That is what a mother is for, to protect and nourish her child. I've been doing that to the best of my ability for the past eighteen years, and right now I will need to be the very best mother I can possibly be. The fear has lifted as I contemplate giving up my life for that of my daughter. I don't want to die, but if it means Mel can be free, then I won't hesitate.

'I'll shout if I need you. Call the police if I'm not out in ten minutes.'

I give neither of the men time to object as I launch myself out of the car and stride calmly down the garden path. It is a small cottage, two up, two down, red brick – nothing like the period splendour of her Horsham home. Probably a farmer's dwelling in days gone by, isolated, hidden behind a hedge on a narrow country lane. Any screams would go unheard out here or perhaps be mistaken for the desperate yells of a dying rabbit clamped in the jaw of a predatory fox. There is a light on in an upstairs window, glowing red behind the drawn curtains. I wonder whether Anna will open the door to me, or whether I will have to enlist the help of Ben and Joe to break in. I tread carefully along the path of large flat stones. I stumble and the calmness dissipates as my already sore ankle makes itself felt yet again. As I take a final three paces to the door, a security light comes on, bathing me in a bright yellow light. I jump and blink hard, trying to adjust to the light. But before I can reach forwards to press the doorbell, the door flings open.

And standing there is Jenny.

## 37

I am so shocked to see Jenny, I can only open and close my mouth like an idiot. What the hell is she doing here? Have I got it all wrong? Has Jenny been behind everything? For a long moment I stand and stare at her, totally confused. I have known Jenny for nearly twenty years. It's bad enough having misjudged someone I've known for four years, but twenty years! And what is her motive? I can't have inadvertently done that much damage to Slate Wilders; besides, it's not even her business, she's only a director. And then the adrenaline kicks in and the fury bites me. In that first long-drawn-out instant, I look at her but I don't see her.

'Have you got Mel?' I spit.

'No.' Jenny's voice is hoarse and she is staring at me with the strangest expression. Her complexion is blotchy and her eyes bloodshot and unfocused. There is something seriously wrong. Jenny opens her mouth as if to say something, but no words come out. Her eyes flicker from side to side. I wonder if she is going to faint.

'What's going on, Jenny?' I put my hand out to touch her,

but she staggers backwards into the small hallway, leaning her back against the wall.

'What the hell is going on?' I step into the dark hallway, and as I do so, the door slams behind me and a voice curls around us.

'Welcome to the humblest of my abodes!'

I swivel around. There is Anna, bolting the door, first at the top and then at the bottom.

'What is Jenny doing here? And where is Mel?'

'Now, now.' Anna speaks to me as if I am a fractious child. 'All in good time. Why don't we ladies take ourselves into the sitting room and have a little heart-to-heart.'

I open my mouth to speak, but Anna is in control.

'Jenny will walk in first because she knows where to go. You, Laura, will follow her.'

I am too shocked to do anything other than as instructed. The space is tight and Anna is so close to my back I can feel her warm breath on my neck.

The room could not be more dissimilar to Anna's living room at home. It is just large enough for a double-seater sofa, which is covered with a scruffy cream throw; a small pine table with three mismatched painted pine chairs; and an old-fashioned bulbous television wedged in the corner of the room. A navy beanbag has been dumped in front of the fireplace, which perhaps once housed a grate and hearth but now stands barren and forlorn. The room has a damp smell combined with something else a bit more fetid. I can't place it. Perhaps it's fear. Cheap cream tattered curtains hang across the window, but there is a sliver where they don't quite match in the centre. Behind them is a wooden panel, possibly shutters, although it looks more like ply used to secure window glass that has been broken. Joe must have got it wrong when he said that this place has five-star Trip Advisor reviews.

Jenny stands by the table, swaying back and forth. Despite

the cold there are large sweat-stained patches seeping out from underneath her arms, marking her navy blue blouse.

'What's she doing here?' I turn to Anna, who is so close to me, I have to step backwards. I trip on the beanbag and collapse onto it. She laughs uproariously. Last month, last week, even yesterday, I would have laughed with her, but now there is nothing remotely funny. But then I check myself. Anna has never been a barrel of laughs. She was happy to mock other people, to laugh at them, but thinking about it, humour was never her strong point.

'I assume you mean Jenny?' Anna says, folding herself elegantly onto the sofa. Jenny's eyelids are drooping.

'Jenny very kindly came to value this little cottage of mine. We had a quick look around; I gave her a cup of coffee with a marvellous drug in it and then explained that she would be staying here. Possibly indefinitely. The thing that is rather lovely about this location is its remoteness. We may only be a few minutes from Petworth, but the mobile phone reception is non-existent, and there is no landline. You can shout and yell and stamp your feet all you like, but no one is going to hear. Isn't that right, Jenny? What premium would you put on that, I wonder? Total seclusion yet within a twenty-minute walk of a delightful town. Ten percent, fifteen percent markup? She's already tried the screaming tactic, haven't you, Jenny love? Doesn't work and it just makes me very, very angry.'

'Why did you lure Jenny here?'

'Lure. It's such a wonderfully powerful word, don't you think? I lured Jenny because I am rounding up your flock. You have forgotten who is the most important person in your life, the person who has been there for you come hell or high water over the past four years. I need to remind you that Jenny here will never care about you like I do. Jenny is a little bit of collateral.'

I don't understand what she's saying, and all I can think about is Mel. My girl.

'Where's Mel?'

'Poor little Mel.' Anna briefly closes her eyes. I think about leaping up and swiping her, but I don't have time. She opens them again, those beautiful blue, pale ocean-coloured eyes. 'Mel's on her way to join Becky. Didn't you get the note?'

'No!' I scream. 'No!' I pounce towards her but stop. I am not a violent person.

'Belt up, Laura. I can't abide screaming women.'

'Take me to Mel!'

'I might, or I might not. Actually, I haven't quite decided.'

'You.' I turn to Jenny. 'Why aren't you doing anything to help?'

It is as if Jenny has turned to stone. My spunky friend Jenny has had all the lifeblood drained out of her, and she can't move, she can't speak, and her eyes flutter closed.

'Don't blame Jenny. She's just a bit player in our little drama.'

'Your little drama!' I yell. 'I know you were there that night Becky died.'

'You don't know anything. That's the thing, Laura. You know nothing!' she snarls, sitting up straighter on the sofa, uncrossing her black trouser legs. I notice that she is wearing flat shoes. Anna never wears flat shoes.

'I know you were there and you pushed her. You killed my sister!'

Anna laughs. It is a blood-curdling, dark laugh with a hint of a cackle. Where has my friend gone? Who has Anna transformed into?

'Becky stepped out into the road. She had her head in the clouds like she always did. Silly, silly Becky.' Anna flicks her hair and rolls her eyes. 'And now poor little Mel is about to step out into the road too. Such a shame for the same tragedy to afflict a family twice. You really must learn to look where you're going.'

'No!' I yell. 'Please don't hurt Mel. She's done nothing to you. She's young with her whole life stretched out in front of her.'

'You should have thought about that,' Anna says languidly. 'Silly Laura.'

'But what have I done? Why do you want to hurt me?'

'If you can't work out that one, then you are even more dumb than I realised. You can be so hopelessly naïve sometimes, Laura,' she twitters. 'Hopelessly naïve. Until you acknowledge the hurt you have inflicted on me, you will continue to suffer. You will be living in fear for the rest of your life because I have it all planned out.'

'I don't understand, Anna!'

Her eyes are almost luminescent, they are so bright; her pupils massive. She licks her lips slowly, suggestively, as if she is about to savour a delicious meal. 'Would you like to say goodbye to your daughter?'

'No!' I scream and leap towards Anna. If violence is the only way to stop this, I will fight with every ounce of strength I have. Out of the corner of my eye, I notice the large cross-body bag she is wearing, a black bag against her black polo neck jumper. I have never seen it before, never seen Anna carry anything except a designer handbag or fine leather briefcase. With one fluid movement, she reaches into it and produces a knife. I scream again. 'No!'

The carving knife glistens as she points it at me, her arm held out straight, her eyes firmly affixed on mine. 'The funny thing is, I don't actually want you to die. I want you to suffer, to live a life of such terror, it simply won't be worth living. You're so weak, you'll eventually take the coward's way out and end your own life. But I will have the satisfaction of knowing that you are my puppet and I have forced your hand. Of course, if you would like to die now too, then I will happily oblige. So what will it be, Laura? Now or later?'

'Kill me now, but release Mel!' My voice is quivering. I have never known such terror.

She shakes her head, her hair shimmering from side to side. 'It doesn't work like that, Laura. I decide who will live and who will die. And I decide when.'

'Why have you told me so many lies? Who is Jim, the good-looking man I saw leaving your house and who was with you at the hotel that night?'

Her laugh has a hysterical edge. 'He's an escort. Sex with no strings attached. A pretty face and a big dick! Don't look so shocked, Laura.'

'My phone, my computer? What did you do to them?'

'Oh, Laura, sad, trusting Laura. I followed you to the pub and took your phone when you so stupidly left it behind. I put some spyware on it so I could see exactly where you were all the time. I got copies made of your keys, and you made it so easy for me to get access to your flat. You really are very careless and dumb to boot. And you lied to me, Laura. Time and time again, I told you not to see Ben Logan, but you ignored me.'

She swivels suddenly to face Jenny. 'And you, Jenny, what have you got to say for yourself? Jenny, who mocked me when we met at your place. Jenny, who claims to be a better friend to you than me. Jenny, to whom you defer. What do you have to say for yourself?'

Something snaps inside Jenny. I watch it as if in slow motion. The pallor in her face morphs into red, her eyes flicker open, she takes a massive inhalation and leaps forwards towards Anna, but when she's still a foot away, she collapses to the ground, as if she's lost all control of her limbs. I hear a scream, a frenzied, horrific sound that deafens my ears, and only when the noise abates do I realise that it came from me.

'Shut the hell up!' Anna shrieks, waving the knife.

The guttural, animal howl emanating from deep inside me halts. Anna kicks Jenny, who lies motionless in a heap on the floor.

My phone is ringing. I move my hand towards my pocket.

'Don't answer it,' she hisses.

'I have to.'

'Do not answer it.'

I let my hand drop to my side. It seems impossible that my terror could notch up even further, but it does. It will be Ben calling, and somehow I have the clarity of thought to remember that we agreed he and Joe would come knocking on the door if I don't answer. That they will call the police. But none of us considered that Anna might have a knife. We never thought that she would be this volatile, this violent, quite so very evil.

Anna steps forwards and points the knife towards my chest.

'You, you're coming with me.'

'No,' I say. 'I'm not leaving Jenny.'

'Fine, I'll kill all three of you, then. I'm quite capable of doing it, you know. It won't be the first time.'

'What do you mean?' My voice quivers.

'Laura, sweet, silly little Laura. I always get what I want. I am strong and powerful, unlike you. How do you think I come to be living in such a beautiful home? How do you think I can afford not to work? I didn't have a rich daddy, but I did have a rich sugar daddy. Luckily for me, he died.'

'Did you kill him too?'

She laughs. 'His life had run its course. Just a bugger that...'

'What?' I say, wondering if I am about to learn a fragment of truth, wondering if she might remember just for an instant that we are meant to be good friends.

'You're coming with me.' She waves the knife too closely. 'Walk in front of me.'

'Where's Mel?' I ask. 'Please, I'll do anything you want, but take me to Mel.'

'You see, she doesn't give a toss about her friends, Jenny! You're on the floor dying and all Laura cares about is her spoiled princess of a daughter. I should have known that both sisters would be the same. Becky couldn't give a toss about me once Joe came into her life. Flung me aside as if I were a worthless toy she had outgrown. At least we know where we stand, hey, Jenny?'

I glance at Jenny. I think she is breathing, but it's hard to tell.

My phone pings. I assume Ben has left me a message. My hand drops into my pocket, my fingers curling around the cool, familiar metal case, but Anna notices and she pounces, jamming the sharp cold metal tip of the knife into the hollow of my back.

'Take your hand out of your pocket.' I remove my hand immediately. 'We're going out,' she announces. 'To Mel and her fate.'

My heart soars. Soon I'll be with Mel, and better still, if we're going out, Ben and Joe will see us. They'll be able to follow us, get the police to track where we are. Soon Mel and I will be rescued, and Jenny will be whisked away in an ambulance and given an antidote to whatever Anna has drugged her with. We will all be fine. But as Anna forces me out of the small living room, we don't turn left to the front door, but we walk right into a kitchen. Although the lights are off, I can make out old Formica-covered countertops and a small gas stove with a hob on top. The fridge hums loudly and there is a pervasive smell of damp rotting earth. I wonder if Mel will be in here; but no. The room isn't even large enough for a table and chairs.

Anna shoves me forwards again. 'Put your hands behind your back.'

'Why?' I gasp.

'Do you want to see little Mel or not?'

'Yes,' I whisper.

'Then do as I say or else I'll stab you and kill Mel.'

I do as I'm instructed and hold my hands behind my back. I wonder for a moment if I should run, if this is my chance. But I am too late. She grabs my wrists and secures them tightly together with something hard, plastic-like. It digs into my flesh.

'Move now!' she says, jabbing me in the back.

## 38

I am standing in front of a back door; the upper section is constructed from a pane of glass, but I can see nothing through it, just the blackness of night. The door is unlocked and it opens with a squeak. She pushes the tip of the knife into my back, and I yelp as the blade cuts through my clothes and pierces my flesh. She shines a torch from behind me, lighting up a narrow path of concrete slabs littered with decaying leaves. I tread carefully, not wanting to stumble, not wanting to do anything that might startle Anna into pushing the blade in further.

'Turn to the left.'

This time she shoves me with a hand. We walk across soggy grass. I can see nothing except my feet, which slurp in the muddy earth. My breath is shallow. I try to listen for the sound of a car, perhaps a siren in the distance, but I can hear nothing except the squishing of our footsteps and the light pattering of rain on the bare branches of the trees. We walk for five or ten minutes perhaps, but time stretches, and with no visual or auditory benchmarks, no stars in the sky to act as beacons or comforting lights from neighbouring houses, I lose sense of distance and time. All I hear is my heart beat. My terror. I wonder if I can take advantage of the night and slip away from Anna, hide beneath a bush, but then I feel the tip of the knife again and realise that would be sure death, if not for me, then, assuming she is still alive, most certainly for Mel.

The torchlight glints off a window and I see a pair of wide, terrified eyes, imploring, desperate. I move as if to hasten towards her, but Anna slaps me hard on the side of the head and the knife in my back jabs in further. It feels as if blood is dripping down my spine. I stumble and she drags me by the sleeve of my coat.

'If you say a word, I will kill you both. Get in the car!' The long sharp blade flickers in the torchlight.

It is a large Range Rover, black, shining, new. I have seen this vehicle before, I am sure of it. I recall the big black car on our tail when Rob and I left the house viewing after Eddy's no-show. And then there was the black car tucked under a tree when I left the new housing estate with Jenny. The third time was the following morning, the morning of the car accident, which now I know for certain was not my fault. No doubt there were other times too, other times when Anna followed me.

She releases the catch on the tailgate of the car. The light that comes on is brutal. Mel is sitting in the boot, her hands and ankles tied together, a cloth tied around her head that forces her mouth open. It is tinged with the rust of dried blood.

'My darling,' I say, shifting towards my shivering daughter. She looks at me with terrified eyes and a ghostly pale face and shakes her head.

'If you touch her or speak to her, you both will die. Get up.' Anna shoves me into the car, waving the blade in front of my face. I clamber in with difficulty and sit as close to Mel as I can without actually touching her.

'I thought you couldn't drive,' I say in a whisper.

'More fool you.' Anna laughs. She slams the boot shut, almost hitting my head, and the car shakes with the velocity.

'Are you ok?' I whisper to Mel in the two seconds we have before Anna hops up into the driver's seat and closes her door. Mel nods her head, but a tear trickles from the corner of her right eye. And then we are plunged back into darkness.

'Lie down, both of you. If either of you sit up or become visible to any cars behind us, which incidentally is extremely unlikely, as I have darkened glass in this car, then I will pull over and plunge the knife into your ribcages. Mel first, then Laura.'

I am hopeful that the roar of the engine and the bright headlights will alert Ben and Joe. But the car purrs softly when she starts it up. I wonder if it has been fitted with a silencer of some sort or another. And whilst I can't sit up to look, the car is not bathed in light. I assume she hasn't switched the headlights on, so she must know exactly where she is and where she is going. She must have parked the car at the back of the house, in a field perhaps, far away from prying eyes on the road. My heart sinks. I wriggle over slightly and position my body alongside Mel's so I can touch her, give her some degree of comfort. She is shivering uncontrollably. I try to curve myself around my girl, to impart some warmth and strength.

The car bounces as if we are driving over rough ground, and then after an indeterminate length of time, there is a big jolt and the tyres move smoothly. We are on tarmac and driving faster and faster, and now I can see that she has switched the headlights on, because the branches overhanging the road are lit up, and when she goes around corners, there is a red glow from the brake lights. But I don't see any car behind us. Where is Ben? Has he not realised Mel and I are in fatal trouble, that Jenny is poisoned and possibly dying on the living room floor?

I remember Joe's description of how Anna treated Becky: like her plaything. That's exactly what she has tried to do with me. The death notices, the emails, the graffiti. She's had fun playing with me, watching my reaction. Trying to stay one step ahead, watching me as my life started to disintegrate around me. As my fear increased, I leaned on Anna more and more and that was exactly what she wanted. I think of the rape and I shudder with disgust as I realise she must have drugged and undressed me.

The car is slowing down now. I must focus, work out how to get attention or jump out of the vehicle. I think back to the numerous crime series I have watched on the television. How did victims or detectives stop kidnappers or hijackers? Murderers even. I can't think straight. All I can hear is the pulsating of blood in my head as if it is blocking the synapses in my brain. And then, with a gasp, it comes to me what I have to do. Talk to her. Get her to talk. Try to rekindle the ashes of our friendship. Try to understand what is motivating her. Why does she hate me so much?

'How did you meet Becky?' I shout from the back.

'Shut up!' she snaps. But I don't intend to give up.

'I'd really like to know. You've never told me.'

'There are a lot of things I've never told you.' She laughs to herself. 'But why not? Yes, I will tell you. I will tell you the story of your little sister. I was involved in a car accident. My husband died. That part of the plan went swimmingly, but my air bag didn't fully expand. I hit my head. Naturally I sued the garage and was awarded a nice little sum that bought the cottage you've just visited. Incidentally, that's going to become your home for a while, Laura. It will be the place where you will grieve the death of Mel.'

Mel starts shaking again. I press my body into hers and whisper as quietly as I can in her ear. 'It will be fine, darling. I won't let anything happen to you. Please don't listen to her!'

'No one will miss you, Laura. No job to turn up to, no relatives that care about you, no husband or boyfriend.' She speaks in a sing-song tone.

But Anna is wrong about that one. I exhale as I realise how very wrong she is, and I allow myself a moment of hope.

'Your job will be to look after me, to do everything I tell you. And so long as you do that, I will look after you quite wonderfully. I may even redecorate the cottage for you.'

'Thank you,' I say.

Mel looks at me, her eyes boring into mine, uncomprehending. I mouth, 'It's ok,' and hope she understands I'm playing the game.

Anna is in full flow. There is an excitement in her voice that sickens me.

'I developed epilepsy after the accident, and it was your beloved sister, Becky, who rescued me when I had my first fit. Quite the little nurse she was, accompanying me to the hospital. I recognised a lost soul in Becky and soon we became inseparable. She told me everything. She needed me. I played the grieving widow, but at that point I was free. Financially set up for the rest of my life, everything was turning out just beautifully. But stupid Becky didn't realise how good her life was. She thought she had fallen in love. Of course it wasn't really love, just an obsession, but she became blinded. It was Joe this and Joe that, and then she began to stand me up for little Joe. She was all set up to announce her engagement. She was going to leave me behind.' She pauses for effect and lowers her voice. 'No one leaves me behind.'

'So you killed her?'

She snorts. 'Silly, silly Becky didn't look where she was going.'

'Why have you got me and Mel? We haven't done anything to you. I've been your friend and you've been an amazing friend to me. I couldn't have got through the past four years without you.'

I look away from Mel to avoid the scowl, the confusion, the fear that I know is written across her face.

'You are right. I have been a wonderful friend and you have thrown that friendship straight back into my face.'

Car headlights fill up the rear of the Range Rover, and for a moment I am hopeful that we will be intercepted, but Anna puts her foot on the accelerator and throws the car around corner after corner, tyres screeching as Mel and I are thrown from side to side. As the lights fade, she slows down and starts talking again.

'How dare you take what is mine! Ben Logan is my doctor, my lover. You stole him and now you will pay and so will he. You rejected my friendship for Jenny's and made me look like a fool. You chose your ex-husband, that weak bastard Ian, over me! It was me who arranged for Becky to be buried in the graveyard of your choice; it was me who arranged the funeral and held your hand through your grief. Yet today, you throw that back into my face for a man who lied and cheated. You have no taste, Laura. But worst of all, you went behind my back. You approached the police to get them to reinvestigate Becky's death. How could you do that just when your grief, my grief, was beginning to settle? You are a fool and a coward and so very far out of your depth.'

The fact that Anna is admitting all of this to me dashes any residual hope. By confessing what she has done, by explaining the depths of her jealousy, she has played her hand. There is little doubt that Mel and I will die. How can we live now that she has admitted her culpability?

And then, as if she has timed her diatribe to perfection, the car lurches violently to the right and we skid to a halt.

## 39

Anna switches off the engine and I can hear her shuffling around in the front seat. I shift away from Mel, as far away as possible, mouthing platitudes at her, hoping that I can give my daughter some comfort and ease the terror. I try to control my breathing, but my heart is thudding so loudly, I wonder if Anna can hear it. The car shifts a little and then a door slams. The internal light fades and we are plunged into darkness. Then the car is lit up as headlights appear, and I hold my breath and say a silent prayer. Let it be a police car. Let it be our rescuers.

But no.

The car drives past, and again we are consumed by the night. A minute or so later, the boot of the car is wrenched upwards and a torch is shone into our eyes. I blink hard, trying to see past the blinding light.

'Mel, get out! Laura, do not move!' she orders.

I watch as Mel struggles to sit. I wonder how long she has been tied up, whether her arms and legs have gone completely numb. I want to help her, but I know all I can do is bide my time and watch as she wriggles around. Anna laughs at her discomfort, and then she reaches into the car and pulls at Mel's hair, jerking her head upwards, forcing her to sit up. Mel is screaming, a scream that is muffled by the tea towel tied around her mouth. My screams are silent because I have to stay strong for Mel. My baby, my darling; I have to save us.

'You are coming with me,' Anna says as she tugs Mel forwards so that she is sitting with her legs dangling off the tailgate of the car. 'Hurry before anyone sees us.'

The knife in her right hand glints in the low light that shines from the open tailgate. Anna pushes Mel, who tumbles onto the tarmac and out of my sight.

'Don't hurt her!' I say.

'Shut the fuck up.' Anna produces a cloth, which she ties savagely around my mouth. I feel as if I am going to suffocate. My eyes are bulging.

'Sit up and look out of the front of the car. I want you to savour every moment of what is about to happen.'

She glances at her watch. 'Between two and five minutes to go. The milk lorry comes past here every night just before 9 p.m. And you, Laura, will be crying over spilled milk!'

Anna laughs, but it sounds fake, as if even she realises her words aren't funny. I am trembling all over, and I can't imagine what Mel must be feeling.

'It's a big lorry. One of those silver tubular lorries filled with lovely milk. Ever so heavy and unfortunately unable to stop quickly. You'll hear it before you see it. It rumbles along the road beautifully, giving me plenty of warning time to get Mel in position.'

She pauses for a moment then slams the tailgate shut. I can't see what she's doing, but I know now what I need to do. My arms are secured behind my back, but I need to bring them to my front. I shift forwards and then press my feet against the lip of the boot, forcing my hands under my backside, and I wriggle until I can ease my legs through my arms. Although I am unfit, I am double-jointed. It hurts, but it is possible. All the while my eyes are on Anna dragging Mel into the centre of the road, further from the car into the inky darkness. As soon as my arms are freed, my wrists now secured in front of me, I have mobility. I throw myself over the rear seat, tumbling forwards until I am in the front, in the driver's seat. Glancing around manically, I look for a key, but it's not there. And then I see the stop/start button. No key required. I don't expect the car to start, but nevertheless I put my foot on the brake and press the button.

To my amazement, the Range Rover purrs to life, the headlights bathing the road in light, illuminating Anna leaning over Mel. As soon as she realises what is happening, Anna swings around. She rushes towards the car, the blade of the knife waving violently, but my foot is on the accelerator, and the car lurches forwards. Can I hit her without hurting Mel? Can I steer with my wrists bound together?

And then I hear it. Anna is right. The wheels do sound like a rumble, as if the earth is being shaken slowly. I see the lights flickering between the trees, but it's impossible to tell how fast it is moving and whether there is anything I can do. I accelerate into the road, straight towards Anna, and as I see her eyes widen, I hear a scream and a thud and I'm on the wrong side of the road, just inches from Mel, and I swerve around her, putting the Range Rover between Mel and the lorry. I slam my foot on the brake. The giant headlights get closer and closer, blinding me as terror grips my body, and I wait because I know this is the end and there is nothing I can do to save myself. I pray that the velocity of the crash won't push the car backwards over Mel. That at least my daughter will be spared. And then, because there is nothing else that I can do, I close my eyes tightly and wait for the inevitable.

Even the car is trembling. I hold my breath, lungs burning

with my last gulp of air. I wait for the pain. There is a roar. Brakes screech, metal on metal.

A shudder.

Then there is silence.

And still I don't open my eyes. A few seconds later the light is so bright behind my tightly closed lids. I wonder if I am in heaven, if this is the light that is talked about in books about the afterlife. And then I look. The huge lorry is an inch from the nose of the Range Rover, white light, silver, I can't even see the lorry's windscreen, it is too high up.

I'm out of the car, running backwards towards Mel. There is someone else too, a man, who reaches her before me, lifting her up as if she is a bag of sugar, carrying her to the side of the road.

'What the hell?'

∿

FLASHING BLUE LIGHTS. Male voices. A cacophony of male voices, some familiar, others not. So much noise. Car engines, a helicopter too, so close, just the other side of the hedge.

'Laura!' Arms are thrown around me.

Someone is pulling at the fabric smothering my mouth and it tears free, releasing my screaming voice.

'Mel!'

'She's ok,' Ben says. 'She's fine. Ian has her. He's over there with the lorry driver. You're both safe.'

I am shaking so much, even Ben's strong arms can't quell the trembling.

'Anna?' I ask.

Ben shakes his head and turns me away from the road. But it's too late. I've seen her crumpled in the road, a dark pool of blood seeping from her head.

I did that.

I killed Anna.

I burst into tears.

'Joe, can you get my doctor's case? It's in the rear of the car. I need some scissors, quickly.'

'Ma'am, are you all right?' A policeman peers at me. Another man, not in uniform, strides towards us, holds out his badge and repeats the question.

'I need to go to Mel,' I say.

Ben cuts the ties around my wrists and supports me as we hobble across the road. There are so many lights, I can see now what has happened. Police cars are parked at unlikely angles, blocking off the road in both directions. The helicopter quiets as its blades slow down. The milk lorry is stationary, the driver talking to another police officer, wringing his hands at his sides, his thin face as pale as the milk he is delivering.

When Mel sees me, she bursts into hysterical sobs that rack her body. She is wrapped in a silver blanket. Ian sits with his arm around her shoulders, and a female police officer holds one of her hands.

'I'm sorry, my darling,' I say as I envelop her in a hug. 'I'm so sorry I failed you.'

'But you didn't, Mum.' She snuffles. 'You saved me.'

'How did the lorry stop in time?' I ask.

'He saw the lights of the car. You stopped Mel from being run over,' Ben says.

'And how did you get here so quickly?'

'When you didn't answer your phone, we walked all around the outside of the house and found the back door open. We found your colleague on the floor, unconscious.'

'Jenny,' I say. 'Is she all right?'

'She'll be fine. She's safely in hospital. My guess is she was sedated with the same drug Anna used on you. I've been thinking about what happened. She must have followed us to the pub when we had lunch and then added a date-rape drug to your Irish coffee.'

'She had a tracker on my phone, and she copied my flat keys, so access was no problem,' I say.

'It's all over now. We saw the car tyre marks in the field. I rang the police and they were already on their way after Ian had spoken to them. I guessed she'd be bringing you to the lay-by, so we all raced here. But it was you who saved Mel,' Ben says.

I hold Mel tightly, stroking her hair, kissing the top of her head, her cheeks. Eventually Mel and I stop shaking, and gently, she pushes me away.

'I'm not a baby anymore,' Mel says, smiling at me with her tear-stained face. Mel is going to be ok, I think.

I stand up.

'I'm a murderer,' I say quietly to Ben.

'No, my darling, you're not. You saved your life, you saved your daughter's life, and Anna, well, Anna got what Anna deserved.'

I watch as the police swarm around us. My eyes are drawn to the body crumpled on the road, but then a small white tent is erected, and I realise that I will never see Anna again. Those pale blue eyes have gone, and I shiver as the fear cascades through my body one last time and then dissipates, leaving me free.

# A LETTER FROM MIRANDA

Dear Reader,

Thank you very much for reading I Want You Gone, set in sunny Sussex, where I live with my husband, musician daughter, and black Labrador. It is such fun creating imaginary worlds in familiar settings.

I love writing and I couldn't do it if I didn't have extraordinary support from my family. My husband, who keeps me fed and does the tough techie stuff. Our musician daughter, who astounds us with her creative talents and vision. My parents and sister, who continue to inspire. I am very lucky. Special thanks to coach Emily Tamayo Maher who has supported me throughout the past very fruitful year and to Brian Lynch and Garret Ryan of Inkubator Books who work their magic on my novels making them so very much better.

If you could spend a moment writing an honest review, no matter how short, I would be extremely grateful. They really do help other people discover my books.

Amazon US
Amazon UK

I'm looking forward to bringing you more books in the near future.

With warmest wishes,

Miranda

www.mirandarijks.com

Published by Inkubator Books
www.inkubatorbooks.com

Made in the USA
Monee, IL
06 May 2020